PARADISE

by

MARY-ANN SIMPSON

All rights reserved
Copyright Mary-Ann Simpson 2006

Mary-Ann Simpson is hereby identified as the author of this work, in accordance with Section 77 of the Copyright, Designs and Patents Act 1988

This book is sold subject to the condition that it shall not, by way of trade or otherwise, be lent, resold, hired out or otherwise circulated without the author's or publisher's prior consent in any form of binding or cover other than that in which it is published and without a similar condition including this condition being imposed on the subsequent purchaser.

British Library Cataloguing In Publication Data
A Record of this Publication is available
from the British Library

ISBN 1846854520
978-1-84685-452-1

First Published 2006 by

Exposure Publishing, an imprint of Diggory Press,
Three Rivers, Minions, Liskeard, Cornwall, PL14 5LE, UK
WWW.DIGGORYPRESS.COM

This novel is a work of fiction. Names and characters mentioned in this novel are the product of the author's imagination, and any resemblance to actual persons, living or dead, is entirely coincidental.

Callum hadn't inherited the red-hair of the MacCready clan, but he certainly had their temper. And he was unable to retain office staff on the homestead just outside town because of it. This was the only place left to him since they'd lost the vast cattle station started by his great-great-great-great-grandparents way back when. Even the named haunted him. He'd lost his personal Paradise too, in the debacle following his father's drunken death. Diane had married old man Gough rather than live in straightened circumstances with Callum. The last herd had been rustled, disappearing into thin air, like a column of smoke from a campfire on a clear day. Just the latest in a long line of setbacks, beginning with his mother's death eight years ago. By god, he was determined to hang on to the little homestead. Come what may.

What came was an unlikely alliance with a drifter. Jacq Tregissick drifted from town to town, taking whatever work she could get, *if* she needed to work. It seemed to include various shadowy areas Callum was none to sure about. But the local Police Sergeant recommended her, so who was he to argue? She certainly sorted out the homestead.

But who had planted the little bugs so carefully round his home? Who was delving into his computer? Subtly transferring money out of his Bank account? What could one person do to help stem the tide of despair and insolvency sweeping him steadily towards the abyss? ...   .Especially a *woman*?

I am very grateful to the Committee Men who manage the Gone With the Wind Copyright, for their permission to include the short quote from that book, which is used on page 226.

And, to Land Rover for their prompt agreement to using the various terms indicating the Land Rover vehicle which features throughout.

Mary-Ann Simpson started writing children's stories simply to keep her grandchildren amused, but gradually other voices clamoured for attention, wanting to have their stories told too.

Her adult life has been spent working in various areas, which now provides insightful backdrops to her novels. Mary-Ann feels privileged to have been both a friend and counsellor to families in crisis, and this has given her greater understanding of human frailties and strengths, thus adding an extra dimension to her characters and their busy lives.

Although rooted in Seventies culture, Mary-Ann's novels are firmly based in the modern technological world, having just the right mix of the everyday, laced with various problems that are part of the human condition we call 'life'.

As Mary-Ann says "Every day has provided something, some insight into people, some facet of living that can be used for a book. So thank you, Life, for providing me with so much diversity from which to draw my characters and plots."

About The Artist

The late Alayda den Otter was born and grew up in Brisbane, Australia. Having raised her children, Alayda found an outlet for her artistic talents in acrylics. On her last trip to the UK, she brought me one of her paintings. *That* was the inspiration for this tale, and so, I used the original as the cover.

Thank you Alayda. Still inspiring me six years' later.

CHAPTER ONE

"Jack Tregissick?"

The upward inflection at the end of the two words seemed to suspend the paintbrush. Turning towards the rider, the woman was forced to look up. She frowned, but the man didn't move his horse out of the sunlight, and she could not see him clearly. This then, was the legend called Callum MacCready.

She nodded, but continued to paint. If he couldn't dismount, then she was certainly at liberty to carry on with what she was doing. What she was doing, was painting Tom's fence. It whiled away the hours until she could persuade him she was perfectly safe moving on, …again.

Impatiently Callum started his prepared speech. Jacq nodded, apparently concentrating on her work. Callum could feel himself tensing in response to her casual attitude. Didn't she know people stopped work when he spoke to them? Racking his brains he tried to recall everything he'd heard about Jack.

People always talked in a small town. Always. This one was no exception. He must have heard something. He sifted through Nick's remarks about her. She'd worked for the Police Department, employed for six months by the County to transfer their records to a new computer system. What else? Nothing… nothing! Just Nick's comments, well complaints, more like.

She listened politely, not to say disinterestedly, while Cal explained that Tom Crowthorn had recommended her to help in his office. Unsmiling, she had nodded patiently, as he outlined the set up, continuing to dab here and there at her half-painted fence.

"OK. When do you want me to start?" She eyed the partly finished fence consideringly, waiting for his response.

"Last week."

Looking up sharply at the tone of voice used, she'd asked, "Who else is out there?"

"Few horses. Needed all hands for round up."

Convinced she'd turn him down, Cal's speech got terser and shorter the longer the conversation lasted. He was too busy to pussyfoot around, giving only a passing nod to the social niceties, turning over alternatives while they spoke.

He used to be quite a conversationalist, but now he mostly spoke in monosyllables. Terse short instructions, nothing more polished at all. Because he hadn't got time to waste on the niceties, just wanted to get on with the job in hand. Save his homestead and his livelihood from vanishing down the black hole, which had appeared at the same time his father died.

"OK. Tonight. Teatime. Can you give me a job spec?" She half-flinched from the fury in his face.

"If I could do office work, would I be employing you?" He said it through gritted teeth. "If it looks as though it needs doing, then do it."

"OK." Turning back to the fence, she resumed her painting. Not working any faster or slower than when he'd arrived.

Funnily enough, he'd expected to be offered refreshment. No, no! What he'd expected … … was for her to stop, and concentrate on what he was saying.

Give him her undivided attention. Expected some courtesy. The English were renowned for it, so he'd heard and now this... this... woman had... well, what exactly? She'd treated him the way he'd treated her. Off-hand, casual, dismissive.

He'd had a long, hot, dusty ride into town to find her, when really he could ill-afford the time. And now, she turned away without offering anything.

"The water in the bucket is for your horse. If you want a drink help yourself."

Callum was unused to this, especially from an unsmiling woman. Most women smiled at him. Had done all his life. Most were eager to please big Callum MacCready. Not over-eager as they had been when the MacCreadys owned most of the land hereabouts (and most of the wealth too), but he was a bad man to cross. Certainly his size and his temper carried him into more fights and disagreements than most of the other local notables. Callum might not have the red MacCready hair, but he certainly had the temper and dark good looks.

Crossing to the indicated bucket, he dismounted, watering his horse while studying the covered table close by. Having quenched his own thirst with some juice, he stuffed a couple of little cakes into his mouth, almost as an afterthought. He put two more in each shirt pocket, feeling like a kid stealing cookies from his mother. With his mouth conspicuously full of cake, crumbs fell from his shirt as he swung back into the saddle. Cal was completely unaware Jacq watched him gallop off, unsurprised at the disappearance of the cakes.

❈ ❈ ❈ ❈ ❈

Jacq had been intrigued by her cousin's description of the problems besetting the local people. It seemed such an idyllic setting. Surely you wouldn't meet greed and avarice here?

But, it seemed you could. Tom Crowthorn, the local Police Sergeant, had been quite open. Not wanting to believe old man MacCready had indeed gambled away the family homestead. Yeah, he'd been heartsick when Meg died, but not so far gone he'd have signed over the homestead. Not after five generations, no way. And too, the way the Blackstocks, MacGregors and one or two others had lost their places. It all reeked a bit.

Jacq hated mysteries.

CHAPTER TWO

When the man she'd lived with (oh yeah and loved) for twenty years left her, without a satisfactory explanation, Jacqueline Tregissick had struggled to rebuild her life. Having to sell her home to meet the selfish demands of the man to whom she had given her love, was the final straw.

It had given her the impetus she needed to make a complete break. Well alright, not a complete break, … nearly a complete break. She had stayed on at the Bank, not liking to jeopardise her pension by leaving them altogether. Instead she had taken up an offer to job-swap for a year.

Coming to Australia unprepared for the full impact of its majestic beauty. The vast sun filled (or rain drenched) skies appealed so strongly, that at the end of her year she had quit the Bank, which had been her lifeline. Her one point of sanity in a shifting, sliding world, as her life disintegrated around her. Honestly believing she had enough skills to see her through, Jacq decided to roam Australia, until somewhere called loud enough to become home. The only family she had left was here. Why not stay, as it appealed so strongly?

The tenant of the poky flat, which was all she could afford after David wiped her out, clamoured to have his tenancy extended. Breathing a sigh of relief, Jacq agreed. Glad to be free of the windy city. The crowded suburban trains on which she stood shoulder to shoulder with other pale and wan city workers.

Was she sorry to leave rainy old England behind? No, not really. She was sad for the lost dreams, her lost youth, the wasted years of living with a man who had been entirely self-engrossed.

Twenty years of praying and hoping one day he'd wake up and see *her*. Jacqueline. Recognise he wanted *her*, wanted to marry *her*, wanted *her* to have his babies. But instead, he'd woken up one day and wanted his freedom.

Wanted the days of his youth. Wanted to 'play the field', before Jacq destroyed forever his sense of optimism. He'd said it so coldly, when telling her what he wanted. Never once mentioning Jacq, *her* dreams, *her* lost youth. Only his own.

"I only ever meant it to be short-term."

Short-term…. Short-term?

Had he meant it to be short-term when Jacq had taken out that last bank loan to upgrade to their detached house? Short-term, each time they'd moved to something better, bigger, nicer?

Short-term, when she'd borrowed the money for his latest sports car?

"I was never into that domestic scene Jacq. You knew that. I still kept up my nights out, didn't I? What did you think I was doing, while you were working overtime?"

"I certainly wasn't sitting here twiddling my thumbs. It's been fun, but it's over Jacq. Just give me my share of the house, and I'll move out. See, I'm not even insisting you go. You don't even have to sell up. Just give me my share Jacq, and I'm outa here."

His share? His share…!

Should she just pay him the bare minimum he'd given her to cover his food and occasionally a bit towards the bills?

Dave had never helped with the mortgage, or the utility bills, but had insisted on sharing some of the other bills, *if* they came in over budget. Contributing to the phone bill for example, if he felt his own usage warranted it.

Never as much as half, thought Jacq, in retrospect, in the depths of her despair. Just a fraction really, except for the food. Dave had always been fanatical about paying her exactly half each month for the food she bought.

She'd jokingly set up a spreadsheet because he had been so insistent. Needing to see an itemised list of all the foodstuffs. Never the other stuff; the cleaning things, loo rolls, soap powder, the day-to-day stuff of which life consists. Oh no, too boring, too humdrum for Dave. Oh but, he'd paid for the steaks and other fancy things he wanted when his friends came for a barbeque. Halving *those* food bills and the subsequent drinks bills meticulously on his return. Oh yes, Dave had even done *that* shopping, but could never help Jacq with the bulk shopping she did week in, week out.

His had been the major voice in choosing the house, choosing the furnishings. Knowing just what he wanted. This or that TV, or stereo, or whatever. His own pc, upgraded pcs, his own laptop. Oh yes, Dave certainly knew his own mind.

Why hadn't Jacq realised before? How stupid did you have to be, not to realise this man had been sponging… yes *sponging* on her for over twenty years?

Jacq had supported his decision to leave his dead-end job, supported him through a seven-year course to become a Radiographer. And *this* was her reward.

He'd been qualified just over a year when he decided to move. Had taken a new job in the North of England, where housing was cheap, without telling her.

Jacq had arrived home tonight, her mind full of the quarterly figures. The usual quarterly juggling, which almost caused her nightmares, certainly caused sleepless nights. Trying to balance the commissions and interest. Trying to gauge to a nicety what the customers would accept uncomplaining, against the margin she needed to make to ensure the staff received their annual bonus. Working from her laptop into the wee small hours, and on train journeys as she travelled to and from the Bank, which absorbed most of her waking hours.

His portion of the meal she'd cooked for the two of them, had been cling-wrapped. It awaited re-heating in the microwave, if he were still hungry when he eventually returned home.

Jacq didn't know where he was. Just 'out'. He never liked to be questioned about what he did. She had at least learned *that* over the years of sulky silences, the noisy eruptions when things didn't go his way, the tangible 'frost' he exuded if he was upset.

Looking back, Jacq realised that living with Dave had taught her a lot about secrecy. And, not just about secrecy, but the difference between secrecy and privacy. That had been a hard lesson to learn.

Tonight, he'd caught up with her in the kitchen, as she made herself another coffee, before returning to her figures.

"Ah Jacq!"

She'd turned round at the unexpected pleasure in his voice. Expecting… expecting what exactly? Well, certainly *not* to be told he'd got a job in Newcastle. *Not* to be told it started Monday week.

Certainly *not* that he'd calculated how much she owed him on 'our' house. As if it had been in joint names. With his share of the rise in value of their home, he'd be able to buy exactly what he wanted. He said it so gleefully, casting scornful glances at this home they'd shared for so long. How he had pressed for 'his share'.

Not believing Jacq couldn't simply give him half the increase in the market value. He'd been saving all these years, why hadn't she?

Why hadn't Jacq got a nest egg to fall back on, now that their lives were parting? Why? Because she'd been using her money to keep him in the style to which he was accustomed, that's why!

Those few days before he moved, were filled with bitter recriminations. The twenty-year fabric of their relationship was wiped out, totally destroyed by that one conversation.

When Jacq had turned at the sound of his voice, expecting a loving hug at the very least, and – who knows, - perhaps a passionate embrace? A passionate embrace, well some sex, any sex, would make a nice change, actually. Passion might have offered some comfort anyway, after a long and cold train journey. Huddled over her laptop, working on her knees, elbows pinched tight to her body to avoid offending fellow travellers.

Before he left, in a self-drive van, he told her he'd instructed solicitors to act for him. Solicitors to recoup his money! Dave!

The self same Dave, who hadn't wanted a formal agreement, hadn't wanted to be joint owner of their house. Hadn't wanted anything in writing.

"I trust you Jacq. And you trust me, don't you? Well then, what use lining a solicitor's pockets? We're fine."

Jacq could still see that van, laden down under the weight of all their household goods. Dave claimed half of everything Jacq had ever bought for their home. Blithely packing anything he himself had paid for, without thought, without question. As well as all the things she had bought for his exclusive use.

He'd split the CDs and DVDs, by preference. Leaving her with her own selection of DVDs but no player.

Mystified by her reaction, he'd said, "You're always too busy to watch TV. If you get more free time, then simply buy another. You can afford it. Anyway you never understood how this one worked, did you?"

On and on endlessly, until Jacq wanted to scream with the pain, scream with the selfishness of this man she had been lovingly nurturing. Lovingly cherishing. Lovingly supporting through his career change.

The joint account she'd opened when Dave started at University had always been wiped out by the end of the month. Two years into the course, Jacq stopped topping it up mid-month. She continued to feed it with the agreed figure of £400 per month for his 'personal expenses', but stopped adding little extra amounts here and there, when she spotted how low it was. Dave banked at her branch, naturally. Where he could get free overdrafts, free banking, and other staff perks.

"I don't want to live off you Jacq, but the grant is miniscule." He'd said when talking about the Grant.

Jacq had agreed, happy to be earning enough to supplement his grant. Happy to pay all the bills, all the expenses; happy to pay for a holiday or a short break away from the stresses of his course. Happily planning for *after* he'd settled into his new career. Surely then? Surely by then, he'd be ready to talk about a family?

Her biological clock ticked relentlessly through the long, long days as she beavered away at the Bank. Shutting her ears to the joys of her friends as they started or extended families. Being the loving aunt stopped some of the pain, but not all of it. Oh no. Only one thing could stop, would stop the pain, the anguish of not yet having her own baby to cuddle. David's graduation, and then... *then*... it would be time for Jacq.

Time for the things she wanted out of life. Time to give up full time work, perhaps? Well, until the babies (both of them) started school. Time when Jacq would, could relax for a while. Chill out, enjoy her babies, and then start afresh down the line. As long as she didn't leave it too late, that is.

❋ ❋ ❋ ❋ ❋

Dave wouldn't even give her a new address, or phone numbers.

"Better to have a clean break, Jacq. No point going over and over."

So, ... there she was. 38 and no social life. Not that she really had time for a social life. Most of their friends had been Dave's, who now avoided her like the plague. Looking the other way if they saw her approaching, ...ducking into shops. Would have been quite funny, if it hadn't been so painful, thought Jacq.

Dave disappeared from the radar of her life as if he had never been. Twenty years! Leaving only a deep dark blackness that never seemed to lift. Her antennae had always been rigged to him. For twenty years she had known instantly from a sigh or a nod, exactly what he wanted. Divining what he needed from her without him saying anything. His going left a great void.

Oh yes, Jacq had been busy at work over the years, had worked all hours to maintain their lifestyle. Wanting Dave to be happy, wanting whatever pleased him. But she had still known unfailingly, exactly what Dave needed from her. Jacq had let him decide every aspect of their lives. Thinking they were blissfully happy, she had let him manage their lives, subjugated all her own dreams to Dave's needs. So... that all ended too.

Jacq never knew how she struggled through the quarterly figures that month. Glossing over her pain. Glossing over the loss of her life.

The fact that both Commissions and Interest balanced third time through amazed her. It had always been a struggle, ever since she'd first been appointed Supervisor. Her predecessor had never fully grasped it and, in showing Jacq, had never satisfactorily explained the reasons for the calculations, the alterations. And now, in the midst of the desolation that was her life, everything balanced third time round.

Hell and damnation, I obviously worried too much! Still, while there's life there's hope, Jacq thought.

❋ ❋ ❋ ❋ ❋

The email about the job swap came at just the right time. Oh yes, just exactly the right time, for someone whose life had ended. Someone who didn't now want to keep to all the old routines. Someone fluttering so painfully to emerge from her cocoon. Eager to fly, eager to taste every adventure life could offer. Her wings were singed, but not so badly she couldn't escape.

Never let it be said Jacq had no grit, no determination. She could and would succeed! So there, she added, nodding childishly in the direction of Newcastle.

Yup, Jacq hated mysteries.

CHAPTER THREE

Two and a half weeks after their initial meeting, Callum trotted up the homestead road, weary, hot, dusty and tired. Wanting only a shower, a shave, a proper meal and a fresh smelling 'proper' bed.

The figure reclining in the shade on the verandah surrounding the homestead, reminded him of Diane. That's where she'd always been, whenever he returned from a Drive.

Hell, I hope she kept the staff this time, or there'll be nothing prepared for the lads. Shaking his head to dispel the unsatisfactory memory, Cal was unprepared for the bitter taste in his mouth. That had been four years ago. Hell, how long is it gonna take to forget all that?

Returning to the present, he thought again about this latest drive. They'd worked extremely hard. Steers are a pain to drive. They seem to have a mind of their own. Or, at least, only one good brain between them. Couldn't be rushed either. Seven hours a day sitting on your horse, gently prodding, prodding, prodding. Trying to persuade them to move just a little faster, please. Goddamit! Keep those back ones up, or we'll have them spread across the whole state.

And now this! *Madam* there, reclining on the verandah without a care in the world. Swinging his horse onto the grass, Callum passed nearer to the homestead than he originally intended. He'd been on his way to the stables. Look after his horse. Sort out the showers. Check the kitchen, then see to his own needs. Forty odd years of habit, of looking after the horses, then the men, before seeing to himself, carried him wearily along.

All he really wanted to do, was sit in the shade with a long cold beer, and have his mother wait on him, as she used to. Before she died. Hell, life was a bitch, wasn't it?

Unaware that the deep bitterness in his mind was reflected in the tone of voice he used, he said in passing, "Hey, I pay you to work, not lounge round in the shade."

He turned his horse, heading for the stable area. While caring for his horse, his thoughts continued along this well-worn and bitter path. Callum strode determinedly towards his office. He'd known it was a mistake to hire her. Sheer desperation. Well, she could go just as easily.

Callum MacCready had already tried all the local staff. No one was prepared to put up with his mood swings, his black temper. This woman was a drifter, roaming the Australian outback, taking work whenever she needed to raise some money. Seemingly content to move from town to town and job to job on a whim.

The trailer home she had driven on to his lot a couple of weeks' ago, looked dusty but well kept, as did the small Land Rover trundling along in its wake. He'd finally been persuaded by two factors; she didn't need to be accommodated and she appeared undaunted by the backlog since the last secretary had quit in a fit of tears eight months' ago.

Cal MacCready – as he was more often known – had been far too busy since then, droving more herds to the township. Paperwork was not his thing. As long as he could roam the ranges, sleeping under the vast star filled skies, coming back to the homestead for some soft living in between whiles, he asked for nothing more. Not for him the cosy domesticity of his friend, Steve. Married apparently contentedly, now with twin girls born just over 2 years ago.

Despair blossomed briefly as Cal contemplated a bleak future. He seldom accepted Steve's frequent invitations. Didn't need the constant reminder, the contrast between their happy lives and his own aborted marriage.

He'd been flung into a black bitter pit after the death of his father and the failure of his own marriage. His marriage to Diane, the girl of his dreams, so he thought. The dreams of a happy home life had turned into a nightmare before they'd been married a year. Oh, they'd struggled on for a further three years, but the spark had gone.

Steve and Sheena's marriage served as a reminder that not all marriages degenerated as quickly as Cal's had done. A reminder he didn't need. Wouldn't need, until he met someone who made his blood tingle, someone who would stir his senses, someone who would make it worthwhile arriving home... ... Nope, don't even think about it!

Manoeuvring through the fly screen, he headed for his office, stopping in surprise. His office was clean and tidy. No trace of the mountain of paperwork, which for years had covered every available surface. A steaming mug of black coffee was perched temptingly on a coaster on top of his desk. The chair was free from dust for the first time since his mother died. There was even a shine on the windows.

"Be right there." Jacq came through, clutching a notebook and pen.

Cal's eyes took in her official appearance. The smart divided skirt and neat tee-shirt presented a businesslike and efficient air, which contrasted with the image he remembered. Settling herself onto the chair at the side of his desk, pad and pen poised, she waited.

She didn't look directly at him. Not only had his comments annoyed her, Jacq disliked his attitude. Still, ... she shrugged mentally, I can always quit, can't I? Knowing that she wouldn't, not until she'd seen his response to her discoveries. Hell, none of my business, is it?

Sitting himself down, Cal watched her, while taking a cautious sip of his coffee. Scaldingly hot, but devastatingly strong, a tiny sip of the sticky liquid slipped burningly down his parched throat.

Jacq contented herself with writing the date and time at the top of her notepad, her hand just hovered.

"Yes?"

Her eyes flicked briefly to his face, returning immediately to her notebook. "I thought you might have some letters to dictate."

He sighed impatiently. "Do I look as though I have letters to dictate?" The silence stretched endlessly while he downed his coffee.

Cal worked out to his entire satisfaction that she'd come unstuck somewhere around the end of the first week. Had been sitting here in the shade, watching the world go by, while he'd been working his butt off out there.

Sighing heavily, he said, "OK, where have you got to?"

"Well," Jacq coughed. "I archived a load of stuff, but can't find any reference to old filing anywhere.

Where does it go? I've set up a spreadsheet for that, and the Accounts, reconciled your Bank Statements, typed these by way of response to letters received. Here are some cheques that cannot be delayed any longer if you want to stay in business. Made a preliminary draft of your Business Activity Statements for the last two years, started on the current year. Sent a holding letter to the Australian Tax people explaining the reasons for the delay with that."

She nodded at the fat folders sitting in solitary splendour in the middle of his desk. No smile accompanied her words; she simply waited patiently for further instructions.

Cal opened the first folder. His eyes glazed over as they skipped across the various spreadsheets it contained. Hell, didn't realise there were so many outstanding invoices.

The Statement showed a miniscule black figure at the bottom line. The value of the cheques awaiting his signature exceeded it. He scowled ferociously.

"The Bank has agreed a temporary overdraft, until your invoices are paid. I negotiated a special rate in view of the length of your relationship. The wages bill is in there too, although I couldn't find Bank details to send transfers out. When the cash arrived, I made up pay packets." She waited in vain for him to comment.

The letters folder was daunting.

"I've already posted those. Seemed people were taking advantage …. Eer, so I wrote…"

Cal looked at the letters, headed in red, Reminder. Hell, I never send reminders, just wait for people to pay.

"I've paid in all the cheques I've received so far." His paying-in book was pushed across the desk towards him. "If there is nothing else?"

When he shook his head, Jacq added, "Archiving? Could you just point me in the right direction?"

He looked at her blankly, with his hands still on the letters folder.

"Old stuff? No longer needed? Anything more than seven years old can be destroyed? I really wanted to get that sorted today, while you're here."

He followed the direction of her pointing finger towards three brown cardboard boxes.

"OK, leave that. Not a problem." She moved quickly back to the door.

Thrusting his cup at her, he was about to ask for a refill. She nodded, pointing briefly to the side table where the coffee jug used to stand, back when his mother had everything organised. The coffee jug was plugged neatly into a socket above the table. It stood on a tray with additional mugs, sugar, spoons etc.

"I left it there, OK? Help yourself." She slid out of his office without really looking at him.

Listening to her movements while topping up his cup, Cal was distracted from the arrival of a police car. Where's she off to now?

Jacq's footsteps echoed loudly as she headed for the back of the old ranch house. Cal listened to the footsteps performing a little dance. Oh! The expression on his face lightened, not exactly a smile, but all Cal managed in that direction since his father died five years ago. The dunny flushed.

The footsteps were retreating again, when Nick pushed open the door. "Made it then?"

Cal nodded in response to Nick's words.

Nick moved unerringly to the coffee jug, helping himself. Barely pausing before gulping the scalding brew, he swallowed quickly, gasping air across his burned tongue. "Lose many this time?"

"About the usual for the drive. Nothing unreasonable. Still plenty to fatten up before the train."

Nick jerked his head. "Where is she?"

"Out back."

They sipped their coffee in silence. Cal returned to the folders.

Grimacing at the expressions used in the reminder letters, he was surprised how many showed a tick through and date. Pulling the paying-in book towards him, he carefully checked off the credits. Good response rate at least.

He scanned the letter from the bank. Old What's-it never granted overdrafts, what could have made him change his mind? Accounts? Plan? Schedule of Work? Must be mad, Cal had never offered these before. Had no intention of starting now, either. Still, overdraft in place subject to usual terms. Typical bloody bank. Where had he read that they lent you an umbrella when it was dry, wanting it back at the first sign of rain?

Footsteps returned, heading for his office. Jacq nodded silently at Nick, dumping a tray of fresh scones, butter and jam onto the side table with the coffee.

"Help yourselves."

Gone. No comments, no smile, nothing except the food.

Nick said, "These will be good. Have one."

Absentmindedly helping himself to a scone, Cal buttered it while frowning over the paperwork in his room. Well at least, the *absence* of paperwork in his room. None of the intermediate secretaries had even touched it, and now it had all vanished.

The two friends ate their way through the scones, helping themselves to more coffee, chatting casually about the last drive, what was going on in town, generally catching up.

Cal had been expecting trouble on this drive. The last herd had been lost to rustlers. No harm had come to the riders themselves, apart from the damage to their egos. Fortunately the herd was insured, but the hike in premiums and the loss of reputation were short-term problems to be resolved, as soon as Cal had time. No news on that at all.

"It's as if they vanished. There's no trace anywhere. Without any leads we're stuffed."

Cal nodded. He hadn't really expected there to be any leads. The gang had tied up his crew pretty expertly. Leaving them protected from the burning hot sun, and with enough water to last until they were found.

No one had seen the herd moved out. No one saw which direction the gang arrived or left. They'd disappeared as easily as smoke from a campfire on a clear day. How can you hide a thousand head of cattle in open country? It wasn't good for business, losing a whole herd. Nor was it good for business that he'd doubled the crew this time, expecting trouble.

"Good, isn't she?"

"Hmm?" Cal looked up in time to see Nick jerk his head in the direction of the Secretary's office. "Oh yeah. Well, assuming we'll find anything now."

Nick grinned half-heartedly. "No, she's dour but effective. We've certainly had no trouble with all the stuff she did for us. I just wish she weren't related to Tom. Any word out of line is bound to get back to him, isn't it?"

Neither needed to expand that thought. Cal knew better than anyone the problems Nick had staying on the right side of his boss, the local Police Sergeant.

Footsteps returned, turning left into the office on the opposite side of the hallway. They listened silently, as she walked round the room, and sat at the computer desk. A few minutes later they could hear the telltale clatter of keys as she typed something.

"Well, better get back. Only came to check on you." Nick's words were overlaid with the sound of a large herd arriving.

"OK, see you later. We'll be in to wet our whistles, I expect." Moving together they left the wooden building.

It had been built at the turn of the previous century. The senior MacCreadys had not made any changes. They hadn't wanted to live at the ranch. Had merely taken the opportunity of buying the homestead and sufficient land to enable them to rest their cattle between the drive and the railway, thereby obtaining a better price at market.

Now of course, with the loss of Paradise, the old MacCready spread way out, Cal was lodging in the back half of this homestead, running his transport business from the front – when he could get office staff that is. Twenty miles from town, the place had too few attractions for the local single girls. And, was too far away from town for the few married women still in the workforce.

Cal watched the newcomers. They seemed in fine fettle. Not too tired, either, which was a blessing. Perhaps they could get the earlier train? Recoup his money sooner. He waved acknowledgement to his drivers, turning with a heavy sigh back to his paperwork.

The family clock chimed three as he paused in the hallway. Would she have made a spread for the boys? His mother had always managed something home-cooked for their arrival. He tutted, impatient with himself. None of the intervening office staff even noticed the drovers when they arrived tired and dusty, why would an English woman with a cut glass accent do so?

Oh hell, I shoulda turned on the water. Damn and blast! Never mind no food, they'd have no hot water either. Shower and shave were the first things on a drover's mind at the end of the road. Quickly followed by home cooking, then a beer and a bit of … …. Cal closed his mind at that point.

Didn't apply to him, of course. He'd had enough women to last a lifetime. They only addle your brains and nag all the time. He stomped off to the back, damning all women under his breath.

CHAPTER FOUR

Crossing the yard towards the showers, he noticed a cooking smell. Showers were already being run, and his mood lifted somewhat to find the water had been heating ready for their return. Moving right without altering his stride, he made for the back kitchen, as it was called.

Built at a time when homesteaders had staff, the old kitchen had been sited some distance from the main house, thus keeping it cooler. Mum and Dad had converted it to a big self-service canteen with the latest gadgets. This was where food was prepared and served to all the hands. The homestead had it's own small kitchen, perfectly capable of generating food for the family.

Pushing through the door, Cal expected to find a woman helping. Which woman never even crossed his mind. Women from the local township gave Cal MacCready a wide berth now he'd lost Paradise, the big MacCready cattle station.

No one about. Something was beginning to burn. Tentatively moving forward, Cal was not sure what to do about it.

Jacq burst through the main door, nearly bowling him over.

"Out the way. Out the way."

He moved aside as she launched herself at the second oven, grabbing the oven pad ready. Stunned not only by the speed at which she moved, but that she knew what to do.

"Just in time. Phew!" A tray of Yorkshire puddings was dumped onto a mat on the worktop.

"Right. Sorry, can I help you?" Jacq turned back to her boss, still standing at the door with a bemused expression on his face.

"It'll be ready in about five, can you wait? Did you check their pay packets? They'll be over for them soon enough, yeah?"

Turning away without allowing time to reply, Jacq checked the hot shelf, where two platters of meat were steaming. Picking up the tray again, she tapped it expertly against the worktop. The loosened puddings were tipped on to another platter. A similar sized tray was given the same treatment. Both trays were hustled into the sink and washed immediately. They were left to drain on one of the double drainers, jostled next to roasting dishes.

The plate warmer bleeped as it reached the right temperature. Jacq gave a little nod of satisfaction. Removing two enormous dishes of roasted potatoes from the first oven, she put them either side of the meats. Four vegetable dishes the same size rapidly followed them. Gravy appeared as if by magic.

Cal's stomach made appreciative noises, which Jacq appeared not to hear. The drinks cupboard groaned under the weight of cold tinnies. The freezer shelf supported an array of cold dishes.

"Anything else?" She stopped long enough to consider Cal's face.

"If I've missed something, I apologise. Do you want a plate of food before they arrive?" Her hands hovered busily by the plate warmer.

"No, I need to clean up first." Cal was surprised by the softness in his voice. Didn't sound like himself at all.

"Right, well don't forget their wage packets. I need them checked, because I wasn't sure ..." Her voice tailed off at the impatient way Cal nodded.

"Aren't you staying?"

"Hell no. One thing I sure don't need is a kitchen full of cattle drovers at the end of a long drive. Their conversation is likely to be unedifying, to say the least. They'll be quite randy too, I presume."

Twirling away before he could respond, Jacq whirled out of the back kitchen. Cal watched her run across the yard. King whickered. Jacq hesitated.

Turning towards the horse, she felt in her skirt pocket. Cal continued to watch as she petted his horse. Placing her arms round King's neck, she laughed delightedly when he hauled her off her feet. Restored to earth again, Jacq gently rubbed King's muzzle with great affection. Cal watched them.

King nodded violently at the girl before him. Hey, woman, right? Not a girl, too much trouble. Jack's a woman, must be forty or so, easily.

When she continued to stand before the horse, King lowered his head over her shoulder. The nearest he could get to a hug. A spurt of rage swept through Cal. King reserved that gesture for him. Cal had never seen him do it to anyone else.

King continued to nod, pawing the ground to emphasise something. Too far away to hear what Jacq was saying, it was apparent she was talking to King. King pushed her away, and she retreated. Half turning, she offered the apple from her pocket. King whickered again, reaching for the apple on the hand before him. Cal watched, fascinated, as the stallion lipped the hand concealing his prize, until it uncurled and there was his apple.

He snatched it greedily. Spraying half chewed bits of apple everywhere as he tossed his head and chewed. She patted his nose lovingly, moving back towards the office. Was the scene played out for Cal's benefit? Or was she totally unaware his eyes still watched her?

The screen door banged and the buzz of approaching riders filled the air. Turning his back resolutely on the appetising food, Cal headed for the homestead, clean clothes then shower. Then pay packets, then food.

Grabbing the first pair of jeans to hand, he rummaged for a tee-shirt and socks. His bedroom looked good, smelled fresher too than the last time he'd used it. Puzzling this, he headed for the shower block.

Hey, there were even two or three clean towels still folded on the shelves. Goodo.

By the time he'd finished a thoroughly good shower, not even considering conserving water, Cal was feeling remotely human for a change. Anticipating some good food, he strolled casually into the dressing area.

Jacq was collecting towels, treading carefully over the discarded clothing, humming a tune. "Oops."

The wet towels in his hand automatically moved diagonally down across his body.

A cheeky grin briefly lit the face before him. "You're quite safe, sonny. Nothing I've not seen before."

Leaning passed him, she collected another couple of towels. Turning away with her arms full, Jacq slid through the doors and out of sight. Damn and blast!

Dressing rapidly, Cal headed back to his office. The noise and good cheer in the back kitchen meant the boys were fine for the time being. Better check those wage packets.

A steaming plate of food bore silent witness to Jacq's actions since their last meeting. Stuffing the food down, without really tasting it, Cal's other hand reached for the pay packets. He checked the gross amounts against the running total he carried in his head.

Checking the figures off her list, he noticed she had written Bonus? against the regular crew. Almost as if it was a reminder of his half formed thought on the ride back.

The coffee jug was still in place. Having finished his food, Cal reached for it automatically. Bloody Hell! Blowing on his fingers, he shook his head.

It had never occurred to him she'd replace the bloody thing. And now look! He looked at the smarting hand. Hmmm, not badly damaged. Well, alright. Not hurt at all, just shock. He hadn't expected the pot to be boiling.

Before he could take a drink, the noisy drovers arrived. Paying out the little packets took a good hour.

Footsteps sounded in the hallway, together with a brief knock.

"Anything else you need?"

The grin had gone, to be replaced with what Cal thought of as Jacq's old boiler face. "I'll be in my trailer if you need me. OK?"

Breathing a sigh of relief to be left alone at last, Cal surveyed the letter folder. Right read that in bed. He looked blankly at the empty dinner plate. Seconds? Yes, he'd have seconds, if there were any, that is.

Making his way to the back kitchen, he waved cheerily to the drovers, now heading for town. They'd be back tomorrow about lunchtime. He could manage in the meantime. Hell, they deserved a break after their hard work.

He piled a plate with more food. Sitting in the fly-screened verandah, which ran round three sides of the back kitchen, Cal mulled over his problems.

The Tax Authorities were pushing for returns. His father had always employed an Accountant, well ever since Mum died. I should simply do the same ... except that they cost, don't they? And I can't see them waiting to be paid, not once they get a good look at the Accounts.

Jacq pushed through the screen door, muttering. Scraping the plates clean, she loaded the commercial dishwasher, placing the knives and forks tidily into the special containers. While that whirled to itself, she moved steadily round the room, dumping rubbish into a garbage sack, stacking more plates for another wash load. The leavings were all scraped into the big buckets his mother always used, and dumped outside the back door ready for the dogs.

The cleaned plates were expertly removed and replaced with the second batch. Worktops and table surfaces were scrubbed down while she waited for the second load to finish.

Gazing round the room to check, Jacq caught sight of Cal sitting in the shadows. "Sorry, wouldn't have come in if I'd seen you there. You could probably do with some peace and quiet. Well, I've nearly finished." She nodded curtly, disappearing into the storeroom. She re-stocked the drinks fridge, and left with a short goodnight.

Cal's mind re-traced everything he knew about the stranger. Tom had insisted she was the answer to his prayers, and now reluctantly, Cal was forced to admit she did indeed seem to be. Mind, ... proof of the pudding and all that. Depends whether I can find anything again, once she's gone.

Jacqueline Tregissick was working her way round Australia. She'd apparently been in Charleville six months or so, already. She had a large camper van in which she lived and a battered Land Rover she towed on a trailer behind it. She'd worked for eighteen years in a Bank.

Was having a gap year or two, Tom said. No pressure to return to the UK. No family then, thought Cal, unsurprised in view of her attitude. She seemed perfectly happy with her roaming lifestyle. It wouldn't suit Cal. He was too rooted in this place. Well, not this homestead, but Parad..., the old one that had been in the family for generations. *That's* where his roots were.

She'd been hired by the Police Chief, which hadn't endeared her to Nick in particular. Her relationship to his Sergeant almost certainly meant Police Constable Nick Peters would have trouble with her. But her lack of response to his overtures had been part of the problem too. Until her arrival it had seemed unlikely any female could resist Nick's charms. Still, resist she had, and Nick was never done whinging about her.

Jacq had travelled quite happily between the various Police Stations, transferring all their records onto the new Computer System, demonstrating the systems to the various officers as she went.

OK, so a computer buff... ... maybe. And knew her way round banks, but why would someone with that background want to travel out here? In this wilderness called The Outback, still mentioned with awe in that way. Especially an English gir... woman?

Blast you, call 'em women. Girls are flighty, beautiful but flighty. They knock you down, stomp all over you, leaving you battered and bruised, nursing a broken heart for the rest of your days. Leave it blast you!

Turning his mind resolutely away from grim thoughts, Cal added, she's got to be forty or more to have that much assurance. So no spring chicken then. King's attitude towards Jacq returned to his mind. King's not taken in by anything false, yet he'd seemed really impressed with her. Must be the apples, Cal decided sourly.

In bed, he read through the Letters folder. Surprised, shocked even, to discover she had sent prim forceful reminders to all his bad debts, seeking immediate payment as an alternative to legal redress. In some cases the bills went back a year or more.

My God! What'll they think? Probably that I need the money. Well, I do actually, before the Bank begins to press for repayment of the bank loan.

He rummaged through the Bank Statements. The Loan had been reduced! He'd been away two weeks, well three, if you count the week he breezed in to town and hired her. And she'd made a repayment on his Loan!

Checking the current account statement, he was amazed at the small black figure. Hell, I can't remember ever being in the black, not since the old man passed on. He gazed blindly round his room, thinking about his business, or at least what was left of it.

When his head started reeling with the effort of concentrating, Cal slid the folders to the floor, and settled down. Expecting, as usual, to fall asleep the minute his head hit the pillow.

Pillow, …pillow. My god, it's clean. Bed's fresh too. That was his last conscious thought.

CHAPTER FIVE

Felt good though, to wake up in fresh linen in a fresh room. Luxuriating in his unaccustomed surroundings, he sighed as he wallowed in the comfort of his bed. When the dogs started, Cal leapt to his feet.

Jacq was already running towards the cattle pen. Standing on the bottom rail, she wedged the heels of her boots in place to counterbalance her knees and started looking. She climbed up another rail, pulling small binoculars out of their cover to peer more closely.

Pulling boots over his jeans, Cal zipped the latter hastily as he ran for his herd. The dogs were barking and creating about something, that's for sure.

Everything had been sound last night, when he'd fed the dogs on his last round. And now it was not. What now?

Jacq's head turned slightly in his direction. "It's in the back right hand corner. I can't see it clearly. Do you want the keys for the quad bikes?"

Cal ran for King. Swinging up on to his back, hitching his hands firmly into the rich thick mane, he yelled, "Bring a gun." He didn't stop for her response. Heading directly round the fence towards the trouble she'd located. Hell and damnation!

The quad bike swooped to a stop six feet away, and she loped to his side. "What is it?"

One of the steers was having trouble... calving? Bit late. And too, the drive wouldn't have helped her condition. The stricken cow lay on her side panting.

"Do something," Jacq shook his arm. "Can you do anything? Should I phone a vet, maybe?" Shaking her head, she mumbled, "Stupid. Stupid thing to say with these distances."

"Fetch the bundle of thick twine and a bottle of disinfectant from the storeroom in the stable yard. NOW."

She ran back to the quad bike, keeping the noise down until it would no longer spook the herd.

Cal dragged the cow clear of the other cattle, setting the dogs to keep them back. All the cattle continued to low anxiously. Reaching his arm into his patient, Cal checked his preliminary assessment.

Jacq was back before he'd finished. She knelt patiently by his side, while he finished his examination. Passing over the twine, having doused it liberally in the disinfectant, Jacq moved to the animal's head, and started soothing and calming. Although exhausted, it still lowed nervously.

As soon as Jacq's efforts were rewarded, Cal wrapped the cord round his hand and reached in again. Looping the twine over the tiny hooves, he pulled both ends back out.

"Hold on to her. I'm gonna have to heave a bit, but I have got it facing the right way now."

Jacq nodded, talking quietly and calmly to the cow, while Cal sorted himself out and started heaving. She cradled the cow's head on her lap, stroking and soothing, and slowly the cow relaxed again. The calf was safely delivered and Mum started into the licking that would clean it up.

Cal leaned back on his heels, dragging in a few deep breaths. Jacq handed over a towel she'd brought along. He used it to wipe his face, neck and body, then started on his blood stained arms.

"Everything OK, now?" He nodded. "Right, I'll make some coffee."

Jacq patted King in passing. The horse butted her, nearly knocking her off her feet. The warm chuckle surprised Cal, but not the horse. He butted again. A hand reached into a pocket and withdrew. The horse butted, twice. Cal watched.

The horse whickered gently in Jacq's ear, to be rewarded with one of the little green apples he loved. King followed to the quad bike. Jacq shook her head, brushing her hands together in a "that's it" gesture. King blew down his nostrils, spraying her face. She rubbed her mucky face against his shoulder. King tried a play bite.

"Ah, ah," was said in a warning tone he obviously recognised. King turned away, looking over his shoulder at the woman mounting the quad bike. Jacq nodded, King nodded back.

Cal was fascinated by this byplay. He'd never seen King so taken with someone. He checked the cow, which had been absorbed back into the herd. The others seemed to be taken with the new (and late) arrival. Seems OK. Bonus actually, to bring in one more than he set out with, Cal nearly chuckled. Hey, things *are* improving.

Walking back to the homestead with King heavy breathing in his ear, Cal was surprised to notice yesterday's towels already hanging limply in the still air. While he was trying to work out the implications, Jacq breezed out of the washhouse to collect them. She took the time to fold each towel carefully into a neat pile, before hanging a fresh load onto the drying lines. The basket of dried towels was taken direct to the Shower Block, and presumably returned to the shelves there.

They met up on the walk back to the homestead. "Morning," was said cheerily in his direction. "What time's Steve due?" was asked over his reply, as if it mattered not one way or the other.

"Mid-morning, if he's had no problems."

Jacq nodded, while asking what he wanted for breakfast.

"I can do some toast."

"Righto. Seeya." Turning at the corner of the homestead, Jacq made for the trailer.

The homestead kitchen too had been cleaned. In the early morning light it looked cool and inviting. Coffee was steaming in the jug, bread was stacked in the toaster, simply waiting to be pressed into place. Taking butter and marmalade out of the fridge, Cal was surprised to see steaks de-frosting.

A couple of steaks? Who for? Was she entertaining in his absence? The scowl that lingered permanently behind his eyes grew again. Ten minutes later, Cal was surprised to see Jacq heading for the back kitchen. What's she up to?

Stopping at the shower block briefly, Jacq then disappeared into the kitchen. When she didn't immediately re-appear, the scowl grew.

Glancing at the clock, Cal plunged some more bread into the toaster. He couldn't remember feeling this hungry before. Perhaps it was the fresh food, freshly cooked? Something had certainly improved his appetite.

At ten to nine Jacq hit the ground outside the kitchen door at a trot, hurrying back to the homestead.

She stopped at the dunny on her way into the office. Nine was still chiming on the old clock when she knocked briefly at his office door, coming straight in with the coffee tray.

"Anything else you need?"

"Eeer, we need to talk about the office side sometime."

"OK, do you need a hand with feed or that?"

Cal made for the door. "Nope."

"OK, wage packets when you get back?" Jacq disappeared before he'd considered her request.

In the main barn, three sacks of feed had been loaded onto a trailer and hitched to a quad bike. No sign of the keys.

Lengthening his stride, Cal made for the Store Room. The keys were kept in the top drawer of the old desk in there.

Gone! They'd bloody gone!

Looking blankly round the room, he spotted a box on the wall. "Keys". Inside, there was a hook for each key, above which was the registration number. Each key now had a label printed with its registration number. Huh, no more hunting for the right key. He'd kept meaning to get round to it, just never had any time. Too busy. Still, it sure made life easier.

Taking out the key he wanted, Cal returned to the partially loaded trailer. Why three sacks? He added another one, checked the hitch and drove off. An hour later, having divided the feed between the cattle in the far meadow, he stopped at the Shower Block to switch on the water. Done. Little Miss Efficiency.

Cooking smells were wafting out through the kitchen extract fan, and he sniffed appreciatively. The second batch of towels had been collected.

"We'll talk about the office things this evening in my trailer, please." He hadn't heard her join him on his walk back to the office. Turning towards her, he raised a quizzical eyebrow.

"Hey, you're quite safe. Just need some privacy. Lots to talk about, right?" Jacq nodded brusquely, holding the screen door back for him, going straight through to her own office.

The pay packets sat on the little tray his father had always used. Cal's mind took him back to the years when his father used it. Why hadn't he recognised the tray yesterday? Where on earth had she dredged it up?

❈ ❈ ❈ ❈ ❈

Aged about eight, he'd wandered into the family room on the old homestead. Hell, even four years later he still couldn't bring himself to say the name. Paradise!

His great-great-great-grandmother had named it, when the MacCready's first arrived and bought the land. Paradise. The name was still redolent with the smell of the eucalyptus trees planted to shade the main house. The nearby river had been dammed to provide a pool (well, lake) of water for the animals. He and the other children played in its dwindling waters through the long hot summers.

Back then he'd had no idea the station was in such a precarious position. Could any action by the boy he had been have saved it? Sighing, Cal shook his head. Concentrate on the pay packets.

Yes, that's the only way to get through the black bitterness shrouding his days. Don't even think about those days when he was an eligible bachelor, the prize catch of the local area. Now, in his mid-forties, divorced and virtually penniless, he wasn't much of a catch, even if someone would put up with his temper. The scowl grew again. Dad musta gambled it all away.

All that sweat and toil, gambled away by his father, following the death of his mother nearly eight years ago. How could one man lose so much in four years? The healthy bank balances, the rich pastureland, the massive spread, all gone. Either boozed or gambled away, because his father had lost the will to live when his wife died.

Don't go there, he instructed his busy brain. Pay packets. But his mind continued to play that long ago scene, even while his conscious mind concentrated on this second string of pay packets.

❋ ❋ ❋ ❋ ❋

Mum had been sitting on Dad's knees as they checked the money together, before folding it neatly inside each little envelope. Dad was licking the envelopes, complaining about the taste. Mum kissing him with each one, to take the taste away.

Such a surge of longing swept through that eight year old, and again through the older man he'd become. Cal wanted what they had, what they'd had throughout their lives. Watching their closeness and banter, Cal had mostly felt like an outsider.

On this occasion, Dad had growled some dismissal, but Mum had risen to her feet.

"What is it son?" She always spoke softly, always.

The older man recognised now, the love in that long ago phrase. The child he had been had not seen it. Had felt unloved and unwanted because of the joy apparent in his parents' loving companionship. Turning away, the child poured a glass of cold water from the newly acquired fridge, before retreating to his bedroom.

Had he spoken at all? Cal couldn't remember exchanging any words. The only memory remained that silent acknowledgement of their great involvement in each other. The feeling he was somehow a blot on their happiness. His presence somehow cast a damper over the little cameo he'd interrupted.

Feelings, which had grown, nurtured as they were by his father's gruff teachings. His blunt insistence Cal be better at everything than any of the hired hands. And he was.

It was no consolation at the end of a hard day. Even now, Cal weakly longed to come home to the happy atmosphere his mother always created. Put a sock in it, he instructed himself.

Mess boy. Hell, what made her, he jerked his head quickly in the direction of the other office, make up a pay packet for the mess boy?

He'd just come along. Not been hired or anything formal. Just for the experience. That's what he'd said. "Please Mr MacCready. I'll come for the experience." And now, here was this pay packet.

Reluctantly he admitted the boy had been useful. Jock was getting a bit long in the tooth to be droving. Well, driving the mess-truck. They'd all been glad of the help provided by the youngster.

The scornful noise he made while weighing up the pay packet and the youngster for whom it was intended, caused a temporary lull in the tapping from the other office. Cal paused expectantly. The key tapping resumed. He returned to his study of the pay packet.

Half pay… hmmm… well, reasonable I suppose. We do need someone to help old Jock.

Diverted, his mind added, need to train up a replacement I guess. Speak to Jock. Find out when he wants to retire. Hell, he must be getting on. Hell yes, he's been here all my life. I can't remember him ever being young.

The sound of another herd drew his attention. Standing at his office window, Cal watched the cattle being driven into the near paddock. They'd be going to market first. He counted the shadowy riders he could see. Yup, all present and correct.

CHAPTER SIX

The mess truck turned off, rolling towards the stockyards and back kitchen. Jacq trekked quickly across his peripheral vision, heading for the back kitchen. Cal poured two coffees, strolling casually to meet Steve. Glad to have his best buddy back all in one piece.

A large 4x4 rolled into the stockyard behind the mess truck. He could already hear the two girls chirruping at their mother to release them to greet their father. Steve gave him a quick update, while strolling towards his family drinking coffee. Swinging his twins up into an arc, he smiled at his wife. When the girls ran giggling in the direction of the horses, Steve reached for her.

Cal turned away. Embarrassed to witness the passion these two felt after four weeks apart, even after ten years of marriage. His lips twisted bitterly to recall his own greeting from his loving wife. Listlessly he followed the little girls, intent on keeping them out of danger, at least until their parents were finished.

The usual ritual of safe homecoming proceeded around them. The girls returned to Cal, wanting something he was unable to decipher. Cal told them to ask their Mummy first, irritated that he still couldn't interpret their baby talk. They retreated back to their parents in a rush, and Cal strolled towards the back kitchen.

The first of the hands arrived at the front, and Jacq erupted from the back door, nearly knocking him down.

"Nope, blast you! Just eat, right." She scowled ferociously at Cal. Lumping him in with the cold damnation she used so scathingly on the single word. "Men!" Without apology, she marched determinedly back to the office.

The screen door clattered shut, and Cal was in time to catch a glimpse of Terry, grinning maddeningly.

"What d'y do?"

"I like 'em feisty."

"That's not feisty that's disinterested. What d'y do?"

Marginally embarrassed Terry said, "Pinched her bum as she went passed. Grabbed a good handful, too."

"Listen mate. Leave her alone. Have some fun in town, but leave her alone. She's damned good at her job."

Turning about, the drover muttered something. Cal spun him back quickly. "Say that again. Say it again and I'll knock your flaming block off."

Silenced by the massive fist in his face, the drover muttered, "Keeping her for yourself?"

"Not bloody likely, is it? But I can't get staff to work out here and she's good, so if she says off limits, that's how I want it to stay. Right?" When the drover nodded, Cal added, "Spread the word too. Don't want anyone getting outa line. Right?"

Spoiling for a fight and reluctant to let the guy go, Cal eventually dropped his fist, releasing the shirtfront.

Following the drover into the back kitchen, he was greeted by the smell of food again. His stomach growled appreciatively. Helping himself to a plate of food, he straddled the bench next to Steve. Steve grunted in answer to his questions, while chewing and swallowing food quickly.

"Nearly as good as your ma's."

Cal nodded in agreement.

"Who cooked it?" asked Sheena, Steve's pretty wife of ten years.

"Jack Tregissick."

"Oh, I've heard about her. She's a tough old bird, right? Must be to live way out here with you guys."

Cal shook his head. "Only been here coupla weeks. Was in town before that. Working for the Police Department."

"Nick says she's a right old boot. Po-faced and sour."

"That just means she blew him out. Don't take him seriously, do you?"

Sheena chuckled back. "No, that figgers. If it doesn't fall at his feet, then it's gotta be gay, right?"

Steve said warningly, "Little pitchers."

"OK, OK." Sheena's hand brushed lightly against Steve's.

Embarrassed by the telltale twitch inside Steve's jeans, Cal said, "Better go. Soon be pay-time. Seeya."

He scraped his plate clean, stacking it with the others in the dishwasher rack. Only about half of the guys had done the same. The other plates lay around the tables, littered with scraps and in some cases, stubbed out ciggies. Disgusting, he thought.

Hurrying back to his office, Cal listened to the banter of the crew, hoping Jacq was the tough old bird of report, or she'd be burning with embarrassment at their comments. His presence slowly silenced the men, queuing impatiently for their reward for four weeks on a dusty trail, moving a herd of cattle towards the railhead.

"Listen up. There is to be no further talk of that nature here. Save it for your private time and private places, godit? While you are on my premises, you will treat my staff with respect. Nobody, but nobody, in a civilised world, wants to listen to that sort of smut. If you really cannot control yourselves, then I won't be employing you again."

He waited for acceptance to spread through the waiting faces, before opening wide his office door, in a gesture that spread back in time through five generations. Cal MacCready sure as hell didn't want to be the one to finally lose his grip on this patch of the Outback. It was bad enough they'd lost Paradise, wasn't it? Let alone this small place.

At the end of the queue, he offered Steve his pay packet saying, "Where's MacGregor?"

"Waiting for a lift back to town."

"Right. I'll walk over with you."

❋ ❋ ❋ ❋ ❋

Back in his office, Cal thought briefly about the expression on MacGregor's face when offered the envelope. He'd recognised it. The pride of being able to earn some money, and the loss of face in admitting how desperately he needed it.

"Take it, labourer's worthy of his hire." The boy had blushed brightly, to the amusement of all around. "Come back with the boys tomorrow. Might have a job you could do." The same pleasure washed briefly over the young face.

Hell, I remember being that young, that greedy for attention. Never got it though, did I?

His mind drew him inexorably back to his own youth. His parents had been totally absorbed in each other and running the station. He'd never been able to hold their attention.

Even his Report Cards from school were merely nodded over quickly, before the old man reached for his mother. Cal felt his whole life had been spent watching his father reach for his mother. Still, long time ago now.

Checking his wrist, he found he'd not put on the watch his mother had given him before she'd died.

"This was my Dad's. He'd have wanted you to have it."

Momentarily diverted by the fact that he knew nothing, absolutely nothing about his family, he dragged his mind back to the matter in hand. Shaking his head to clear the sound of his mother's voice from his brain, Cal assessed the level of sunlight around him, gauging it was nearing tea.

Wandering into the back kitchen he found Jock and Jacq in quiet conversation. On the serving area, one plate was piled with sandwiches, another two held biscuits or cake. An enormous teapot rested on the corner of the hot plate. Mugs stood nearby, together with milk and sugar.

Not liking to interrupt, Cal sat separately, eating his way through his tea, working out a routine for the upcoming week. Jacq and Jock argued amicably about who would clear up and set out breakfast for any early birds. He listened absently to their banter. They were obviously on the same mental wavelength, which was odd, after all they'd only just met, hadn't they? He ransacked his memory again.

No, no they must have met at Tom's. After all Jock had barely been at the spread this last few months. That's why Cal thought Jock was retiring ... because he'd spent a lot of time in town recently.

Jock rose, rolling towards the door. Long years spent with horses had rounded out his legs, giving him a rolling gait like a sailor. Jacq chased after him, tucking her hand under his elbow.

"OK, OK. Do it together then."

They went off towards the stock. When the taller woman leaned towards the bent old man, Cal felt again that sense of exclusion, which seemed to be his lot in life.

❋ ❋ ❋ ❋ ❋

"Oh," Jacq stopped in the doorway. "I was just coming to do that."

"Done now."

"Thanks."

Just as if it were her place and not his. Unaware that his face lightened briefly, even though his voice remained sour, Cal turned quickly away.

"Jock's checking on that calf. He says he'll give a hand with the feed tomorrow. Do you expect them all back?" In answer to his nod, Jacq added, "Maybe I'll put out some salad as well tomorrow. I'll leave the chiller shelf set up. Must be cheaper than keep re-cooling it."

Turning to leave, she raised her voice to say, "Anything special you need tomorrow?"

The screen door slammed behind them as they made for the homestead.

"What time?" she asked, as soon as they were striding out.

Cal normally had to adapt his stride on those rare occasions when he walked with anyone, anyone at all. But on the walk back, Jacq kept pace effortlessly, despite the height of the heels on her sandals.

"Wha..t! Oh yeah, eeerm soon as, really."

"Now, if you like. What time are you meeting Nick?" He arched an eyebrow questioningly. "Nick said you always go out the night after a drive. I just assumed it'd be tonight. Still, if we don't finish, we can carry on tomorrow. Seeya in five."

Jacq wheeled off in the direction of the Shower Block. Cal noticed the towels, now blowing gently in the breeze, which always sprang up towards evening. He blushed recalling her visit to the Shower Block yesterday. Yeah, she musta cleaned up while they ate, again.

Half watching the neat efficient way Jacq swiped the towels off the line and into the basket, seeming to fold them in four as they floated through the air, Cal strolled towards King. They'd be back on the shelves soon at this rate. Patting and petting his horse, Cal talked with a freedom he'd never experienced with a fellow human.

CHAPTER SEVEN

"Come in, come in," she said impatiently, at his tentative knock on the trailer door.

"Tea, coffee?"

They sat opposite each other in the compact kitchen divided from a miniscule lounge area by a bar. For the first time Cal spotted Jacq was embarrassed.

"Look," glancing briefly at his face and away again. "Look, this is marginally awkward. So if you want me to but out, that's OK. Just say so, and I'll but out. Move on, as soon as you find a replacement. No probs, no hard feelings."

"OK." Cal wondered what was coming.

Jacq tossed a small black electronic square across the intervening space.

"What is it?"

"Transmitter."

Cal looked up, catching her eyes briefly, surprised by the troubled expression they showed. "You mean…"

She nodded.

"Where was it?"

"Your office. I've just taken it out. Hope they won't realise they're off air. Put it back later before Nick gets here."

"Before Nick…"

"Yup. Don't know who's at the other end. Could be anyone, couldn't it?"

"But… Nick? He's my oldest mate."

"Hmmm."

In the long pause which followed, she watched Cal uncertainly.

"Well, someone surely installed it, right? There's two in my office, one in the lounge, another in the kitchen. I'm hoping the three in the back kitchen are out of commission." She tried a light-hearted grin. "Don't want the Equal Opps people after your men for their conversation, do we?"

Cal looked bemusedly at the chip in his hand.

Jacq coughed nervously. "There's one in your bedroom too."

She was saying the homestead was bugged. His homestead! But who? And why?

"What should I do? How did you find them?"

"Eerch, spring cleaning, y'know and just uncovered them. I thought we could try to track down the people who planted them. What do you reckon?" He shook his head. "They've not got a huge range, must be somewhere local. There's a couple of storerooms I couldn't get into. Might be there. Finding the recordings won't help that much, really. Although there might just be some clue to their identity."

"What does Tom say?"

"Not told 'im. Your homestead, your livelihood. Why would I tell Tom?" Jacq eyed Cal belligerently.

"He said you could sniff out trouble. Is this why he wanted you out here?"

She smiled grimly, which made no difference to the expression in her eyes. "Nope. He wanted me out here, *safely* out of the way, but where he could still check up on me. Won't let me out of his sight, now." She sighed as a memory flitted through her mind. "Oh well. I suppose it's nice someone cares. And it's a nice town. Wouldn't mind staying on a bit. Once we've sorted you out."

Cal's eyes returned to the transmitter he held. "How do you know about these?"

"Iffy past. Ask no questions, you'll be told no lies," was said with an air of finality.

"And you'll simply refix it?"

"Sure. Don't want them to know we've cottoned on, do we?"

When Cal continued to look blankly at the small piece of surveillance kit, Jacq said, "Right, leave that. Discuss it once you've had time to come to terms with the wider implications. In the meantime, we have a ... *you* have a more serious problem with your business."

Retrieving the kit, she tossed it lightly in one hand, while watching him. "Bear this in mind, won't you, with whoever you talk to in the homestead?"

Once he had nodded, she took him through his business problems. Explaining clearly and succinctly, that failure to comply with recent regulations meant he was in serious danger of finding himself in jail. She walked him through the regulations and the remedial action she had taken. It seemed he had just caught the deadline and was safe.

"Unless of course, your silent listeners were hoping you'd not understood the regulations?" Jacq waited for a comment.

"They'd be right." He said eventually. "I just kept brushing it under the carpet. Hoping it'd go away."

"OK, fixed now tho' eh? Just don't go mentioning it to anyone at all. No one, right? If you do get trouble, we may get a bit nearer to finding out who is behind all this."

Moving on, unembarrassedly discussing his finances in an impersonal way, Jacq said, "There seems to be a massive overspend somewhere. I'm not quite sure… … it all seems *very* vague. But even allowing for inflation, your outgoings have risen considerably over the last four/five years. You need to cut down your wages bill. I can appreciate why you took on extra lads, but really… well…. Two reasons for sticking to your regulars, one is that they might – only might – be more loyal. The second is, fewer people gossiping about what they see and hear. So, stick with your regulars only. No matter what. We have ways round your probs without hauling in extra mouths to feed. Long term you need to replace Jock. Keep on young MacGregor. He's sound, I'd say. Needs the money for a start, but also a good cook. He'll not chouse you out of the food quality either. Point to bear in mind. OK?" She waited politely until Cal nodded.

Jacq seemed to have grasped the salient features of his business in the time she'd been here. Certainly she'd understood more than Cal had about the regulations he'd missed. His mind was distracted again by his initial impression on arriving home yesterday.

"OK, no need to pay me until I finish up. And, you don't draw much either, so that's good. My major problem has been finding out who is checking your computer. They also seem to have switched some funds out of your accounts. Er, did you know your wife still has…"

"*Ex-wife,*" was said with a barely suppressed growl, but a return of the bitter tone Jacq had first heard when Cal arrived at Tom's.

"Alright, *ex*-wife still has access to your bank accounts?"

The growl became a roar.

"I… that is… I instructed the bank to suspend all drawings unless they had your signature, until you sorted out a new Mandate. I hope that was OK? In the meantime, I keep niggling away at those transfers. Haven't got very far yet. Any questions?"

Unable to keep up with the various items, and still trying to sort things out in his mind, Cal muttered, "Computer? Over spend?"

"Yeah, not protected is it? Anyone can get into it. Look at all your personal stuff. I'm fairly sure some large sums are missing. I need to have a proper look, not just bits. Haven't been able to get down to it properly, yet."

Cal shook his head. What could he say? Nothing. While he'd been looking the other way, someone had been bugging his home, switching money and generally playing in his private stuff? He'd never spotted it, yet this woman had! How come? How come, when she'd only been here two/three weeks?

A warm tanned hand hovered over his.

"Don't worry about it now. Have a good time with Nick."

The warm chuckle he'd heard yesterday when Jacq was talking to King, echoed through the trailer at some thought accompanying the words. Cal wished he could ask what had prompted it, but hesitated too long.

"Sleep on it. We can speak again tomorrow. Nothing's going to happen tonight."

They stood together.

As she showed him out, Jacq said, "Try not to worry. I have already put some solutions in place. The rest we can talk about. Go shower for your night out, while I restore your lodger to his rightful or should I say, wrongful place." The conspiratorial smile warmed Cal in places he didn't want to know about.

Jacq snuck into the house silently, in the wake of Cal marching firmly along to his bedroom. He hoped she'd be alright to sneak out again.

Meeting Jock in the showers, Cal was relieved to hear him say, "Have a good time boss. I can manage the stock. Seeya tomorrow."

Good, gave him a chance to let off steam.

CHAPTER EIGHT

Nick's car drew up. Nick might have been responsible for his lodgers? Nah, they'd been mates since school. They'd started in the same class and stayed friends no matter what. Nick Peters was six months older than Cal, but had never married.

Always steered well clear of the Parson's mousetrap. One of the politer expressions Nick used to mean marriage. Nick seemed never to have calmed down, was still pretty much the man he'd been in his teens and twenties. Was still volatile, determined, opinionated, not to say pig-headed, which caused him a whole heap of problems especially with his Sergeant, Tom Crowthorn.

Cal would bet his life on this particular mate. As he would on Steve Collins. There weren't too many people fell in that category, were there?

Yeah, there'd been a crowd of bright rich young things, who had gathered round his wife whenever she held court. But they had vanished as the marriage become more and more acrimonious. They certainly never saw Cal if they passed him in town. Not that it bothered Cal, well, not much. He'd never had anything in common with them, having more to turn over in his mind than the latest fashions, the latest electronic gadgets.

Tonight, for the most part, Cal managed to forget about the implications behind Jacq's words. Well, at least, he hoped it wasn't too obvious to anyone else in his circle. His evening settled into its normal channels. Plenty of cold beer, plenty of female company – well, if you weren't too fussy, that is.

Actually, he was having a good time, until Nick said, "Hear you've been reading the Riot Act to your troops. Tom kept on about Equal Opps while Jacq worked at the station, so she musta nagged him about it. Can't say I'm that keen myself. Seems she's a right old boot. Equality? Barefoot and pregnant, that's where they belong."

Cal looked at his friend with fresh eyes. Nick really meant it. Oh, Cal paid lip service too, but niggling at the back of his mind had been the pattern of his parents' lives. Their happy companionship. Alright, it was based on sex. You only had to recall the gleam in their eyes after a drive, but they seemed able to keep control of that, and still organise the business. Each taking responsibility for their own area of expertise, but overlapping in some way to build a seamless, thriving enterprise. Partnership is what they'd called it.

Sounded about right to their son, many years later. But hey, women don't want that, do they? They just want a meal ticket.

Look what happened when he lost the old place. Zilch, all the pretty butterflies vanished on the breeze. Didn't seem to matter who they married, as long as he was rich enough to keep them in comfort.

Looking back, Cal was conscious that the vague unhappiness he'd always felt with Diane, had crystallised. Discovering he'd never been happy with dreamy Diane, caused another frown to appear on his face. Cal had always put the difference in their personalities down to the ten-year age gap. Diane, she'd been pretty and perfectly turned out for every occasion. Local Beauty, Riding champion etc, etc, but she seemed to have no heart underneath it all. Brittle and arrogant, convinced she held a special place free from ordinary worries. The best of everything was hers by right, without effort, without thought.

Another of his father's expressions came to mind. Neither use nor ornament. Hell Dad was always winding Diane up. Is that why she hated him so? Why didn't I see it at the time?

A hand snaked down his shirt front. He stopped it quickly in its downward thrust.

"Hi Cal. Want some company?"

As if his thoughts had conjured the girl out of the crowded bar, Diane was working her way onto his lap. He stood quickly, almost overturning his chair, in his anxiety not to have her so close.

"What's the matter hon? Don't trust yourself?"

A burst of merriment greeted this sally, but Cal wasn't in the mood. Sitting the drunken girl on his chair, he jerked his head towards the dunnies, saying "be right back."

Unable to delay his return any longer, he breathed a heartfelt sigh of relief. Diane and Nick had both vanished.

It was short-lived when Nick came back with fresh drinks, saying "Diane's in the Ladies. She'll be back."

"Oh, I thought you'd gone off together."

"No mate. She's your girl."

"Hey, she's married. Oughta remember it too. Not behave like she is."

"You had her first. Hey, actually you didn't. Anyway, when did you become a prude? You've been sniffing around her since the divorce."

Trying to work out when his attitude had changed, Cal realised he was too drunk to make the effort. But hey, she was, wasn't she? Married! I mean, married to old Gough, not me. Should stick to her vows. He stored Nick's words away for later... when he wasn't drunk. What did he mean? I *didn't* have her first?

Diane continued to pester and tease until Cal finally made it clear he was no longer interested. He didn't want Diane, ...he didn't want *any woman* upsetting his life again now. He'd reached a period of calm after four years of anxiety and loneliness. He could certainly manage his life without help, especially female help.

"You'll be sorry."

The drovers looked amazed as Diane stomped out on the words.

Nick said, "I thought you were storming that citadel?"

"Nah mate. Gone passed that stage."

Shocked to discover that somehow, during the past few weeks when he'd not been into town, he had gone passed that stage. He was much more interested in what Jacq had discovered about his business. Much more interested in rescuing his inheritance, than in pursuing the girl who had broken his heart way back, when he first lost Paradise.

He'd lost the girl he thought he loved and Paradise in one fell swoop. The idea appealed to his drunken brain. Fancy carrying a torch for her all these years! She was certainly no better than she should be. Mind you, he'd not helped by sniffing round like a dog. Limping heartbreakingly along, gut-wrenched every time she looked in his direction. Waiting to rush back in at the merest sniff of her petticoats, the slightest of smiles. He'd not looked at another woman since the divorce!

Four years with no sex? Hell longer, Diane had been real mean with her favours even when married. Various old fashioned tenets brushed into his mind, as he sat steadily drinking.

Quietly watching his drovers get even drunker, he thought, one of them could be working against me? He sat in a haze of smoke and laughter, pondering this thought.

Nah mate, trust them all. They were hand-picked by either Dad or me. They must be sound, must be.

❋ ❋ ❋ ❋ ❋

Cal ended up on the couch at Nick's, which was why they always used Nick's car. If Nick made the grade, that is got lucky, then Cal caught a ride back to Nick's place to sleep it off. He could catch the crew transport back to the homestead the following day. A habit set up in their teens and resurrected following Cal's divorce.

Nick after all, was still happily single, pursuing any bright butterfly that fluttered his way. And there were many. Nick seemed to have made a golden progress through the local single girls, and even a few of the married ones as well. No wonder he'd been unimpressed by Jacq's ongoing refusal.

Cal stirred restlessly. That isn't how he wanted his life to be. But then, this celibacy wasn't what he'd expected of life either. Surely there was more?

Today young Macgregor was driving. Tam grinned happily at Cal, who was peering blearily through the red mist in front of his eyes. The chorus of groans from the bus, as it bumped and rattled its way back to the homestead, only served to make Cal feel greener than he did already.

Following the trail of hung-over drovers and riders into the back kitchen, Cal's nostrils were assailed by the flavour of bacon frying. Jock was cooking up a storm. There was nothing like the smell of frying bacon to cure the loudest of hangovers.

Standing blissfully under the shower later, Cal contemplated his feelings about Diane, his feelings about his marriage. Cured, yes he was cured, …well, half cured. He no longer dragged around a leaden weight on the end of a chain; a leaden weight that had been his heart, way back, when he knew how to feel. Inordinately cheered by a brighter prospect, he whistled softly under his breath while dressing.

Towels were again hanging to dry as he made his way out to King. Jacq was standing silently, arms round King's neck, hugging the horse. At his approach, King snorted his normal welcome, causing the woman to step away.

"Hi. Good night?" She was turning away before he could reply.

He put out a hand to detain her. "Do you ride?"

"Yeah, not in a while tho'."

"Well if you want a ride, let me know. I'll fix you up with something suitable."

"Thanks."

Cal was unable to read the expression in the eyes, which had flicked all too briefly across his face. They'd been heartsick and troubled he thought, but was unable to check or even discern where the thought sprang from. He watched as the figure retreated.

Silently grooming King, Cal turned over the problem of his Bank Account. He'd no recollection of ever giving his wife signing authority. Not even when they'd first been married had he been besotted enough to do that. And certainly later... later, when she was running up debts halfway across the county, it would never have occurred to him to do so.

Oh, if she'd helped in the business like Mum used to, she'd have had a wage, but not when she only sat around all day moaning. No way! Dad had always said, don't work, don't eat. Life had been that simple. Still is, Cal ruminated.

Half an hour later, he heard the sound of an unfamiliar engine as the Land Rover swung out of the yard, and looked up quizzically.

"Church, boss. She's staying at Tom's for lunch she says, be back about tea time."

Jock joined him at the rails, having checked the two herds. In answer to Cal's nod, Jock said, "Now don't go getting lippy with me, boss." Moving away, the old guy chuckled to himself.

Cal reflected he'd not usually have acknowledged anyone at all, much less bothered what the crew did with their day off. Talking of day off, what had she done the last two weekends?

The spare trail horses had needed to be fed, had she done that? His head came up again, and he scowled. Well, presumably, because they were still standing in the corral, eating their heads off. She'd also looked after

King. Must have groomed him too, judging from the state of his coat.

He narrowed his eyes, to study the corral in the distance. Yup, they looked neat too. Dusty, but neat and tidy. Yes, they'd obviously been groomed several times. Takes some doing, he reflected.

The trail horses were often semi-wild from not being worked, and these had been left behind for just that reason. Hell, better get some of the boys to re-train 'em, Cal thought, tearing his mind back to the job in hand.

King was never used for trail work. He wasn't suited to it. King was for Cal's free time. Glorious gallops to the waterhole and back, with the possibility of a swim. Long slow hacks in the evening twilight, or in the moonlight at the end of the day, or in the pre-dawn hush, when the Outback was beginning to stir back to glorious life. King was his leisure and pleasure.

It was King who listened to Cal's hopes and dreams, and then to the bitterness as those dreams faded and died. Truth be told, it was King shared Cal's life these days. Not a happy thought.

Racking his brains, Cal tried to recall anything else about Jacq. Sifting through Nick's various complaints about her, he delved for the kernel of truth. Visualising again the figure he'd first seen painting Tom's fence.

He'd heard the gossip whenever he was in town, but dismissed it. She was nothing to him, would be nothing to him, and so was easy to dismiss. As all matters unrelated to Paradise and regaining it, had been for several years.

On that morning, she'd been dressed in a scruffy old tee-shirt and paint stained dungarees. Both were over-sized, having obviously seen better days, not to mention a more robust figure. Her hair, despite being shortish, had been held back from her face in a band. Dabs and steaks of paint on her nose, forehead and chin showed where she had been wiping sweat away. The band was presumably for that purpose, and there was one on each wrist.

She'd straightened up when he approached, then returned to her task. Her attitude had irritated him for some reason, and yet he could now recognise that she was only reacting to his own mood. Anyway, who said everyone had to bow the knee to the MacCreadys? This, after all, was egalitarian Australia, not some outpost of Britain.

❈ ❈ ❈ ❈ ❈

Grooming King again at the end of a relaxing day, Cal became aware of Jock watching him.

"Hey old fella. Save me the job section from the paper. I need to check something."

"Gotcha boss. Any partickler job? Mess Cook, for example?"

Cal shook his head. "Nah, you're safe for a while old timer. Just let me know when you want to go, OK?"

Looking at the face of the old man who had been working for Paradise since before he was born, Cal surprised a tear sliding down the wrinkled old cheek.

"Nowhere else to go, boss. 'Druther stay where I know, than go walkabout."

Cal nodded in acceptance. "Thinking of taking on young MacGregor."

"You asking me or telling me?"

"Asking."

The old man chuckled toothlessly. "My, something's changed you. Can't just be that girl you was chasing."

Cal stopped switching King's legs with a handful of straw, and turned.

The old boy scuttled away. "Just messing boss. Just messing."

"Need to check office pay for your lady friend. She's been working free so far." Cal raised his voice, so it carried across the yard.

"Better check more than office pay, son. She's been doing the work of three while she's been here. The homestead's cleaned as if your Ma were still alive. The storerooms have been cleaned and re-stocked. And, she seen to the trail horses while you've been away. Yup, mighty useful fella, *my* lady friend."

Tea was once more spread on the counter, when Cal arrived in the Back Kitchen. Same as yesterday's he noticed.

"How d'you mean, old timer? Stocked the store rooms?"

"No food, boss. That's what I mean. Cleaned it right out to set up the mess trucks. Couldn't have fed the boys when they got back without re-stocking. Clean forgot about it."

Something of Cal's surprise must have shown on his face. Jock chuckled again, before clearing the tables used by those 'boys' heading for town again.

Cal sat on, pondering what he'd heard. Adding it to the facts he had faced last night and again this morning when he surveyed his room.

Why? That's what he couldn't understand. Why? Why had she done it all? When did she find the time? She'd only been here two and a bit weeks. She'd cleared up ten/fifteen years of rubbish, sorting out all the things Cal never got round to, and certainly weren't done if he didn't see them. So, why? Why would a stranger... indeed, *how* would a stranger know where to start?

He'd given her no information. Sitting here in the shade, drinking tea in great greedy gulps, Cal silently accepted that. No information, not so much as a please. Yet she'd driven out here at the time she'd said, waving casually as he rode away on a trail horse. He'd not spared her either a backward glance, or even a thought while away, and yet here was his homestead. Clean, comfortable, and being run efficiently by a complete stranger.

"She's back boss. My lady friend."

Raising his hand in acknowledgement of the information shouted from the back, Cal was standing by her trailer home as she parked up, totally unprepared for the vision climbing down.

CHAPTER NINE

Hell, those legs went on forever. Clad in something shiny and sheer, which sparkled and spangled as they followed a pair of strappy shoes over the sill on the driver's side. His eyes followed up, up, up.

There, at last, a skirt, which had obviously shimmied up those impossible legs as she drove. The skirt was followed by a wisp of a top, which moved with the body beneath, revealing yet concealing at the same time. Cal's throat tightened.

He quailed before the bitterness on her face. Reaching back into the Land Rover, she pulled out a hat, which must have knocked the other churchgoers dead, and a bag of groceries. Jacq slinked her way into the trailer.

"I'll just get changed. Seeya in five."

She was back in five, saying seemingly without a pause, "Yes?"

The legs were respectably covered in black denim, the wispy top exchanged for a more hard working cotton polo shirt, in vivid blue. Into the pause, while Cal tried to think of something intelligent to say, she asked, "Have you eaten? I'm having tea. Would you like one?"

He followed her back inside, waiting silently while she made and served mint tea.

"I should have said, it's all found. No need to feed yourself when working here."

"My day-off, I expect to feed myself." Still no smile, not even a noticeable thaw, although the tight bitter expression had been controlled and was no longer visible.

Cal tried again. "Thanks for all your hard work... ...."

She was already making a negative movement, saying over the end of his words. "No problem. Can't stand mess."

They sipped their tea in silence, then Jacq relaxed against the seat. "And?"

"How were things in town? Have they fixed up the fans in church yet?"

"*Things* seem fine. No. Was very hot and uncomfortable. But have to put on a show, don't you? Prove we're not all Philistines?"

Having drained her cup, Jacq rose silently to replenish it. An eyebrow arched at him over the work bar as she pointed her teapot in his direction.

"No, thanks. Stick to proper tea."

A brief nod of the head was all he received.

"Did you want to speak about the coming week? Tell me what's happening?" Jacq sat down opposite him, with a quizzical expression firmly in place rather than the bitterness he'd previously seen. Drawing a notepad towards her, she rummaged in her shirt pocket for a worn down end of pencil. She licked this encouragingly, entered the date and time, and waited.

"Errm. I realised we'd not talked about pay. Need to sort that out..."

Both eyebrows rose with the polite "Oh?"

"Yes, eerm... not sure what rate..." Cal floundered to a halt.

"We spoke about it yesterday. Agreed I'd wait until we'd got things sorted, more organised." Jacq waited impatiently for his agreement. Cal had great difficulty recalling yesterday's conversation. His mind was locked on to his vision.

"Why? You'll need to live... ..."

Her hand came up in a stop motion. "That is my concern, I think. I've said I'm fine until the end of this job. Your cash flow won't support any additional expense."

She studied his face for a minute or two. "We can discuss it now, if you prefer. Agree terms if you wish. But I am quite content to wait until matters are resolved."

Stunned by her casual dismissal of pay, Cal stared in disbelief. "If you think you'll wring more out of me, then disabuse your mind right now."

"That's it. Reduce everything to the lowest common denominator, why don't you?" Jacq bit her tongue to stop the bitter flow. Drew a steadying breath, and managed to say reasonably calmly, "How much do you normally pay? I'll take that. I've been keeping time sheets, obviously. Wouldn't do to overstep the mark, would it now?"

Unable to restrain himself, Cal asked the question he'd been turning over in his head since he'd worked out exactly what she had done in two and a half weeks. "Why? Why? Dammit, why all this?"

His arms swept wide in an expansive gesture, sweeping glass ornaments from the nearest shelf, swooping over a pile of books resting on the floor, and nearly toppled the laptop by the side of his chair. The glass broke noisily in the sudden silence.

Eyes brimming with tears, Jacq stomped out for a dustpan and brush. She'd recovered herself on her return. Moving him aside brusquely.

"Mind your hands, for goodness sake. Mind your hands with all that glass. Here. Sit!"

Pushing him back into the one armchair, she swept up the big bits, brushing fruitlessly at the smaller shards. Throwing away the debris, she pulled a sign from under her seat. Stood it carefully over the area of breakage. A warning sign over the broken glass? Cal watched in amazement.

"I'll clean up later."

"I'm sorry. Were they valuable? I'll replace them obviously …."

The hand made its stop motion, and tears loomed again.

"Rubbish, if you must know. Just rubbish. You've done me a favour really. I… I… haven't been able to part with them. And now… well, good riddance."

She moved shakily to sit down again, then gestured wildly and left him alone. On her return, she'd recovered somewhat.

"Sorry, had to wash… wash my…." Looking vaguely at her hands, Jacq took a deep breath. "Where were we?"

Cal sat open-mouthed, as she glanced round seemingly at random, gathering herself together. "Pay? Well, what did you pay my predecessor, whoever she was?"

"I can't, simply can't just pay you that amount. You've done so much."

"I apologise if I've exceeded the job spec."

The bitter tone of voice had returned. Jacq looked round again. "I'm sure I wrote it... aah."

Opening a small desk diary, she flipped through to the page for the 16th. Handing it over, she pointed at the entry.

Cal read, "Job spec? If it looks as though it needs doing, then do it."

"I took you at your word. As I said yesterday, say the word, and I'll but out. You should find someone fairly soon, now everything's straight. If that's all?" She stood again, looming over the taller man, sitting in the one armchair in her trailer.

"Hey look. You can't quit half way through. You said you'd help..."

"And..." was said aggravatingly slowly, when the pause Cal left lengthened.

"I... I... I'll replace your treasures. I'm sorry I broke them."

Jacq dismissed his words and the implied gesture with a weary wave of one hand. "Is that all? I am very tired. If you've finished, I'd quite like to get some sleep."

The tight frozen expression on her face gave no ground before his glare. Most people backed off when Cal MacCready glared like that. Not this girl.

They were interrupted by a quick knock at the open doorway.

"OK, you two. Time out. Back to your corners. Missy, the Shower Block is clear, if you want to use it. Should be OK for an hour or so. Then you get some rest. Must have been quite hectic on your own round here. We'll see you tomorrow, after breakfast. OK?"

Jock hustled the astounded woman into her bedroom, and Cal over the steps. "Come on boss, never did no good arguing with a lady heading for the showers, did it?" He hustled and chuckled.

Cal grabbed his arm impatiently. "We'd not finished!"

"Seems to me nobody was saying nothing. Must have been finished."

"I broke some ornaments…"

That did get Jock's attention. "Not her paperweights? Say it wasn't them fancy paperweights?"

"I'm a clumsy oaf. Shouldn't really have been sitting anywhere so small and dainty." Cal flushed to have expressed his thoughts out loud.

A whirlwind swept passed them, heading for the shower block.

"Ain't nothing gonna stop her. She's only got a dinky shower in her truck. Been waiting for a peaceful spell to have a proper shower since we got back."

"She could have used the homestead one."

"Does she look the kind to take advantage?"

Shocked by accuracy of the old guy's words, Cal shook his head. He could think of nothing to say. Nothing!

Ashamed now, of his outburst. And too, …to have broken those ornaments of hers. She was obviously fond of them to have carried them with her from her previous life, and now he'd broken them.

They walked in silence to the Back Kitchen. Jock started cooking some steak. "Took these out of your fridge, boss."

Placing the plate before the younger man, he added, "I saved the other for her, but she won't be back until you go." He made a hurry up motion.

"She could do with some sleep, she's been a tad busy, I reckon." His nodding head seemed to encompass not only the Back Kitchen, but the whole of the homestead and range.

Cal considered his words, while gulping his meal. "Why were the steaks in my fridge?"

"Case you and Nick wanted a barbie, I guess. She's been listening to a lot of chat from Nick since she arrived. Hell, has no time for him, but listens real polite to all his fine words and fancy ways. If he's aiming to wear a body down into a date, I reckon he's on a loser." Jock chuckled.

"I'll do this piece of pie, you can eat it at your place. She's eating before she sleeps. Trust me." He snorted. "I've no time for all that fancy diet stuff. She's eating today, or I'll know the reason why."

Trying to imagine how Jacq would feel to come across him now, Cal picked up the plate of pie and headed home. He powered up the computer to open his mailbox, while gulping pie.

Started reading through the stuff piled up in his absence. Opening the big diary kept on his desk to record the herds, dates and times, he was amazed it was already logged. How come? These were his personal emails, addressed to him, yet logged already. His mind fretted at this mystery. She'd said his computer was not safe. That's how Jacq knew they'd be home 'til Wednesday.

Is this what she meant? She'd been able to access his private stuff? She'd simply opened the computer on the side desk in his room, and read everything. Bloody nerve!

❋ ❋ ❋ ❋ ❋

Turning it over in his mind for the umpteenth time before resolutely physically turning over in bed, Cal was startled to realise Jock had been right. Jacq had been busy enough on the homestead even before they'd all turned up. She'd still done a bloody good spread, not once, but twice. He'd never said thank you. Just accepted it. The way he'd accepted the clean towels, the hot water, the clearing up. And then, broken her precious ornaments. God, what a shit he was!

He'd gone to the trailer to invite her for a ride. Hoping to talk a bit more about her discoveries in the privacy of the open countryside. Her trailer was far too small for a big bloke like him. Suited her somehow. Small and delicate, … not that she was small or delicate, just somehow contained within herself. Shipshape too. Cal snorted in the privacy of his bedroom, wondering what the silent listeners would make of the sound. Hope I don't talk in my sleep.

Tiredly he wondered what apology he could offer, so Jacq wouldn't run out on him now. Just when he'd got an ally, … someone he trusted to help him. That thought kept him awake.

When had he first realised there was no one he could trust with his innermost thoughts? Before his father died certainly. Oh yes, there was no one on either spread Cal could tell his secret fears too, as he watched the family fortune drain away. Certainly not Nick or

Steve, his greatest friends. And, definitely not the bitter woman who refused to sleep with him.

The knowledge Jacq was an outsider had been an additional factor in his decision to go with Tom Crowthorn's suggestion and ask his cousin to work in the office. Although why he would listen, or indeed be speaking to Tom, with all that stuff from Nick going round in his head, Cal couldn't explain. Maybe at forty-four he was finally getting mature? Getting some judgement? He snorted again. Unhappily aware that there had been enough gossip about the MacCreadys over the last few years.

His own outbursts of temper after drinking himself legless were responsible for that. Following as they had his father's drunken debauchery since Meg died. Wide-awake, Cal puzzled just why he'd want any help. Big Cal MacCready needing help? How likely was that?

But… she'd found out something really useful. Something he'd never have thought of, never. Sighing impatiently, Cal rummaged under his bed. If he couldn't sleep, may just as well do some paperwork.

Cheered immensely by the idea his listeners wouldn't know what he was looking at, he was diverted from the office files by a vision of the porn books he had sneaked home as a teenager. He'd certainly never have stored them in the house. His father would have beaten him black and blue. Had done frequently when Cal was younger, despite his mother's pleadings. Don't go there.

Concentrate on these facts. At the end of the letters folder was a clear plastic pack containing a list of everything Jacq had found in the various storerooms she had cleaned, together with a diagram of the homestead showing his lodgers. Only one thing stood out.

Mrs Meg MacCready's diary. It was starred in red, and shown as being in the trailer. Why? Odd thing to move, wasn't it? The diary of a long dead woman. Someone completely unknown to you. Why had Jacq moved it outside?

Cal eventually fell asleep in the middle of the really rather dull list of the various bits of broken equipment, or damaged and irredeemable oddments in the last Store Room Jacq had been able to clean. The papers slid and slithered from the bed, as he finally settled into his normal sleeping posture.

Trying to work out just which of his workers, or heaven help us, friends, would have been trying to get him out, was his last conscious thought.

❇ ❇ ❇ ❇ ❇

Dragging himself out of a heavy sleep, Cal thought he could hear somebody moving about in the office. Grabbing his jeans, he staggered and nearly fell, trying to force his sleep-sodden legs into them as he ran for the front hall.

Swearing robustly in his sleep filled daze, he was staggered to find Jacq moving quietly around her office. Looking up as he entered the door at a run, to say, "Yes?"

For all the world as if it wasn't... 5 o'clock? 5 o'clock, goddamit! What's she doing at this time of the morning?

Cal stopped in confusion, waiting while she uncovered the computer screen and keyboard, placing both covers over the back of her chair. The room was piled high with more of the brown cardboard boxes. To be honest, there was only a narrow corridor between her desk and the doorway, which at least explained why she seemed to parade round the office before resuming her seat. Having now seated herself before the computer, she waited politely.

"Errm, what's going on?"

"Jock said you wanted me to stay. I'll stay then." Jacq glanced only briefly in his direction before powering up the computer.

Cal was still standing in the doorway. He looked as if he'd got up in a hurry. Hair still tousled, bare feet, jeans which had been hastily zipped when he spotted her cool, suave, professional appearance. He watched her dazedly. She was staying? Because Jock asked?

A frown appeared on her face.

"What? What is it?"

Her left hand made the stop motion he remembered, before moving to her lips. Lodgers. Whatever it was, she wouldn't say because of the lodgers.

"Do you want coffee? Cookie will have made some by now."

Cal scowled. "Bloody dishwater. Yours is better."

"Careful. No sense going over the top. I'm only staying for another month." Sighing dramatically Jacq rose, retracing her steps to the door.

Waiting for Cal to retreat, she said, "It'll be ready by the time you're dressed. If you've finished with the folders, I'll file them." The wriggle of her eyebrows was presumably to indicate the lodgers still listening.

"What's this lot?" Pointing at all the brown cardboard boxes.

"Archiving. You must have a stack somewhere. You obviously don't rent space anywhere else. I need to throw away the oldest to make room for this lot."

"*This* is the mountain of paperwork from my office?"

"Yup, and anywhere else I found it. All sorted and filed. Listed on spreadsheet. All present and correct." Heavy emphasis was given to these last phrases, which distracted Cal momentarily.

"Right, see you in five mins." A silent nod was the only response she received.

Sorting and re-stacking the paperwork in his bedroom was beyond Cal's limited powers. The bundle of paperwork and its accompanying folders looked nothing like the neat stack he had taken from his desk, when returned to her outstretched hand. Jacq made no comment about it.

The coffee jug, mugs and some damper were sitting on the side table in his office. Cal looked at the oasis of calm Jacq had created in his room, at the expense of the space in her room, and felt a niggle of guilt for his treatment of her.

"Both herds are fine. The Stockmen are beginning to move about. Have you booked space on the train?"

Sipping the hot brew, made as if to his own specification, Cal shook his head.

"I'll get on to it."

His hand scratched at the two-day stubble of beard growth. The only red he'd inherited from his father. Yeah, a red beard. No sense growing that to protect from the heat of the sun. It never looked right against the dark brown hair he wore brushed straight back from his face. Right, coffee and damper, then shower, shave, instruct men.

Look at Firefly. She may be suitable for Jacq to ride. This afternoon, we'll hack to the waterhole and maybe... well maybe I'll start by apologising for my behaviour.

CHAPTER TEN

Swallowing the last mouthful of cake whole, Cal rushed after Jacq. He caught up with her half way to the homestead.

"Hey? Could take a ride tonight, if you like?"

She eyed him assessingly. "Righto. Don't make a habit of this. Will give the watchers pause for thought."

Turning abruptly away, she left Cal staring after her. He checked his watch. She'd been on the go since five this morning.

King whickered, attracting his attention. Patting and petting his horse, Cal whispered a promise of a gallop tonight. His words to Jacq last Friday rushed though his mind.

It was perfectly normal to take a siesta if you started early. You catnapped or something from 11 til 1. Even on the trail, they never drove the herds during that peak time. When had he started behaving like his father? Criticising first, complaining second?

Horrified at the vision of himself repeating all his father's mistakes, turning into the old man he still wasn't sure he loved, Cal cringed. He liked to think of himself as happy-go-lucky. Sure he had a temper, but mostly he was happy-go-lucky, wasn't he?

Ribald comments and lewd jokes filled the air as the stockmen returned to feed and water the herds before setting off for the railhead. The space had been booked. They needed to leave tonight to arrive for the early Wednesday train. Steve would take them. Stay overnight in town with Sheena and be back out here, say Friday to start again.

Terry sidled up. "Fancy your chances, boss? They're running a book on who gets into her knickers first. You or Nick."

A sudden stillness stopped the man's chatter. Not many survived one of Cal's brooding glares. One of the others took up the teasing remark. "Got some catching up to do, boss. She's been in town with Nick this whole year. Running round on police business, he says."

The comments and laughter of the other stockmen nearly drowned this out. The searing heat of Cal's glare spread round the whole crew.

"Good luck to him then. I'm off women for good."

An outburst of laughter and mickey taking greeted his words.

"Turning the other way then boss? Have to watch our step on the drives now boys." Terry muscled in on the conversation once again.

Cal thought, I'll have to be more careful. Don't want any gossip. Jacq's right, we don't want to warn the hidden watchers.

The men moved slowly about their chores, before washing and changing to drive the herd to the train. The extra men had all been paid off, leaving only the regular hands at the homestead.

"I'm gonna take Jacq up to the waterhole boss. That OK? Young MacGregor'll be here."

Cal nodded slowly. At least the old boy still had a modicum of sense. I can head out the other way, cut back to the waterhole, catch 'em there.

When had he realised Jock was in cahoots with Jacq? She must trust MacGregor too. But not Steve, and not Nick. I wonder why? Hell, I wonder where she learned about the bugs? Banking doesn't seem to cover it somehow!

Jacq mounted by the simple expedient of climbing the paddock rails. Firefly was no real height. Cal hadn't expected the anxious air the woman showed. Still, English riding is not the same as out here, he shrugged and turned back to the job in hand.

Diane would simply have swung herself into the saddle. But then, she'd had years of practice. Cal was convinced Jacq had not had so much leisure as to enable her to excel at outdoor pursuits. That thought led him to ponder how she had managed the stock. Surely office work didn't give that much scope? The memory of Jacq comforting the cow returned to his mind, as it would many times in the future.

Watching her departure with Jock, Cal became aware of MacGregor at his side. How'd he get there so quietly?

"Trouble boss?"

"Nope, don't think so. Might go for a gallop myself. Shake the kinks out. You alright alone here?"

"Yup, we had a spread like this one. Feels nice, like coming home." The youngster turned away, as if embarrassed, adding as he walked away, "Thanks for the job boss. Makes a real difference."

Cal watched him go. Liking the way the boy made no sound, as the dust scuffed up from the heels of his trail boots. Thinking again about the sound of the high heels tapping to and fro in his homestead. Why'd she make so much noise? Didn't make sense when viewed against the silence, as she'd removed then replaced his lodger after inspection. Shrugging, he went for King's tack.

Tacking up out of long habit, swinging effortlessly into the saddle, Cal headed towards the mountains in the far distance. He trotted and cantered for a while, before giving King his head.

Far enough out from the homestead, he turned inexorably towards the waterhole. Two figures were sitting on the bench placed just there by long dead settlers. They were etched against the skyline as he approached. Dropping King's reins, he dismounted to creep forward.

"Come out boss. We've heard you this past mile or more." Jock chuckled, pinching his companion's hand. "Give me a minute or two to get outa your way. Come in as if you've been for a piss. Oops sorry."

The last bit was said to the woman. "Us men get mighty crude without any civilising influence."

Jacq patted the hand releasing hers. "Away old man. None of your blarney here."

Cal waited while Jock stood and stretched, saying more loudly, "I'll just check the plumbing. Be right back."

Trying to make himself the same shape as the departed man raised a smile from Jacq, as he approached.

"Sit, sit! I've no wish to twist my neck looking up at your great height." A slight smile accompanied the words, soothing the troubled feelings Cal had been experiencing all day.

They watched the sunset sliding its gold and crimson colours over the waterhole, before the sun disappeared, apparently forever, behind the mountains in the distance. In his anxiety to cover as many of his questions as possible, Cal totally overlooked that he also wanted to apologise.

Listening to the cautious replies, he wondered what made her so cagey.

"Banking. Makes you afraid to raise your head above the parapet. Even if it's not bullets flying about, it's likely to be brown and smelly."

Looking at the relaxed face next to his, now tinged with the colours of the setting sun, Cal smiled for the first time in years.

"I'm cagey because I don't know who to trust. I'm sure about Jock and Tam, but the others… just not sure yet."

Going over the conversation in bed later, Cal realised she hadn't included him in the list of trustees. Was that so obvious it didn't need to be stated? Or, was it simply that she didn't trust him? How did her apparent distrust affect their relationship?

❄ ❄ ❄ ❄ ❄

Around the homestead he continued to act as if she irked him. Jacq too, took every opportunity of stressing she was leaving, as soon as a replacement was found. Their bickering became part of the background, but on their trips into the Bush, Cal became increasingly relaxed. Finding someone who could (and would) take an intelligent interest in his business, someone who sparked ideas, who challenged his stereotypes, made Cal re-think his life. Viewing it objectively for the first time ever.

Even King quickly accepted Firefly. Sharing his paddock without any animosity, taking a proprietary air with the younger mare. Jacq groomed both horses impartially, saddling up Firefly whenever she wanted a ride. Caring for Firefly afterwards.

She was mounting up one evening as Cal finished his tea. Strolling casually towards her, he said, "Where's Jock?"

"Busy."

"You're not going alone."

Jacq nodded brusquely.

"Lady, no one but no one rides alone."

Settling herself into her saddle, she rejoined, "I'll go direct to the waterhole and straight back."

Jacq needed, really needed to have some time to herself. Far away from the homestead, with its doubts and uncertainties, where she could just be herself. Think through the problems she'd uncovered, work out a plan and then... ... she'd come back and put it into execution.

"Five minutes and we'll go together."

"I do not need a babysitter. I'll go direct there and direct back. Along the track."

"You're going no where alone."

Stockmen drifted casually over to see what the fuss was about. Jacq's face said, bloody men, with a return of the bitter look Cal had seen before. Something inside Cal melted. Hell, she looked so hurt. Poor little thing.

He watched her toss a mental coin, breathing out on a sigh of relief, when she finally nodded briefly.

Tam came forward with King's kit. "Let me help you boss."

They rode in silence. All along the track, Cal waited for her to make some comment. He could see she was seething, and waited for it to boil over in his direction. He knew he'd been high-handed, but hell, no one did ride alone, ... well, none of the men rode alone. He did, constantly. But then he'd been born here. Knew the countryside like the back of his hand. He'd really welcome an opportunity of telling her so.

Firefly seemed to be itching for a gallop, but Jacq settled her competently. Riding side by side, in the ground-eating lope of the good Outback horse, he waited for an eruption.

After fifteen minutes of silence, he said, "Gallop?" A nod was his only reply. Their heels hit the sides of their horses at the same moment and they both surged forward.

The evening breeze teased her hair out from under her hard hat, bringing high colour to her cheeks. They slowed of one accord on reaching the waterhole, still neck and neck.

Sliding down from Firefly, Jacq hugged her horse happily. "Thank you."

Cal thought she addressed the horse. Standing lost in the shadows, Jacq continued whispering to the horse, with both arms wrapped round its neck. Lost in a private world. For some reason Cal felt again the same sense of desolation he'd experienced with his parents.

The two horses gulped noisily at the water, and Jacq drew half a dozen really deep breaths. "Wow! Needed that."

Cal took the reins for both horses, ground hitching them before offering Jacq a place on the bench. Instead she squatted on her heels, then sat quickly, with her legs straight out in front of her. Leaning back on her hands, she studied the evening sky. Gazing round and round, giving a little nod from time to time.

"Which one's the Southern Cross?" Startled, Cal pointed. "Right. Thanks."

"No social chit-chat then?"

Her blank face turned in his direction. "No." Settling herself flat on the reddish earth, Jacq gave herself up to her thoughts.

Cal watched her, wondering what she was thinking about. King and Firefly cropped grass noisily, crickets whirred restlessly, Jacq gave a deep, deep sigh. Gradually the calm quiet exerted its usual influence, and before long Cal was asleep. When he woke, Jacq seemed to be calculating on her fingers.

"What's that?"

"Hmm? Oh, just working something out. Sometimes the old fashioned methods are best, aren't they?" The relaxed chuckle sounded nice. Friendly and … nice.

Cal checked the time. They'd need to ride back soon, and he wanted to ask her about things… …. The girl who had set out had seemed cold and unapproachable, but this one, well you felt you could ask anything.

He started on his questions. The first thing that came into his head was about Bank Authorities.

Sighing, she sat up. Curling herself over one knee, Jacq gave a brief dissertation on Bank Mandates in general, then his in specifics. She'd picked up copies in town this morning.

"The copies are in my trailer. I don't want them in the homestead in case... well, in case anyone else sees them." Jacq waited for Cal's answering nod.

"I've completed a new form. Just sign that. I'll slip it in with your letters tonight. Don't let it out of your sight, please."

She'd leapt from the bench on to Firefly, before he could ask if she wanted a leg up. Surprised that he wanted to hold a woman... any woman... even briefly, while throwing her up to a horse.

Jacq was five seven or eight to his six four. The protective feelings aroused earlier had not entirely disappeared, Cal found. He didn't now want her to manage on her own. He wanted to be the one she turned to for help.

She seemed to manage very well on her own. Was it an act? Some learned behaviour? Did she have a past? The tight bitter expression appeared fleetingly in his mind. Yes, some bastard had caused that.

Turning his mind resolutely back to what he'd learned about his Bank accounts, shocked by that and even more by the implications behind the words, Cal was silent on the ride home.

Surprised that Jacq groomed Firefly without any of the normal chatter between riders, Cal was watching her moodily as she strolled to her trailer. She had declined his offer of tea and supper with a brusque shake of the head.

"Regular chatter-box, ain't she?" Jock cackled to himself, as he leaned against the rails, watching the horses frolic, now they were free of their tack.

"Didn't see you there, old timer. How long you been there?"

"Too long, I reckon."

Momentarily distracted by the lights coming on in the trailer, Cal nodded dismissively.

It was only later, in bed, he wondered if other eyes had been watching him and Jacq return from their ride. Relieved to reflect there was nothing to indicate any closer connection than boss and crew. Certainly nothing companionable in the silence as they'd cared for their horses. Hey, there was no closer connection than boss and staff, was there? Cal was surprised by the sense of desolation left in the wake of that thought.

Jacq had developed the habit of leaving a folder of letters on Cal's desk at the end of each day. Anything she was unsure about he signed, if he agreed with. Routine letters she simply signed on his behalf, posting them in the box at the main entrance to the spread, leaving a copy for him to read. He'd become used to the fact his correspondence was dealt with so efficiently. Unsurprised if there was nothing waiting for him, as on the last two nights.

Tonight however, he nearly bumped into Jacq as she moved silently into his bedroom, carrying the Letters folder. It hadn't been on his desk just now when he looked.

Cal jumped nervously, not expecting anyone else to be about the homestead. He'd certainly heard nothing. Her finger covered her lips as she came through the door. Lodgers, of course. She patted the folder, before placing it direct into his hands, and he nearly laughed out loud. It was so very cloak and dagger. A grin appeared briefly. Jacq thinks so too. Comforted by this sign of allegiance, Cal nodded back.

Jacq disappeared as silently as she'd arrived. He looked questioningly at her feet. Socks. Clever girl.

The bare facts he'd learned earlier, didn't prepare him for the forgeries in the folder. Hell! Diane had been signing on his account since the wedding. No wonder the money didn't seem to go far. And, on the business, she'd been signing, ... what was it Jacq called them? Instruments. Yeah, Diane had been signing instruments on the business account since the old man lost it, and Cal had taken over.

He closed his mind to the painful scene he'd had with his father. The old man was so drunk his speech was slurring, but he'd still had the sense to hand over the business stuff. Insisting it would be safer in Cal's hands than Col's own.

His right hand struck against his forehead, why hadn't Cal thought of it before? Perhaps the old man hadn't been paranoid? Perhaps someone really had been out to get him. But who? And was it the same someone now?

❋ ❋ ❋ ❋ ❋

It was a sombre Cal who silently replaced the file direct into Jacq's hands the following morning. She stamped briskly about in her office, before slipping off her shoes. Opening a drawer, she pressed a switch. The normal clattering sound filled the air. She sure typed fast. Grinning, she slid passed, to replace the file in her trailer.

On her return, he was still standing there, gobsmacked. That's why she made a noise. To distract the listeners from something else she was doing.

Slipping back into her shoes, switching the machine off, she carefully locked the desk drawer.

"Oh boss. Didn't hear you arrive. Checking on me huh? Anything I can do?" Was said in near normal tones, despite the grin.

"Just coffee, thanks."

The note on the coffee tray read, "Thanks indeed, as if."

❈ ❈ ❈ ❈ ❈

Once a week they'd ride out and meet up. Tam or Jock always accompanied her after that first spat, disappearing from sight as Cal came in view. Not always at the waterhole. As she became more familiar with the countryside, Cal reluctantly agreed to change their rendezvous to further confuse the Watchers. Not that either was convinced there were Watchers as well as Listeners.

The search of the remaining Storerooms had revealed nothing foreign. Jacq had been most disappointed when reporting the results of her Spring Clean.

'Spring Clean.' Cal was still unused to the euphemism Jacq used to cover the work she'd done around and about the Homestead.

She continued to maintain that the range of the little bugs was insufficient for the Listeners to be far away, but short of searching the cabins used by the Stockmen, she was stumped for the time being. They waited patiently, or as patiently as they could, sieving every conversation for clues.

Having asked for and received his permission, Jacq patched a power cable to the trailer, making a minute search of the hard drive on the homestead pc via her own computer. Carefully tracking and checking each and every abuse she could find. As far as Cal was concerned she found nothing.

In fact, the abuses added to the confusion Jacq felt. It almost seemed as if Cal were the person hacking into his files, but from his comments during their talks, she rather doubted he had the ability. Unless of course, he was simply a better actor than he seemed on the surface?

Jacq continued to pace cagily round him. His reaction to the Bank Mandates might have been false. Then again it might be that '*ex-wife*' was the culprit on the computers too. Wonder who suggested they install computers? Knowing that might help. Get Cal in a good mood, ask him, Jacq thought, hoping she'd remember in time for their next ride.

Cal was acutely conscious of the silence falling as he pushed into the Back Kitchen whenever the other three were together. Almost as if they were ashamed of their camaraderie in the face of his well known bad temper. It emphasised the sense of isolation Cal still felt.

From time to time he noticed how the other drovers treated Jacq, … were treated by Jacq. The happiness she spread seemed contagious, seeping insidiously round the homestead. Hell, when did the guys start whistling again?

✻ ✻ ✻ ✻ ✻

Cal slumped moodily in his office. Jacq had left his Tax Returns in a folder on his desk. A bright pink sticker on the front proclaimed, "Get out of Jail Free CARD", bringing a smile to his lips briefly. Underneath, it also said, "These must go off by the end of the week. If you need a hand inputting, then yell." He'd never seen the complete form before, and was grappling with this hideous vision of officialdom.

High heels tapped closer. Hell, Cal didn't want or need any help. 'Course he could fill in his own returns. 'Course he could.

He sat up sharply as the heels hesitated before moving away again. He'd been so sure she'd be out of the way all morning. Had planned to spend this morning privately figuring it out. The memory of his father's Accountant flitted through his head again. Most people who knew him would assume he employed an Accountant. Not Jacq. Seems she expected him to do it himself. Perhaps he should just give in gracefully?

What does she mean? Inputting?

Groaning, he turned to the first page. It felt a million miles from the happy bush meeting yesterday. Yup, name and address, correct. OK, that wasn't too bad, was it?

He flipped over the page and moaned aloud. The door to his office opened silently, and he looked up. He'd not heard anyone approach … Didn't matter who they were, they'd be a welcome distraction from this …

The card in her hand read, "Do your Tax forms in the trailer, if you want?"

Stunned, Cal paused. Why was she offering? How did she know he was having problems? He nodded quickly, about to rise and follow her.

The card flipped over quickly. Siesta. She looked sternly in his direction before slipping out as silently as she'd arrived.

Ashamed of the relief burgeoning with her offer, Cal resumed his place. Yeah, that's best. He grinned. The Listeners never knew of these silent exchanges. The three or four times a week, he'd find Jacq before him on some secret mission or other.

He sighed happily before flipping through the rest of the form. What's that?

The form had been completed in pencil with a note cross-referring it to the entry on the spreadsheet. He studied the form more closely. Yup, all filled in, with clear indicators showing the source of all that information. Cal only had to ink in her figures. Great!

He stopped at the Trailer to thank her, saying he'd not need more help, surprising her into a smile.

"Actually, I thought you might want to curse and swear while you completed it, and not want the Listeners to know of your problem."

Jacq thought he worried about his standing? No way! 'Course he didn't! He never even considered other people, much less cared for their good opinion.

No, no that isn't true. It's not! Cal cared only too much that he was in reduced circumstances; that he could no longer spend so freely, and that his wife had left him to flounder in a pit of debt rather than be poor herself. The ink was barely dry on the divorce papers before she was married to old man Gough. 'Course he cared! He just preferred not to let others see it.

Dragging his thoughts back to the present, Cal realised he was preventing Jacq entering her trailer. She stood to one side waiting patiently.

"I don't need to disturb you. Seems I just need to ink in your figures."

"Yeah, hope so. Need to check 'em too of course. But stay here if it helps at all."

Jacq nodded casually at the inviting interior. It always smelled good. Tempting Cal as he rushed passed on his way to or from somewhere, ... something.

Rushing from pillar to post. His father's expression sprang to mind, together with the knowledge that Cal himself no longer did so. No longer needed to do so – because Jacq had everything under control.

They went through the Returns sitting side by side at the breakfast bar. Conscious of her closeness, of the lavender fragrance that seemed to waft around her, Cal kept a tight rein on his physical reactions. He kept on telling himself, that's all it is. The proximity of a sweet smelling female after years of enforced abstinence. Trouble is, he wasn't sure he believed it!

Things were going well, until he met her eyes just as she chuckled in response to his comment. He'd felt exposed, pinned down in some way by the innocent expression on her face. The suddenly stark realization that she saw him as an ally, not as a man, just an ally. His ego smarted at the thought. He'd never before been treated in this casual jolly way. Sure, she got riled if Cal annoyed her, but she said so immediately. None of the sulking which used to epitomise his marriage. Jacq treated him as if she were his equal, even though she only worked for him. Worked for him! Hell and damnation, he'd still not set up a pay scale!

"Leave them here. I'll put them through on my laptop later. OK?"

He nodded, entranced by the silky smooth hair near his face.

"I'll keep the forms out here too. I know the background is on the mainframe, but just to be on the safe side, I'll keep the forms here. OK?"

Cal nodded again. Relieved not to have to make decisions on these aspects of his business. More than relieved that most aspects of his business, *all* aspects of his business, were in safe hands while Jacq remained.

❄ ❄ ❄ ❄ ❄

Jacq was on the trail of the money lost from the Bank Accounts. Apparently chafing at the time it was taking a) to find it, and b) to identify the final recipient.

Staggered to discover over two hundred dollars a week had been secreted out of his accounts for the past eight years, Cal hadn't known what to say in response to her question of how frequently he checked his bank statements. Never, would be the honest answer, he admitted, but he didn't like to say that, in the face of Jacq's open conviction he would do it much, much more frequently. Like every month!

The Bank also dragged its feet over producing the original instruction to transfer the funds. Cal pressed Jacq to cancel it. He wanted the Bank to reimburse all his monies stolen with their active participation. Jacq was reluctant to do so, saying their best hope of retrieving the funds was by not alerting the fraudsters they'd been rumbled. His very powerlessness added just the right edge to Cal's voice when he spoke to Jacq.

He was, however, forced to concede to the changes Jacq wanted to make to his computer. She had shown him the times his pc had been accessed. Identifying some of them to him – but by no means all.

Some were from the Stockman's lounge and some were from the pc in Cal's own office, while he was away. Cal was left with the impression it was impossible to trace all the unwarranted intrusions, but this was far from the case. Jacq was simply not sure how much to trust him.

Stunned, and feeling violated in some vague way, Cal agreed to each and every one of the proposals she made. Fielding the enquiries from the Stockmen by glossing over the problems. Glad Jacq had the forethought to provide an innocent sounding reason for these changes. Only one thing puzzled him.

Terry. Terry would not leave matters alone, kept pestering for a clearer description, more detail of why these changes were being implemented. Cal shook his head every time it came to mind. He'd employed Terry for just over eight years now. Must be sound. *Must* be.

Over the next three months, more herds arrived then departed for the rail station. Jacq continued to work in both the office and the stockyard, as well as maintaining the homestead to his mother's demanding standards. She was already working on a plan to get some help with the extra work she did round the homestead. Not that she had mentioned it to Cal, yet. Time enough when things are running a bit more smoothly, and he's not so harassed for money, she thought.

Most Sundays she escaped into town. Church, she said, or Tom's.

❋ ❋ ❋ ❋ ❋

They'd had another highly vocal dispute, which rumbled on for a couple of weeks. Jacq wanted the men to be paid by direct transfer, saying, rightly too, that it was much safer. It also ensured that wives and children had access to money – if the transfer was phrased appropriately.

Jacq had angered both Cal and some of the older men by holding a public meeting about it. Hecklers were dealt with severely by a new version of Jacq Cal had never yet seen. He wouldn't want to get on the wrong side of her!

This feeling was compounded when he discovered a file under the few letters he still signed from time to time. It contained a thorough briefing on all aspects of wages, with the automated transfers neatly highlighted. Jacq had even researched cash cards and debit cards ready for the questions the Stockmen would inevitably ask. Bloody nerve! What do you mean we could have a cash point here for them? Bloody nerve!

❋ ❋ ❋ ❋ ❋

Cal strode confidently into the tented arrangement housing the Land Rover. The bonnet slammed loudly in the oppressive mid-summer silence.

"You want me?"

Jacq put down a spanner, wiping her hands carefully on a grimy cloth, walking determinedly towards him and away from the vehicle.

"Yeah. Wanted a quick word."

"I'll be through in a minute. Take the weight off. Trailer or office, whichever."

Surprised she'd been working on the Landy, Cal asked, "Anything I can do?"

Jacq's eyes followed the direction of his hand, back towards the vehicle.

"Nope. Just changing the air filter. Sure do get clogged up out here."

"I'm considered quite handy with vehicles if...."

Jacq silenced him with a quick hand movement. One Cal kept seeing. It seemed impatient, not to say curt, almost rude.

"Thanks, but no. Wouldn't get too far depending on men, would I?"

The tight bitter expression was back on her face. Cal wondered what caused it. Why was she so down on men? Probably some bastard in her past.

They walked together towards the trailer, while Cal explained why he'd called. It was the siesta time, and Jacq was, or at least, should have been, enjoying a well-deserved break. It was apparent though that her mind was not on Cal, but some other problem. She'd managed to smudge oil and grease on to her nose. Catching sight of herself in the mirror, Jacq grinned suddenly.

How Cal wished they could have met without all this... this... going on. A relaxed and happy Jacq could have been just what he needed. Some light-hearted company to get him back into proper courting. Needed to keep his hand in, if he wanted to continue the MacCready line.

Suddenly, against all the odds, against the bitterness of his unhappy marriage, Cal realised he did want to continue the MacCready line. Hell, it had run on for five generations, almost as important as holding on to this bit of Outback. Almost... well maybe, ... with the right girl.

Mentally reviewing the local single girls, Cal dismissed each one out of hand. Too silly. Too young and foolish. He needed someone mature, able to hold their own.

Cal continued to call her Jack as if she were male, or even 'lady' in a sarcastic tone, and she continued to call him "Boss." He wondered if Jacq were happy with this arrangement. Clamping down hard on a sudden image of Jacq – he always thought of her in the softer version of her name Jock and Tam used – kissing him responsively back. No, nope. Don't even think about it!

CHAPTER ELEVEN

It had taken a good deal of persuasion to convince Jacq he could be trusted, but Steve had eventually been issued with a satellite phone. This enabled the herd to be tracked all along its route.

Neither Cal nor Steve knew Jacq had given Tam a more powerful transmitter than the lodgers, to go on the ear tag of the lead critter. Or that she was in touch with young MacGregor in the mess wagon periodically. Too secretive by half.

The drives were arranged so that the drovers would be either in their respective homes or at the homestead over Christmas. Out again in the New Year, obviously.

Cal had seen nothing of Diane since their altercation at the end of August. He didn't seriously expect any repercussions. She didn't live at Paradise, although it belonged to the Blaumfelds, well her brother Denis. Besides, what could Diane do?

❊ ❊ ❊ ❊ ❊

Bumping into Tom on one of his infrequent trips to Town, Cal didn't know what to do with the information Jacq had not visited Tom in maybe three, four weeks, to use Tom's own words.

"She must have moved heaven and earth out there for you in that time. I hope you're paying her well."

Jogging back to the homestead on King, Cal turned this conversation over and over in his head.

Adding it to the information dropped by Nick, that he was busy with a new out of town date, Cal felt very uncomfortable. Sometimes Jacq was too secretive for her own good, he thought again, unsaddling King.

And …. Hell, I've still not done anything about any pay scale. Goodness knows what rate she should be on … …. His mind went over the range of skills she used to help him run his business. Readily admitting that his business was running more smoothly simply because she was there, organising him, releasing him for those aspects he enjoyed.

He'd begun to look forward to their meetings. Even when there was nothing to report, even when they just sat in quiet contemplation of the beauty of their surroundings, he was pleased for the time alone.

No, NO. Not *with* her. She could be a block of wood for all he knew, … all he felt, … all he cared. It was just so peaceful. Jacq was not one for incessant chatter. If something needed saying, she said it, but if not, she was silent. This gave an air of tranquillity to their meetings, which had eluded Cal all his adult life.

❋ ❋ ❋ ❋ ❋

Today, trotting along whistling softly to himself, Cal too was looking forward to Christmas, in a way he hadn't since very young. He'd picked up the post while in town, carrying two bags of assorted mail with him. He'd be back in town in a couple of weeks to pick up the cash for those drovers not swayed by Jacq's powers of persuasion.

He handed the two bags to Jacq, who had been strolling casually from the back kitchen to the homestead. It certainly didn't occur to Cal she had been watching out for him. They never exchanged commonplaces. Cal sometimes missed holding proper conversations.

His mind wandered over the books on show in the trailer, wondering idly if Jacq had read all of them. Maybe they could talk about them? Cal, like many another cattleman, read voraciously. There'd not been too many other distractions while he'd been growing up. The range of books had been limited, but even now he could still lose himself in some story or other.

True to the illusion they'd created, she didn't linger, simply accepted the bags on her way back to the office. By the time he'd seen to King, and had a drink, the mail was sorted.

A coloured and scented envelope sat in solitary splendour on his desk. He was sniffing appreciatively at it, when Jacq stopped in his doorway.

"Common as muck." But the grin belied the tone of voice she used. "I'll just take these over to the boys, boss," was said in her usual way, for the benefit of the listeners.

Cal experienced a great longing to be done with all the subterfuge. It seemed to be taking forever. The note was unsigned, undated and crudely written. "Beware who you trust. She is not what she seems."

Wha-at? Staggered, he pored over the envelope, looking for clues. He'd show Jacq tonight, see what she made of it. Hard on the heels of that thought came the question, what if Jacq is the 'she' referred to? Suppose Jacq was the 'she' he shouldn't trust?

Uncertain, he stuffed the letter back into the envelope and into the bottom drawer. The writing looked suspiciously like Diane's he thought, after some calm reflection. Could be her, trying to stir up trouble.

❋ ❋ ❋ ❋ ❋

Stopping once again in his doorway, Jacq said, "Have to go to Brisbane, boss. Problems with my passport. Got to go to the High Commission. If I catch the Friday train, it won't impact the homestead will it?"

Reluctantly Cal allowed himself to be talked into Jacq taking some holiday. He'd miss her, actually. No, you're kidding, right?

Despite the rapport of their meetings, there was still an element of uncertainty, not to say distrust in their 'banter'. A needle sharp point, in the chat flowing back and forth between them. It sometimes seemed to Cal Jacq still didn't like him, for all her help with his problems. Not that he ever considered his own feelings for her.

She was just an ally. Someone useful to have on his side, while sorting out the problems he'd faced since his parents' deaths and his divorce. Unsurprising in view of Diane's continued connection to his Bank accounts, and presumably to his computer.

Now the unauthorised invoices had been stopped, the small black figure at the bottom of the statement was growing. Not by much, but it was growing. And, maybe, who knows… if we can reclaim some of the diverted funds, perhaps then, I will have enough money not to be worrying about it 24/7?

Cal paused at this point in his thoughts. Didn't want to get ahead of himself. We're certainly no nearer finding out who bugged the homestead or who was behind the diversion of funds. Walk before you run, please.

But still, some spark of something, was giving Cal an inner glow, absent for a good long while. Yeah, a good long while.

At Jacq's request, the MacGregor family had been removed from town, and now lived on the homestead. Jacq had insisted that the housework, washing etc was too much for Tam and Jock to manage, especially as they both disappeared for each drive.

Saying at the time, in answer to Cal's query, "We can also train up Patience to provide you with office help. That'll save more cash."

He was intrigued by her efforts to recoup his funds, and as ever minimise his expenses. He'd arched an eyebrow at her.

"Able to help in the office and in the laundry?"

"Yup. You must have realised by now I'm only spinning out the office work so I don't have to leave." She rubbed her hands together gleefully. "Coining it in, that's me."

❋ ❋ ❋ ❋ ❋

In reality of course, Jacq wasn't sitting doing nothing, as was obvious every time Cal rode in. The homestead had been painted with surplus paint, 'found' in one of the storerooms. The windows all shone. Even Mum's garden was slowly being restored.

Riding up the drive each time he returned, Cal could hardly believe the difference one woman could make in such a short time. Over the months of her stay, Cal had gradually worked out exactly what she had achieved in her first two weeks. And... he still hadn't worked out a pay scale... .... After all, what could you offer someone who seemed able to do so much?

❋ ❋ ❋ ❋ ❋

The reason the Store Rooms had been empty of food back then, was because Suppliers had refused him credit. This information was among the backlog of letters he'd been ignoring.

In her second week Jacq had marched into each of his Suppliers demanding to know the background. Issuing a written guarantee that bills would be met in future on demand, Jacq had re-instated those supplies, starting with the critters as she called the various animals, and then the humans.

By dint of comparing the local suppliers with the invoices in her Ledger, Jacq had uncovered a selection of fraudulent invoices. Smiling grimly, she listed the total of those goods separately. Another fine mess. Look where it gets you if you don't 'do' office work.

Keeping her eyes open for these Suppliers, she tried to track down their Bank accounts. Where's the money really going?

Jacq had researched the legitimate local Suppliers, transferring to cheaper sources where she could. She also arranged for some of the food to be supplied ready prepared, rather than starting from scratch each time she cooked for the drovers. Apologising to Cal for the slightly higher costs, but explaining she had insufficient time to prepare all the vegetables.

The food was back to the standard Mum would have accepted, a surprised Cal thought. Jacq seemed to know instinctively what the men needed. Knew what Jock and Tam could achieve with the Mess Trucks.

She even steam cleaned the Mess Trucks on their return from a drive. Something which hadn't happened in a long time.

Cal and the 'boys' enjoyed coming home at the end of their drives, now that the water was hot, and the food healthy and wholesome again. The drovers even whistled as they went about their chores, and *that*, a shocked Cal realised, hadn't happened since Mum was alive.

Jacq had also changed the way things were done. Every item coming onto the homestead, now had to be physically checked before the delivery note was signed off.

❄ ❄ ❄ ❄ ❄

An unwilling smile curved his lips, as Cal was diverted by the memory of catching Cookie on the trip before last. Cal had wandered into the Mess tent, looking for a coffee. The coffee seemed to have improved and now here was Cookie, listening to a tape.

Cal stopped. Jacq! Cookie was listening to Jacq. Surprised, Cal listened to the end of a recipe for damper.

"What's this?"

Jock jumped nervously. "Sorry boss. Jacq gave it me. Helps when I lose track of a recipe. Memory's not what it was."

Jock continued to react nervously round Cal, convinced he'd be getting the sack for not being up to the job.

Two or three days later, when Cal had finally worked it out, he looked for Jock.

"You're OK, old timer. As long as you can hear the recipes Jacq records for you, after that tho', out. You hear me?"

He'd been unprepared to be tackled by Jacq over his treatment of Jock. Hell, how'd I know she'd be upset? She had though. Had stormed and yelled at him at their next bush meeting.

Stamping impatiently round him, forcing him to turn in a circle while she ranted at him. Telling him Jock deserved some respect, some concern, some consideration. Had been working for the MacCreadys since the early nineteen-forties. Working since he'd been five for them.

How would I have known that? Little hellcat! Wouldn't like to get on her bad side.

Cal frequently turned over all this information in his head, whether out with the critters or back on the homestead. There was nothing to show a thaw in their relationship. No seismic shift, nothing tangible really. So why did he feel more hopeful about the future?

❇ ❇ ❇ ❇ ❇

At their meeting before Jacq went to Brisbane, she asked Cal to keep a strict eye on her trailer.

"I don't want to find any lodgers when I return. Also, quite a lot of your stuff is on my pc now. Guard it carefully. Promise? Without it, we have no evidence for when we find the culprits."

Cal nodded solemnly. Glad now that he would be round the homestead rather than on another drive.

Impulsively she'd clutched his hand. "You'll be alright with Pru and Patience, won't you?"

"Yup. Her cooking's not up to your standard, neither's her coffee… …"

CHAPTER TWELVE

Jacq gave the trailer keys to Tam, saying, "The Landy will be at Tom's. There's a silent alarm on the trailer. You'll get a text on your mobile, right? If you get one, wait a good half hour before going to see what happened. Promise me. I don't want you tackling any burglars."

"We won't know who it is, if I don't check."

She nodded reassuringly. "They'll show up on the CCTV. Don't worry. Just, I'd prefer you to check and re-set the alarm, once they've gone." The youngster grinned happily. "We'll meet up when I get back. OK? Review the tape together, if you like."

The MacGregor youngsters quite often collected in Jacq's trailer in the evenings. Giving their mother some welcome relief, now the family were getting back on their feet. No longer quite so harassed about providing for six children, Prudence MacGregor was gradually coming back to her looks. Tam had been but the start of Jacq's campaign to help. But what Jacq really loved was having the little ones to herself, to hug and cuddle.

Returning from a drive, Cal found she'd requisitioned part of the verandah. Just outside the kitchen door, not near his office or his bedroom, she'd said, nervously. Here Jacq helped them with the messy stuff they never got to do at home. There were still two green footprints on Cal's steps where the youngest had been 'hand' painting. Jacq didn't realise Cal smiled every time he stepped over them.

Cal grinned to listen to all the happy noise on his verandah. Sometimes sitting silently, just listening to their squeaks and squawks. It was real nice to hear their happy noises. He'd missed having brothers and sisters. Oh yeah, he'd had friends about the station, but once they'd returned to their own homes, he was alone. The odd one out, in the happy partnership that was his parents' marriage.

❋ ❋ ❋ ❋ ❋

Leaving the Landy at Tom's, Jacq said, "Now keep a good ear to the ground, coz. I want to hear all the tittle tattle on my return."

Apart from idly wondering why Jacq hadn't mentioned she would be spending this week in Brisbane with Nick, Tom simply nodded. He'd spent some time wondering how they'd come together. Things hadn't seemed too promising when Jacq first arrived. She and Nick seemed to strike sparks off each other, and the tension between them had been palpable. But ... well, if it meant Jacq wouldn't be moving on, Tom wouldn't complain. He loved his younger cousin.

Had done so since his teenage years, when she had arrived a small blonde toddling bundle at his grandparents. Instructed by his own parents to look after the little girl, Tom had done so with great pride and joy. Caring and protecting her in a way the young Jacq had never known before.

Jacqueline blossomed under his loving tuition, and had been devastated when he announced his decision to emigrate. She'd been with Dave nearly three years by then, and didn't want to sacrifice the love of her life for the imponderables Tom's would contain, once he moved his wife and daughter to the Outback.

It had been a struggle for them to part. Only the weekly gossipy letters they exchanged had maintained their relationship, before the advent of emails. Until the debacle in the UK, they had been in constant daily contact with each other. Part of each other's lives as they had always been.

It was obvious she didn't want her Landy tampered with. Tom was the only one who knew exactly what kit it contained, having been shown proudly over it once, when Jacq had been trying to get his agreement to continue her travels.

She'd said, "Not much of an epic voyage, is it? If I stop at the first place I find?"

But Tom wouldn't be swayed. He'd known about her childhood, known about Dave. He was Jacq's only link with her past. Did she really want to jettison everything?

Now, he asked, "Don't forget that stuff for the grandkids, will you?"

"Don't fuss. Do I ever let you down?"

No, these cousins never let each other down. Not since they'd been kids together back in England. In a hostile environment, Jacq knew she could totally, totally trust her cousin.

They hugged and kissed on the platform. Tom returned to his house, wondering where Nick was joining her. Perhaps at the next stop? What's that? …
…Morven.

Neither Nick nor Jacq had ever seemed overly friendly, even recently, but, ... if you believe the books, that's often the way this thing called love worked. Be good if they did get together. She'd be close enough to keep an eye on then.

Having planned Jacq's future to suit himself. A future of living close at hand, Tom smiled happily. Maybe it would even calm Nick down too!

❃ ❃ ❃ ❃ ❃

The week dragged for Cal, well nine days all told, with the travelling. He wished he'd thought about setting up a system for checking with each other. Gradually deducing that as the homestead was bugged then so could the house phone. Oh well. Be back soon.

Having had the happy thought he could meet Jacq, talk privately, before returning home, Cal was standing on the platform when Jacq and Nick descended from the train.

Nick kissed the laughing woman before they spotted Cal. Neither seemed to notice the anger Cal was suppressing.

Unembarrassed Nick hugged him, saying "Good of you to meet me. Do you want to carry my bag?"

Tom screeched up in the Police car, sirens wailing, swirling to a halt yards from where they stood.

"Tom."

Tom too was hugged. A kiss landed near his ear.

"Am I holding you up, old son?"

The cousins set off together arm in arm, leaving the friends standing stock still, while Nick considered the thundercloud that was Cal.

"We met up on the train out. Been seeing each other, off and on, y'know. She's a good laugh when you get her alone."

A grunt wasn't quite the answer Nick expected. Cal's mind whirled with the happiness evident on Jacq's face, and the feeling of exclusion, which had re-appeared with Nick's words.

Perhaps Jacq was Nick's 'out of town' girl? The one with whom he had what sounded like wild sex sessions? Well,… allowing for the natural bragging that was part and parcel of male conquest, of course. The image on the platform continued to play behind Cal's eyes.

Cal had never again seen the Jacq who had stepped down from the Landy that first Sunday. She mainly wore trousers of some description. Although whether Jacq herself would be happy to hear her wardrobe so described, was not Cal's concern. Did she take care not to appear too feminine, surrounded as she was by all those men?

Here, before him on the platform, was that vision again. In a floor length skirt of some soft fabric, the matching (extremely brief) top moved with the wearer, revealing a smooth tanned waistline.

Nick's hands had been on the bare skin beneath the top, softly, subtly caressing. And Nick, yes *Nick* had been kissing her. More importantly, in Cal's view, Jacq had been kissing back. And, Jacq had given Nick one final squeeze before letting go.

Hurt and disappointed, Cal meant simply to drop Nick's bags at his place, and return to the homestead. Nick wouldn't leave it, planned a boozy night, which turned into a boozy weekend. Didn't matter to Cal what the hired help got up to on her week off.

❋ ❋ ❋ ❋ ❋

Jacq showed Tom each and every one of the heap of presents she'd bought on his behalf. It certainly didn't occur to him, she was using it as a diversionary tactic.

They lingered over a snack, but eventually Jacq decided to leave. Certain in her own mind that Cal would have been home for hours, simmering gently.

Saying, as she started her Landy, "Look, if I leave now, the littlies will be in bed. Pru and I can hide their presents before they wake up. I'll be back for Church. OK?"

Tom had to be satisfied with that. He knew in rough outline what Jacq had hoped to find in Brisbane, and now she wouldn't tell him. The bright happy look on her face might have something to do with that. Or, again, it might have something to do with his Police Constable, who also looked to have enjoyed his holiday.

CHAPTER THIRTEEN

Tom wouldn't have felt quite so pleased with events, had he seen Jacq's face as she drove towards the homestead.

How dare he scowl at me like that? He set it up for Nick to follow me around, then has the nerve to scowl. Jacq continued to rant at Cal in her head.

Truth to tell, she'd found it unnerving to be the object of Nick's pursuit. Always before, she'd been able to handle it. Been able to divert or deflect his overtures. But, confined together on the train, she had been overwhelmed. Overwhelmed not just by Nick's physical presence, for he matched Cal in size and shape, but by his proximity in a crowd of strangers.

By dint of claiming legions of friends in Brisbane, Jacq had managed to shake him off and pursue her own ends, but she had still found herself spending the last two days with Nick, alone. He'd insisted on showing her the Gold Coast and then the more exotic delights of the Ginger Plantation out towards the Sunshine Coast. Surprised none of Jacq's friends had thought of taking her there.

Unable (and unwilling) to confess that actually she had no friends in Brisbane, Jacq was left to pretend great pleasure in other touristy venues she had not yet seen. Praying there was sufficient information in the various booklets she picked up, to enable her to get by, without revealing any woeful ignorance.

And now, *now*, Cal looked at her so scornfully. Nick had let slip that Cal had asked him... *asked* him, mind you... to keep an eye on her. Bloody nerve!

Jacq slipped quietly into Pru's with the various gifts. Pleading a headache and great longing for her own bed, Jacq escaped quickly.

Baulked of her quarry, and sitting sleepless in her trailer with her angry thoughts still reverberating in her head, she decided to watch the CCTV footage. A sharp intake of breath was the only sound as she watched the two intruders who visited the trailer during her absence.

Unable to bear the idea of sitting in her personal space while it felt so violated, Jacq stormed out to Firefly. Saddling her quickly, they tiptoed away from the homestead, then galloped hell for leather to the waterhole.

Skinny-dipping! I can't believe you're skinny-dipping.

But she was, and what's more it cooled more than her hot sticky body. It calmed the confusion and tumult in her head.

Drying herself on her polo shirt, Jacq trotted more gently back. Arriving just as the homestead was coming to life. The pace was much calmer with no herds around. Mind you, the crew would be back Tuesday. Better make the most of the peace.

Jacq was greeted with such raptures, it eased the tension she'd been under since meeting Cal at the station.

Having despatched the MacGregor clan to church with a message for Tom, Jacq was pleased to sit with Tam, learning what had happened in her absence, and how the drive was going from Jock. She took Tam with her back to the trailer, showing him the film of the intruder Tam reported.

The alarm showed it had not been physically re-set after the first intruder. Had simply buzzed silently to itself, then been re-set by the second intruder, less than an hour later. Happy not to have to explain the first intrusion, Jacq skipped over the explanation of why Tam had two messages and only one intruder.

Jacq continued to wait patiently all through that long Sunday. Determined to give Cal a piece of her mind. Not just for the scowl, ...not just for Nick's constant presence during her 'holiday', but also for the intrusion into her home. Feeling uncomfortable to have trusted someone so patently untrustworthy, Jacq began to question her hard won ability to judge people.

She shook her head vigorously. No, of course, I don't fancy Cal. I mean, as if, right? Bad-tempered, disagreeable, overbearing, chauvinistic. Just, it's disappointing when your judgement lets you down like that. Good job I wasn't more explicit with some of my discoveries. Can't be sure he'd not be passing it on to the other side.

Actually, Jacq needed to get back to Tom. Give him a full frank Report, fulfil her job spec in that area at least. If she went now, she could be back before Cal was. Couldn't she?

In the end, in dithering and changing her mind, Jacq did nothing but sit around, contemplating what she'd do when this particular job was finished.

She knew why Tom was so anxious for her not to go a-roving, but hey, why stop at the first place you find? If the first place is this good, there must be better, and better places surely? Places where the men aren't quite so... ...in your face? Places where they are quite happy to have a partner, and not a doormat?

Jacq nodded to emphasise her decision to move on, soon as.

Monday dawned with no sign of Cal. Not worried, no she wasn't worried, Jacq repeated to herself.

But when she checked on Firefly there was no sign of King. That did worry her. She started the transmitter fixed inside King's head collar. Checking the signal was being received, she noted its position and gave a little nod.

Oh! Cal had evidently sneaked back, picked up King and was now heading for town again. Late morning she rang the bank with various queries, checking in passing that Cal had picked up the cash for the wages. He'd left just after ten, she was told. Hmmm, she pondered.

Checking the signal again, Jacq was surprised it had veered off and was disappearing in the direction of the drovers.

When the signal stayed still for about ten minutes, Jacq started changing into riding gear. Something's up. Something's definitely up. Cal wouldn't just ride off with all the wages like that. Picking up a pocket version of her receiver, Jacq set off for the back kitchen.

Tam was heading her way. "You've heard then?"

"Heard what?"

"Jock says they've been set on. He was expecting them for the midday break. When they didn't arrive he went back looking for them. The men were tied up at the overnight stop. No sign of the herd at all. Jock's released the men. They'll walk to his midday site, pick up spare horses then come home. Do you want him to call in the police, he says?"

"Steve's done that, surely? On the Sat phone?"

Tam shook his head. "Didn't sound as if he had. Shall I call back and ask?"

Jacq was already running for her Landy.

"Where you off too? The boss'd never forgive me, if I let you go out alone."

"I need you to stay here to co-ordinate things. OK?" Jacq bit her lip, while weighing up whether to mention Cal had been diverted with the wages money. "Look, I have a signal from King, who isn't going where I expected him to go. I have to just check it out. I'll be back before the crew are. An hour at most."

While Tam hesitated, his phone rang again. She pressed the pocket receiver into his hand. Taking advantage of his pre-occupation, Jacq turned on the ignition and was off before Tam could take any other action.

Taking the shortest route towards King's signal, Jacq tried to calm herself. Things had obviously moved quite fast while she'd been in Brisbane. Hell, maybe she should have contacted Tom after all?

But her mind was fixed on the problems Cal might be having and not on the lack of current feedback from the police. I'll check on King, then call in.

Maintaining the maximum speed for a Series III until they were out of sight of the homestead, Jacq reviewed her tactics.

The doubled up crew were OK. Bruised egos maybe, but they and Jock were fine, and would be home later today. Steve would have called in the police, who would be there by helicopter shortly. OK, so nothing more I can do in that direction.

Cal? Well Cal, for some reason best known to himself, was heading for the drovers with a whole stash of money on him, and could run into trouble any minute. While apparently watching for potholes and ruts that would trap her wheels, Jacq wondered what had diverted Cal. What had stopped him calling in at the homestead, and then chasing off wherever?

For one heart-stopping, breath-stealing moment, she considered again whether Cal could have been behind all this... this... stuff all along.

Dismissing the thought with an angry toss of her head, she used one hand to clear the tears blinding her vision. Checking again on the signal she was receiving, Jacq flicked various switches on the central console, speaking briefly but urgently to Tom and Control before switching the radio set over to receive, and concentrating on her search.

❋ ❋ ❋ ❋ ❋

King's signal had been stationary for over an hour, before Jacq crawled up the slope and found him. There was no sign of Cal.

King was heading for a collection of horses, held in a makeshift paddock towards the rear of the valley they were in. Tucker's Gap had many little valleys like this. It would be impossible to search all of them, except by air. Thousands of cattle could be here for months, before anyone spotted them.

The smell of wood smoke distracted Jacq. Perhaps Cal's there? She changed direction. Going slowly towards the campfire she could smell, she counted the gang – well she presumed from the snippets of conversation they were the gang. They were talking about dividing the money. Their boss had told them they could keep the cash, just so long as Cal couldn't use it.

For another heart-stopping moment, Jacq thought they'd killed Cal. Resolutely turning her mind away from that, she concentrated on what she could learn. There was no trace of him in or around their campsite.

She retreated towards the Landy. The signal from the moneybag was stationary in the direction of the campsite. Wishing she'd taken the precaution of tagging Cal as well as King and the money, Jacq thought out her problem.

Deciding that as King was here, then maybe he could lead her to Cal, she slipped back towards the horse. Making the low whickering noise he usually responded to, she was pleased to see King making his way towards her. Voices came in her direction, and Jacq cowered behind some scrubby bushes when two of the gang headed towards the horses.

"Shame we can't keep the horses. But it would be too obvious."

"What shall we do with MacCready's horse? Have to shoot it I guess."

Jacq slipped back to the Landy. They'd not kill King. No way!

Blessing the mechanic who'd worked on her vehicle, Jacq silently started the ignition. Driving back along the track, she headed for their campsite. Eight there, two more with the horses.

Parked up beneath the brow of the little slope, she announced through her loud hailer.

"You there. In the camp. There's a big search under way out here for a herd of cattle and the gang who rustled it. Assuming you are that gang, you should know you have five minutes to hightail it out of here before the guns surrounding you commence firing. The clock starts now."

She waited, watching cautiously over the hill, as the men dithered and danced while deciding what action to take. Crawling back to announce, "Time's a-wasting. Anyone still there in two minutes will be arrested for murder and rustling."

That settled it. They ran as if demented towards their trucks, and lit out as if the hounds of hell were chasing them. Jacq was relieved they stopped for the two by the horses. OK, now Cal.

Quartering the ground round the campsite, Jacq eventually came across an area showing where a party of horses had waited. Moving more cautiously now, Jacq checked the ground, following the direction they had taken.

There! There! Blood, plus what appeared to be one horse loping quickly away. Following that sole horse, Jacq tracked Cal.

He was lying unconscious on a pile of rocks in the blazing sun. Taking off her shirt, she moistened it from her canteen before covering his face. Give him some relief, until she arrived with the Landy. Tying her bra to the tallest nearby bush, she ran back to the campsite.

She donned a tee-shirt, before driving back. Restoring her bra to its more usual position Jacq gently checked Cal.

Despite being badly battered and bruised from hauling himself across the landscape, the only major injuries Jacq could find were a possible broken ankle, and the ten or eleven inch gash along his thigh. That had stopped bleeding, although it lay wide open, and was already beginning to look angry. It marked the passage of a bullet, and caused the bloodshed Jacq had found and tracked.

She parked the Landy as close to Cal as she dared, to give them some relief from the scorching sun. Moistening the shirt still over his face, she left that in position. He'd be better off unconscious while she straightened him out.

Cutting speedily along the seams of his jeans, Jacq hesitated. She'd read somewhere that stockmen didn't bother with underpants and blushed as that snippet of information slipped through her mind. Not wanting to face anything... *untoward*... she blushed again at her thoughts, before cutting them off near the tops of his thighs. Cutting the leg sections in half lengthwise, she set them aside.

The ankle would be better off inside his boot, and anyway her scissors wouldn't go through the leather. OK. She drew a deep breath that might have been a sob.

Slipping on a pair of sterile gloves, Jacq washed the thigh wound gently. Feeling for and removing any bits of grit she found. Biting her lip, she poured some neat disinfectant over the gaping cut, sweeping it off as quickly as she could, when the man started moaning. He slipped again into unconsciousness, and Jacq drew a deeper breath. No way out, she'd need to stitch it before she could move him.

Rummaging in her first aid box, she withdrew an evil looking needle and some button thread. She sterilised these by tipping some of the disinfectant into the bottle lid, leaving them to soak in it, while she mentally geared up for the next bit.

Checking his face again, Jacq leaned over briefly to kiss Cal's lips. Right, sooner started, sooner finished. Picking up her needle, Jacq threaded a length of the twine.

❋ ❋ ❋ ❋ ❋

She'd not win any prizes for needlework, but at least it would keep his leg together while they got to hospital.

Her radio squawked. Checking her patient before answering it, Jacq was able to give details of the riders and their last known direction. Repeating at the end, Cal was OK, and she'd take him straight to hospital.

CHAPTER FOURTEEN

King wandered up, breathing noisily in her ear, while she tightened the last strip of fabric round Cal's legs. He snuffled anxiously around Cal, before letting Jacq relieve him of his tack. The saddle was placed into the Landy, with the reins and bridle thrown into the back with the surveillance kit.

Gearing herself up to lift the heavier, taller man, Jacq was surprised to hear him speak.

"'N other kiss'd be nice."

"Hmmm? Touch of the sun, I expect."

Cal studied her blushing face, before shaking his head. "Nope."

"I need to lift you into the Landy. Might shake you round a bit, OK?"

"You seem to have lost quite a few clothes, lady. Or do you always strip like that to attend patients?"

"I... I... er... needed the jeans to fix your legs. My shirt's long enough..."

"Only if I let you have it back," Cal chuckled, reaching for the woman. He pulled her down towards him, stopping with their faces only inches apart in response to the resistance he could feel.

"Shy?" He queried. "Seems to me if you can kiss an unconscious man, you can kiss the same man conscious."

Jacq weakened. When Cal's tongue started probing her lips apart, she drew back with a sigh.

"Need to get you to hospital."

Cal's hands smoothed the same skin Nick had been touching, heightening the blush. Capturing the hands, she smiled. The first proper smile Cal had seen.

"Not much wrong with you, is there? Let's see how you feel after we get to hospital."

Jacq stood astride the taller man. "If you could put your arms around my neck… Then I can grab you and lever you into the Landy."

Cal's eyes roamed over the semi-naked body. His hands brushed the insides of her thighs on their journey to her neck.

"Hey don't handle the goods,… … …"

Cal gently touched the blushing face inches from his own. "Thanks, Jacq."

"No probs. We'll soon have you fixed up properly."

Once he was standing, Cal surveyed Jacq's handiwork. His jeans were now cut-offs. The strips had been bound tightly round his legs, to prevent as much movement as possible in the damaged ankle. Jacq's socks were preventing rubbing at various strategic places, and her own trousers were binding his thighs.

"Good job you didn't go any higher with the jeans, Jacq."

"Oh?"

"Yeah, more man inside them than in Nick's."

"I wouldn't know, and am unlikely to find out." Jacq averted her eyes from the telltale movement inside Cal's jeans.

"Jacq?"

One eyebrow arched in his direction.

"Need a pee. Sorry."

Jacq turned a chuckle into a grunt. "You'll have to lean on me then. I'm certainly not doing more to help."

Cal leaned into the smiling face so near his own.

"Hey. Don't get diverted, or you'll not be able to manage it." Still chuckling, she moved behind him turning her back, resting lightly against him, while he fiddled with his zip, taking more of his weight against her own back as he shifted awkwardly.

Cal hadn't realised quite how difficult it would be to relieve himself in the present circumstances. Embarrassed and uncertain, Cal waited expectantly. God, I hope she's wrong! Visions of requesting a stop for an embarrassing non-pee every half hour, skittered nervously through his mind. They did nothing to help the present situation he found.

There was a trickling sound as Jacq deposited some water from her canteen. "This'll give you a start," was said with the delicious chuckle Cal had first heard for King.

By the time Cal was safely inside the Landy he'd swooned again. Relieved to have him unconscious, Jacq manhandled the bound legs on top of the saddle. It wasn't much, but was the only way she could rest his legs throughout their journey. She didn't want to bend his knees too much.

Jacq retrieved her shirt, fastening the buttons as quickly as her shaking hands would allow. It was a good length, covering her thighs modestly nearly to her knees. A burst of hysterical laughter was bitten off nervously.

King stood beside the Landy whickering.

"Sorry. Sorry old son. I can't take you with us. Go home. Home." Her arm was flung out as if instructing a dog to return home. Jacq watched the horse retreat a few paces and return. In the end she did a pantomime of Jock with the water buckets, and King nodded.

"One week, King. I'll give you one week to get home, then I'll come looking for you."

The horse moved off leisurely, taking a mouthful of scrub here and there as he wandered away.

Cal chuckled. Jacq brushed her hand brusquely across her eyes, before turning back to face him.

"Let's get this show on the road."

Her hand trembled as she checked him before closing the door.

Once Jacq was settled into the driving seat, Cal put his rough hand over the top of hers on the gear lever. "All right lady?"

She nodded without looking at him. The hand caressed again, before slipping sideways to caress her thigh.

"Hey stop that! Being a patient doesn't permit any licence. Goddit?"

Cal sighed, but removed his hand.

"Right, this is going to hurt you more than it hurts me. Hang on."

The radio squawked again with the news Cal's crew had arrived back at the homestead. All in one piece. Was she all right?

"Affirmative. Did you catch the gang? What about the herd?"

She listened silently to the voice at the other end. "I reckon we'll be say four hours or so. Have to drive slowly because of MacCready's injuries. I'll report in again when I'm near town."

Cal was studying the central console. "No wonder nobody got to look inside this. What's all this stuff?"

"This *stuff*, sir, is state of the art surveillance and tracking systems, specially built into the Landy for me."

"Sir? Sir? I never warranted sir while you've been sorting out my life. Why now?"

"Because Sir, I am a public servant, doing a job for my ultimate paymaster."

The onboard computer started up. "Head east, forty minutes for the highway."

Patting his hand, Jacq said, "Would you like some pain relief before we start? I've not got much, but I could give you something. Just stop the worst of it. They'll sort you out properly at the hospital." Her voice caught on the words.

"Something might help. Keep me conscious at least. Kiss is best."

Her eyes flew to his face, then her hand checked his temperature. The hand slid down his cheek gently.

"OK, couple of tabs, and some water." She smiled weakly, but Cal felt the trembling she was trying to suppress.

Jacq settled into her seat and swung east. Cal concentrated on not making an exhibition of himself. Feeling curiously vulnerable to be sitting beside Jacq both only half dressed, he surveyed her handiwork on his thigh. Good job.

Suppressing a groan, he sneaked a look at her. Apparently nerveless, she was concentrating on not bumping her patient too much, but he had felt her trembling and knew she was shaken.

Driving steadily along the highway, Cal asked the question he'd been holding back. "Have a nice holiday?"

"What? Didn't Nick fill you in?"

He shook his head. "Nick?"

"Yeah. He confessed you'd sent him to keep an eye on me." Jacq glanced briefly in his direction.

Cal could think of nothing to say. Jacq thought Nick was spying on her? At his request?

"Say, do you know all the vehicles locally? Can you see who that is, coming up behind us so fast?"

Levering himself up and round in the seat, Cal couldn't suppress a groan.

"Alright?"

He nodded, but Jacq saw the blenched face and bitten lip.

"Pain relief should be through in a while. I can let you have another tablet if it's not enough. OK?"

He nodded through gritted teeth, trying to identify the oncoming vehicle.

"Blaumfeld, I think."

"OK, settle down and brace yourself."

"Brace myself?"

"Yeah, he's in league with Diane. I'm going to go for it. Wedge yourself as best you can and hold on."

Jacq glanced briefly at him, giving a twisted smile on the word. "Sorry."

The Landy drew to a standstill to enable Jacq to press down the little lever Cal knew engaged low drive, and the engine gave a deep growl, as if clearing its throat. Something caught hold of them and thrust them forward.

An hour later, Jacq said, "There, that should do it."

"Top speed is 70 on the highway. Didn't you know that?"

"Not with some galoot chasing you, it's not."

"How'd you get that speed out of this old crate?"

"This old crate, mister, just saved your life. Bit of respect, please."

"Yeah but how?"

"V8 supercharged under the bonnet." Jacq chuckled at his low whistle of surprise.

Cal winced as they hit a bump and then a hollow.

"Alright?"

He nodded, busy suppressing the pain. Satisfied they'd thrown off the pursuers, Jacq stopped to issue more pain relief.

"Sorry, this is all I've got. Now remember, you've had 600 at 1530 and another 300 now, what's that 1700. The Doctor will need to know." Jacq stood, patiently waiting for him to swallow the tablets and hand back the cup.

"Kiss?"

"Hardly appropriate, is it?"

"More effective than any tablets. Trust me?"

Oh Cal, if I could have trusted you, we might not be here now. Jacq kissed him, quelling the thought prompted by his words.

It calmed Jacq, but did nothing for the bulge inside Cal's cut-offs.

"You'd better get that looked at too, while you're there." The cheeky grin appeared briefly, before Jacq resumed her place.

Each busy with their thoughts, nothing further was said until the town rose in front of them.

"Jacq?"

"Hhm?"

"We need to talk."

"Yeah, maybe. Once you're better."

"Oh shit!" Cal sat up quickly, bumping his head on the roofline handle.

"What?"

"The money! They took the money!"

"Nope." Jacq indicated the back.

Peering over his shoulder Cal could clearly see the moneybag.

"Phew! Who else was with you at the camp?"

Shaking her head, she said, "No one."

"I heard a stranger's voice, male. Saying it was surrounded. They'd got five minutes to leave."

Nodding, she smiled briefly. "Just little old me. Good isn't it?"

"You're one helluva woman, Jacq. One helluva woman."

Cal was unconscious again shortly after. Too much medication.

❋ ❋ ❋ ❋ ❋

At the hospital, Jacq borrowed some scrubs trousers. Feeling decently dressed for the first time all afternoon, she sat with Cal as they waited for the x-ray. The Doctor towered above Jacq while checking the plates.

"Not broken, just badly sprained. I'll get it strapped and you can go home."

Cal eyed him assessingly. Well over six foot, built to match, full black beard and moustache, and bright blue eyes which shone encouragingly. Drop dead gorgeous. He seemed unconcerned with his patient, talking direct to Jacq while his eyes roamed over the vision in front of him.

Indicating the cut, Jacq said, "What about that?"

"There doesn't appear to be any grit in it. I'm gonna leave it as is. Should be sound. Someone did a good job." Jacq blushed. Turning reluctantly back to his patient, the Doctor asked, "How's the pain? Do you want another shot?"

Jacq spoke up quickly. "He's OK, I think Doc. Said a kiss was more effective. I'm not qualified to administer medication, but you are. Just kiss 'im. I'll leave you to it." She backed off and was gone before her words registered fully with either man.

"Shot, or shall I get Sister to administer a kiss?"

The Doctor's eyes followed the sound of Jacq's footsteps retreating. A twinge of jealousy surged through Cal, and had to be suppressed. Wouldn't do any good starting a fight with the Doc, but he should watch that expression when looking at Cal's girl.

Cal waited nervously for someone to strap his ankle, and slip something over the gash. When Jacq peered through the curtains, he sat up, reaching towards her.

"Wait for me, please?"

An eyebrow arched in his direction, but she came right up to the bed.

"Jacq, wait for me please?"

Jacq's face said, "Please. As if."

A nurse came in, saying as she replaced the curtain, "Do you need a sedative, shot of some sort?"

To Cal's relief however, Jacq did wait while his ankle was tended. She even found a wheelchair to get him back to the Landy.

She blushed as she stood astride him to hoist him out of the wheelchair, swinging him easily this time into the car. Manhandling his legs in after him, caused a movement in his cut-offs, Jacq pulled back for a minute, blushed, then carried on, without comment.

Once he was settled, Jacq returned the wheelchair.

"Have to stop at Tom's. He's an old worry wart, but he won't rest until he sees me."

"I can understand that."

She peered anxiously at him. "You must have a touch of sun stroke."

"Nope, first time I've felt sane in years."

Jacq was greeted with hugs and kisses at the Police Station. Cal had never seen the older man so shaken.

Shocked to hear Jacq say, "I'll finish up at the homestead. Should be back next week, perhaps. Have to see what happens."

She was leaving? Jacq was planning to leave? Stunned, Cal couldn't think what to say, as they rattled slowly back to the homestead.

❊ ❊ ❊ ❊ ❊

In the melee of welcoming him home and learning what had happened to the crew, Cal didn't at first realise Jacq had slipped away. He caught up with her at the paddock. She was leaning into her horse, sobbing.

"What's up?"

The figure stiffened. He'd surprised her. She obviously felt safe enough to have let her guard down. Cal had never been able to sneak up on her before.

"Er, do you think King'll make it?"

"Sure. Knows his way around."

Jacq remained inside the railings, patting and petting her horse.

"Someone out here could do with some of that."

"Oh?" Turning in his direction, Jacq surreptitiously wiped her eyes. "I see no one."

"Me, Jacq. Me!"

Shaking her head vehemently, she said, "Cal MacCready's too smart for that. You ask anyone."

"He's not as smart as he likes to think."

Jacq's phone set off. "Scuse me."

Turning away, Jacq walked along the paddock, briskly answering the questions she was obviously being asked.

Cal remained in the shadows watching, but although he listened carefully he could not hear any details.

Finally, she was finished, and restored the phone to her shirt pocket, wiping her hands across her eyes surreptitiously. She climbed through the rails next to him.

"Do you need anything else before I go to bed?"

"Hug?"

"Nope. Business relationships don't stand that sort of messing." She wouldn't meet his eyes.

He let the silence grow, just watching the drooping figure before him.

"Boss, I... I... have to go into Charleville to finalise some stuff about this job. Then I'm all through. Patience is probably not up to..."

"You'll be back to finish your work here, won't you?"

Her head shook.

"You have a job to do."

Tearfully, Jacq said, "Nope. All done, Boss. Crooks in the bag, prosecutors building a case. Whatever property or cash can be recovered and identified will be returned...."

"No, lady. *I* employed you to do a job of work. That's not finished..."

Jacq's eyes flashed to his face briefly. "Cal, I won't be allowed to stay. I have to go right out of the area. Right away, until after the Court Case, assuming there is a court case." An air of weary finality settled over her.

"Not until you've explained one or two things to my satisfaction."

He studied her face in the moonlight. She looked exhausted, dead on her feet, not surprising, given what she'd been through today. Balancing all his weight on his crutches, Cal kissed her gently.

"Get a good night's sleep. We'll talk tomorrow." Turning her about, he smacked her behind awkwardly, pushing her in the direction of her trailer, while maintaining his balance.

Ten weary steps away, she turned back, "Do you need help?"

"I'll get Tam to help me, or Jock. Go. Go, get some sleep."

He waved her away. Astounded that tired as she was, she had still checked her horse and would have tended him too, before finally getting some sleep herself.

Alone in his own bed, Cal reflected on what he could remember of events since he'd set off from town this morning. She is something else.

CHAPTER FIFTEEN

The following day brought Diane in a welter of dust and spinning tyres. Her brother had been arrested and was awaiting questioning. The rustlers had been rounded up and would be back in town shortly.

Jacq left her office as soon as she heard who'd arrived, heading for the MacGregors' where she was sure of her welcome. She'd spent the morning making up pay packets, hoping Cal would be too busy this afternoon to remember what he'd said last night. Feeling more in charge of herself today, she was reasonably confident she could deal with the problems, which seemed to have arisen yesterday.

Cal too, seemed to have returned to his normal self. Distantly formal during breakfast, and again when she offered the made up pay packets. Not realising that the bleak, blank look on her pinched, washed out face was the cause of the grim expression Cal's showed.

He was sitting on the old day bed on the verandah, out in the open while still resting his gammy leg. The bed Diane used to use, and Jacq too had occupied briefly, while awaiting Cal's return.

Tam and Jock had spent the morning clearing the lodgers out of their resting places. Cal hadn't had a minute alone with Jacq and worried about that and her, while facing his ex-wife. He didn't want Jacq to leave. Definitely she was not to leave before he'd spoken to her. Sorted something out.

Unsurprisingly Diane was in one of her moods. Cal listened in silence to the long and involved explanation, of how *someone* had been trying to frame her for the problems locally. He didn't believe her. Part of his mind continued to worry about Jacq, while apparently listening to Diane's angry tirade. Busy complaining bitterly about Jacq and all her doings, Diane seemed not to realise Cal wasn't paying any attention.

She'd always been able to command attention, had known instinctively how to play up to the men in her life. She was unused to a man who not only ignored her, but cared not a jot for her problems either. That had been the root of the dislike between herself and Cal's father since the wedding.

Col had been unimpressed by her wiles and impervious to her blandishments, causing Diane to go to extreme lengths to attract his attention. Collum MacCready's behaviour irked Diane, in some obscure way she hadn't been able to rationalise. Hence she tried the harder, finally making the attempts to push him into bankruptcy, or suicide. Something, anyway to prove he noticed her and her presence.

But no, ... for the most part Col had ignored her. Swatting her away as if she were as inconsequential as the flies that abound throughout the year. He'd even ignored her attempts to seduce him! No man had ever done that before, no man!

A police car swirled to a stop, and Nick dashed up the steps onto the verandah. Nick escorted Diane back to town, where she too was formally charged with the series of frauds being perpetrated locally.

Relieved but anxious, Cal tried to get Jacq alone. She was having none of it. Fixed him with a glare to rival his own.

No, she wasn't going for a ride. No, she had plenty to do in her office, in the trailer, in the back kitchen. Somewhere, anywhere Cal could not be. Could not be until he could use his bloody leg again. He felt like... what did he feel like? Only half a man, that's what.

Unable even to walk quickly enough to keep up with Jacq in her restless pacing, Cal stomped around on his crutches, noisily venting his renowned temper on anything and everything in his path. Jacq appeared not to notice. Seemed to be lost in some silent sombre world where nothing could touch her.

The homestead settled back into its normal routine. The calm serenity of his surroundings gradually eased the panic Cal was beginning to feel.

Firefly was gone one morning. Standing at the rail, wondering what the hell she was up to, Cal was tempted to take a trail horse after her. But hell, he knew better than anyone how she could cope. Knew as well as Jacq did herself, where she'd gone. Real quiet, real early too.

Pacing up and down the boundary fence for the rest of the day, Cal felt something of what Jacq had been through when he'd not turned up with the cash. Wryly acknowledging that if he'd had a tracker he'd have been off after her in a flash. As it was, there was nothing he could do, except wait as patiently as he could, for her to return with King.

She trotted up the drive, leading King behind Firefly, just as dusk was settling across the land. The expression on her face eased somewhat to see Cal at the rail.

"Sorry, didn't worry, did you?"

Dismounting, Jacq pulled the reins over Firefly's head. Cal moved to stand behind her. Leaning into her, he raised his arms out of the crutches to hug her. Jacq had to hold him, had to take his weight, but he heard the sharp intake of breath, felt the trembling start again.

He'd not been wrong. Kissing her neck was a reflex action, given his fears this day. Cal knew what he wanted. It wasn't going to slip through his fingers. Not now. Not now he'd finally found her.

Jacq struggled, pulling back from the embrace she had initially welcomed. "Sorry boss. No!"

Waiting until Cal was steady again on his crutches, before removing the tack from Firefly.

"See who I found, boss? Brought him home for you." Tears threatened to break through the seemingly casual tone. "Could do with an apple, couldn't you boy?"

Leaning into her horse, Jacq was crying again, as she carefully brushed Firefly down.

Cal rummaged in a pocket. Apples? Bloody apples? At a time like this, she can talk about apples? Patting and petting his horse, Cal reached a sudden decision.

"Meet me at the waterhole tomorrow Jacq, sundown. Please, please? Jacq, we have to talk."

Jacq gave a brief nod, hoping Cal wouldn't notice her tears.

Her Landy had gone the following morning. Jock and Tam shook their heads. They had no idea where she was.

"She'll be back boss. Trailer's still here."

Neither seemed too perturbed by her continued absence.

❋ ❋ ❋ ❋ ❋

Tam took the tack out of his hands, silently saddling King and waiting patiently for Cal to mount. Firefly was still munching hay in the paddock. Would Jacq show up?

Turning his horse, Cal made for the waterhole. No pretence, was going direct to the waterhole, … hoping, …hoping Jacq would be there, … waiting for him.

Jacq helped him dismount, smiling gently into his face as he slid down. His hands automatically reached for her, cradling the face haunting his dreams. "Jacq! Jacq!"

With a happy sigh, she settled into his arms like a homing pigeon. They shared a passionate kiss, gulping for air, before kissing again.

"Hey Cal. Sit down before you fall down."

The light-hearted laughter encouraged Cal to pull her after him. He felt fabric under his hand, as he reached for the woman he loved, unconsciously echoing the movement he'd seen in his father all his life.

Bad ankle, gammy leg did nothing to slow them down. Tenderly undressing each other, they kissed and clung, exploring the textures of each other.

Her hands gently caressed the leg she'd stitched. Moving lower Jacq kissed it again, as she had when she set each stitch, moving slowly up his thigh, on beyond the stitches.

Nothing had prepared Cal for these sensations, this passion, the feelings flowing through him as their gentle lovemaking continued.

This then, was what he'd missed, what he'd missed through the years married to Diane. This... this... bli –iiiiiiisssss! He sank back onto her.

Cradling her head in his hands, Cal looked directly into her eyes, "I love you Jacqueline Tregissick."

Jacq kissed him, preventing further speech. When she wriggled slightly he rolled off, pulling her with him. Settling herself onto his chest, Jacq sighed happily, before placing little kisses across his face.

"Jacq? Jacq? Need to talk sweetheart."

The kisses continued, even while she shook her head. "Plenty of time to talk, love. Busy at the moment."

Aeons later, the moon rose and sank over them. *This* was Paradise!

Cal had Paradise here in his arms. His homestead was also safe, his livelihood was safe, and he had the woman he loved in his arms. Great. Cal sank into a deep sleep.

※ ※ ※ ※ ※

He was unsurprised she'd gone when he woke with the dawn of a new day. Hell, didn't want any gossip yet.

Cal struggled to rise. Struggled to tighten the cinch on King's saddle. Struggled to mount. Heading back for the homestead. Back to the love of his life.

Back, to find the trailer had vanished. Vanished after last night! How could it be gone? How could Jacq have gone?

He roared and rampaged, knowing it would do no good.

Tam drove him into Town, to the Police Station, out to Tom's. And all the time, deep, deep inside, Cal knew she'd gone. Knew she'd left him. Knew what she'd said last night was the truth. They couldn't be together until after the Court Case.

"If you still want to, Cal, only if you want to. The day after the verdict, I'll be here my love. Waiting here for you."

He thought he'd dreamt it, but he hadn't. She'd really said those words. Really meant those words.

There was nothing he could do. Nothing *they* could do now, but wait for Justice to reach a conclusion.

CHAPTER SIXTEEN

Three months later, Cal sorted through yet another bag of mail for the drovers. That's funny. First time he could ever remember it happening.

A letter for Jock? Who couldn't read? Had to have recipes dictated onto a cassette player. Who the hell would write to someone who couldn't read?

Leaving the mail in the pigeon holes Jacq had instituted in another life, Cal headed for the back kitchen. Out on the verandah, Jock was dozing on the daybed.

"Hey, old timer! Post!"

Surprised by the pleasure in the old eyes, Cal waited patiently for the envelope to be ripped open. Postcard. It contained a postcard.

"That's real pretty, ain't it boss?"

"Brisbane, Cookie. Who's writing to you from Brisbane?"

"Only one person would write to me, boss. Real good fella, my lady friend." The chuckle caused a coughing spell.

Cal hitched the old boy higher up the day bed. Jock was showing his years now, and Cal was glad he'd succumbed to the anger Jacq had expressed. She'd been right too, Jock had been a good and faithful servant and friend to the MacCreadys through the years. It was only right they should look after him in his old age. Hell, Jock had no family other than the MacCreadys to do that for him, did he?

Jock's initial resistance to taking things easy, had soon given way to an increasing need to spend his afternoons on the daybed, where he could still oversee what was happening, feel he was important.

"D'you want to read it, boss? See what she says?"

Cautiously Cal turned the card over.

"Hi Cookie. How're y'doing? Keeping things tidy for when I return? I don't want to have to start from scratch again Cookie. Love to my old buddies. J."

"That what it says, boss?" Jock chuckled again. Tracing the writing with one rheumy old finger, he repeated Cal's words.

"Said she'd write boss. Said she'd write. Seems she's not allowed to communicate with us until after the Case. Tom says the same, so must be true. She misses us tho', don't she boss? Misses us."

Cal watched the happiness fade as Jock slipped back into another doze. Picking up the card, he carried it to the fly screen. No hint. Nothing for him.

What did you expect? Some faded message? Face it, she used you to scratch an itch and has moved on. His heart refused to believe what his mind was saying.

Sighing Cal turned the card, to look again at the picture of Brisbane. Why Brisbane?

People send postcards from places they've been, to show those at home where they are. Brisbane. Jacq was in Brisbane. And she'd be home after the trial. That's what she was saying. A hint. A message. Not communicating with Cal, a prime victim, but getting a message through.

There was a number pencilled underneath the picture. Glancing at the sleeping cook, Cal peered closely at the number, copying it onto his hand from habit. Leaving the card on the table next to the daybed, Cal returned to his office.

Taking the Sat phone with him, he went over to the paddock. Sitting apparently aimlessly on the top rail, he weighed up what he knew.

Jacq knew Jock couldn't read, so why write to him? The message could be read by anyone at all, there was no significance to it. And yet... it seemed to mean something. His brain whirred with activity.

The pencilled phone number could also have been written by anyone, someone in the shop maybe, and not noticed when the card was sold. Didn't need to be Jacq did it? Cal studied the Sat phone cautiously. Another legacy of Jacq's time here.

She'd loved it here, hadn't she? There was no mistaking the signs. Once the Outback has trapped you in it's spell, you can't break it. Don't want to break it. Just want to stay forever. His slow smile spread, as he punched in the numbers. He'd take a chance.

A well-remembered voice said softly, "Hello?"

Cal breathed her name.

"Ahhh!" The warm chuckle came down the line to him, releasing the tension he'd felt since her departure.

"How're things?"

"*Things* are fine. Better now, but fine."

"Ja..."

"Shush sweetheart, walls have ears."

"I need to know you're fine, love. OK for money, please?"

"I'm fine. Promise. Got a new job."

Cal's heart skipped a beat. "Not dangerous! Please, not dangerous?"

Again the chuckle calmed him. "No, no sweetheart. Nothing dangerous. Boring, boring, boring."

"I love you!"

A sharp intake of breath greeted his words. "Shush my love. We have to get through this. How can I... ... How can I if you say that? Please sweetheart. Don't say it."

"Can't stop me thinking it. Thinking it 24/7 lady, do y'hear?"

A single sob reached him. "Have to go, sweetheart. Can't stop. Can't..." The line disengaged.

Hell and damnation! Cal tried the number several times. Knowing that she wouldn't answer, hoping that she would answer. Hoping what? Hoping she'd say the words back to him? Hell no, just wanting to know she was safe. Somewhere in the world and safe. Not worried. He didn't want her to be worrying. Was she really managing just fine?

Eventually the phone was answered by a rough Australian voice, saying, "Shit! Didn't know this thing worked. If you own this then come get it. I'll put it in the trash bin at the entrance to Mount Coot-Tha Lookout." The phone went dead again.

Mount Coot-Tha was on the outskirts of Brisbane. Was one of Brisbane's beauty spots, and a great tourist attraction. So, Jacq *was* in Brisbane, *was* safe for the moment.

Had needed to hear from Cal so desperately she had come up with this plan just to listen to his voice, and he'd thrown that effort away by his thoughtless reaction to it. If only he'd not said those words, perhaps she would have spoken to him for longer? And now, ... Cal had no way of reaching her, none. His hasty actions had cost him time talking to his love, time listening to her voice. Time checking more closely what was happening to her, what had been happening to her in the long weary months since she'd left.

Jacq had thrown the phone away. Storylines from his favourite books came back to him. Yeah buy a pay and go phone, untraceable. That's what she'd done, simply to have a few words with him. Jacq must feel it's still dangerous here, somehow.

Cal searched out the postcard, erasing the pencilled numbers, just in case. But their conversation repeated in his head throughout the long lonely nights. Taking turns with scenes from their time alone together in the Outback. Some nights he'd turn towards her, reaching blindly for her in his sleep, only to meet the usual blank, blank nothingness of his marriage bed.

He'd never felt this way about Diane. How could he have been so blind?

His mother's words also haunted him. "Don't marry her son. Diane's not right for you. You don't love her. You're in love with the idea of her. The idea of someone like her."

But, he'd gone ahead and done it anyway. Pleased to think Mum would have some help as her illness progressed. Pleased to think the homestead would continue to revolve in its regular pattern, despite Mum being desperately ill. What a fool he'd been!

As if Diane would do any of it. She'd been totally self-absorbed. Diane could never have undertaken even half what Jacq had achieved.

❉ ❉ ❉ ❉ ❉

Two months passed with no word. Nothing! Cal's stomach and nerves twisted themselves into knots worrying, …worrying. The disclosures and the gossip in town did nothing to still the worry nagging at his insides.

Initially neither of the Blaumfelds were granted bail. Old man Gough moved heaven and earth, but to no avail. Finally big name barristers arrived from Brisbane, and eventually they were freed on a massive bail amount, with the proviso they must stay well clear of this area. Not visit their homes or their families until after the trial. No formal trial date had yet been set. Regular three monthly reviews was the best they could hope for.

Cal listened respectfully to Tom's explanations of these facts. He'd never been in enough trouble to require legal action. Hadn't realised it would take a good year and more to reach trial readiness

The fact the Blaumfelds were in Brisbane hiked up his worries for Jacq. He couldn't ask for any information without divulging that he knew where she was. An action which might endanger her life more than the Blaumfelds being in the same town.

Alone, and desperately worried for someone else's welfare for the first time in his life, Cal didn't know what to do, where to turn. He roamed further afield on King in an attempt to clear his mind, calm his thoughts, soothe his nerves. But it made no difference.

He'd never known so much angst. Angst! He said the word aloud, relishing it on his tongue. The books all wrote about angst, and here it was in his life. Angst! It wasn't a pleasant feeling, he found, surprised to discover exactly what the characters in his favourite books had been experiencing.

❈ ❈ ❈ ❈ ❈

The typed envelope addressed to Jock caused a momentary tremor. Leaving the other mail on his desk he flew across to the back kitchen.

"Here old timer. Post."

Jock savoured the envelope until Cal thought he would scream with the suspense. Fought to control himself. Fought not to rip the thing out of those old, old fingers and read the card.

Opera House, Sydney. Thank God! Thank God! Is that where you are my love? Sydney?

"Hi Cookie, Still fine. Could do with some of those old recipes here. Take care of yourself. Love."

No signature, no pencil marks. Nothing. The letters were block printed, giving no clues Cal could discern. Hell!

Teary eyes surveyed him. "She's fine boss. She says so. She'll be back, soon as. You'll see."

One of the old hands reached out to pat the younger one. "Wonder why she mentioned your Ma's book? We copied all the recipes out. They're on that little cassette I listen to. Just like to hear her voice. She was something else, wasn't she boss?"

The old man chuckled again. Prudence came through with some coffee, and her glance flickered from one to the other.

Cal was viewing everybody suspiciously these days, he found. Well, except those Jacq had trusted. He reviewed them again, Tam, Jock, Pru … yeah, if Jacq said she was OK, then she was. Not prepared to take any chances while things still hung in the balance, Cal was relieved Jock fell asleep without saying anything further.

Cal shredded the envelope. Another legacy of Jacq's time here. A big shredder, capable of eating plastic cards, cds and things, as well as paper. Thanks Jacq! Briefly he felt again the comfort she had given him, the support she'd provided unstintingly for his business.

Grooming King that evening, Cal heard again the old voice. "Wonder why she mentioned your Ma's old book?"

Old book... ... old book? Meg's Diary? Meg's Diary. Jacq would never have kept it. She hadn't wanted anyone else to read it, but she'd have put it somewhere safe. Somewhere for Cal to find, if he looked... Oh yes, *if* he looked...

Treading cautiously into Jacq's office, (it was still called Jacq's office, even though Patience worked there now,) Cal opened the drawer. The silent glide reminded Cal of the sound of those high heels tap-tap-tapping their way round his homestead. Those busy fingers clattering. What wouldn't he give to have those days back?

Gone! Well, naturally, she'd not leave it behind, would she? Not leave the recording for someone else to find. He touched the brown paper lining. Touched again. Carefully removing the lining paper, he discovered a brown envelope marked Private and Confidential addressed simply to Cal.

Replacing the lining paper, he sighed. The drawer was now the same depth as the others. Not that he'd spotted it previously. Surprised anyone had thought of such a simple hiding place, Cal retreated, clasping his package.

Opening the book at the bookmark, Cal was entranced to see Jacq's writing. But this was not one of the formal little notes she'd left on his business correspondence, the clear details of every telephone conversation. The minutiae of his business had been clearly recorded during her sojourn in his office.

Little Miss Efficiency, he'd called her sarcastically at the beginning, but gradually he had succumbed to the perfection enveloping his business and personal life while Jacq had been around. The seemingly effortless way everything had been organised, with minimal input from himself, he now recalled. Hell, he'd just accepted it as his right! And ... damnation, he still hadn't paid her, not for any of her hard work!

"Boss, I hope you will find this book. Protect it well. Others could do serious damage with the information it contains. When you've read it, re-seal it and give it to Tom. He is safer than the Bank of England. Trust me." On the reverse, scrawled as if at a later time, a later date, she had written. "Much as I love you Cal, I cannot stay. Cannot speak with you until after the trial. It could look like collusion. If they think you are in this with me, they might get away with it all. You might still lose everything. Be patient." Staggered to think there was still some problem lying in wait, Cal paused.

Did Jacq mean it? What she'd whispered over and over as they lay together out there? What she'd written in his Mum's diary? Finally convinced, he scanned the book before him.

Just a diary. His Mum's thoughts recorded over a period. Interesting but hardly vital, yeah?

When no further cards arrived for Jock, Cal wondered if there was still some problem. Who was Jacq most afraid for?

❋ ❋ ❋ ❋ ❋

Terry turned up, in Town fortunately. Knew better than to come back to Cal for a job. After his treachery, he'd be lucky to get any job in town.

Tom waited and watched. Mulling over the latest development, Tom reported the bare bones back to his superior.

Worrying about his cousin didn't help him. Oh yes, letters he wrote could reach her, but… but… why couldn't she contact him? They'd always stayed in touch. All their lives they'd been *there* for each other, at the end of an arm, at the end of a phone. Listening, advising, helping, whatever …. The alliance they'd set up in their youth still survived. *Would* survive even this enforced separation.

Sitting on a bar stool still seething from yet another refusal when Cal arrived, Tom said, "Don't ask old son. Don't ask."

They sat in silence over a couple of cold ones, before walking back to Tom's place.

Tapping the re-painted fence Tom said, "I'd give anything to have her here, right now, painting that."

Side by side they sat on Tom's verandah in drunken contemplation of his fence. More empty cans collected round their feet.

Pleasantly tipsy Tom said, "I miss her. Sure she was a thorn in your flesh if you didn't agree with her, but by god, she'd got some spunk."

Cal nodded. Talking about her was OK. Not as good as talking to her, but... OK.

"I never thought I'd say this. But I'm sometimes grateful to the bastard who made her come out here."

Cal nodded sagely. Drunk enough to know he was drunk, but not fighting fit, as he normally got.

"Yeah, bastard. She lived with him for over twenty years. Knew him before then. Years she gave to him, bastard. Then he ups and leaves just like that."

Tom tried to click his fingers. Clicking and clicking over and over again, until he finally performed the simple manoeuvre.

Lost in his own misery Cal didn't really listen. He heard but he didn't listen. Heard all about Dave. About the Degree. About the hell Jacq's life had been.

Tom sobbed. "Should have made her leave here. When she first uncovered it. Should have made her leave. She wanted to stay, wanted to help you. Can't understand it. Don't understand. What is it with you anyway?"

He turned belligerently towards Cal. "You didn't touch her, did you? My gal. My poor little girl."

Tom sobbed again. "Heartbroken she was when she first arrived. Heartbroken. Yet wanted to help *you*. Arrogant, headstrong Cal MacCready. Said you'd been hurt way down."

Dazedly he looked at the fists Cal was shaking in his face. "Whassa marra?"

Nick pounded up the steps. "Come on Tom. No sense going on like this is there? They won't let you speak to her. That's that."

Cal left the other man to put Tom to bed. He'd ride home and get to bed himself. While he was pondering King's whereabouts, Nick returned.

"He'll sleep it off. Be ready for his next shift. It's just the worry gets 'im. Hey, where d'y think you're going?"

"Home. Sleep."

"Not yet buddy. Sleep at my place, right?"

Gripping Cal's arm tightly, Nick tucked him into the police car, and set off for his own home. Indoors he made coffee.

Cal sipped it, tipping it straight down the sink. "Want Jacq's coffee."

"Well you can't have it, can you old son? Have to wait for the trial." Nick laughed. "We need to work out what danger is still hereabouts that threatens her. Want her to feel safe when she comes back, don't we?"

"What's it to you?"

Cal remembered talk of an out of town girl, remembered the kiss at the station. Eyed his best mate assessingly.

"Pru said I should tell you. Said I should tell you at least, that it wasn't Jacq I was interested in."

"What's it to her?"

"Poor old Cal, always the last to see. The last to recognise what's under your nose."

Nick's chuckle seemed to attract Cal's fist. Perhaps that's why, this time, Cal managed to black Nick's eye. Cal surveyed his erstwhile friend blearily, thinking, first time I've done that since school.

"Calm down fella. Calm down."

Cal had to wait until Nick had placed a pack of frozen peas over his eye, to learn Prudence and Nick were planning to marry. Had been meeting in secret for a year or more.

They'd met when Nick investigated MacGregor's death. Uncharacteristically, Nick had remained in touch with Prudence, helping out when he could. They intended to live in town with the younger children. Tam and Patience wanted to stay at Cal's. That was fine with Nick apparently. The details slipped off Cal's mind, and he shook his head, too drunk to work it out now.

Nick's phone rang.

"Hey, hey calm down. He's fine. Just sleeping it off."

Cal waited and watched. Trying to work out all the confusing facts he now possessed.

"Here, here is someone else desperate to speak to you."

The phone was thrust into his hand.

"I'm outa here." Chuckling to himself, Nick headed for the door. "Seeya."

"Cal! Cal!" The receiver squawked loudly.

Cal shook his head. Wishing immediately he hadn't, when the room swayed around him. The voice on the phone grew sharper.

"Have you been drinking? Drinking with Tom? I don't believe you two. To do this to me now! How could you?"

"Sweetheart?"

"Don't you sweetheart me. I... I..." Sobs prevented her from speaking.

"Sweetheart? I'm sorry. I just didn't know what to do."

"Oh, so drinking's the answer is it? Is it?" The voice sounded cool, but still angry. "I don't think so. I so don't think so. Wouldn't you be better employed checking the homestead? Keeping things ticking along out there? Make sure no one else is helping Diane and Denis? Make our lives safer for the future? Oh no! Not the two great brains I love. No, they must go out and get drunk together."

"I love you sweetheart."

"And…" was said in the deceptively gentle way she had.

"Just I love you. Can't wait for you to get…" His arm swept wide, meaning to embrace the homestead, the town, the Outback.

"Mind the ornaments, Boss. For pity's sake, mind the ornaments when you get expansive. Get some sleep, then plan. Do y' hear me? Plan for the future, please? Please?"

"Sweetheart, I need to know you are safe. Can't we set up something? Please?"

"Love, it is not safe. I daren't even write to Jock again. Don't want him hurt on my account. Please sort it out, Cal, please." He listened to her heartbroken sobs. Wishing just to hold her, just hold her while she needed comfort.

Jacq drew a deeper, steadying breath. "I can sort something out for Tom, but not you, boss. Check with Tom. I… I… can only contact him. Sorry boss. Love you. Bye!"

The line went dead again, leaving Cal staring blankly at the receiver in his hand.

Jacq phoned Nick? She could phone Nick but not him? Not Tom? When they both loved her so. Why?

He settled himself to sleep with that question reverberating round his head. Meaning to settle it with Nick once and for all tomorrow.

But in the morning somehow, the whole thing had become clearer. Cal could focus properly. Jacq was saying someone else might still be trying… …. Someone *apart* from the Blaumfelds was lurking and needed to be stopped before they finished… or hurt anybody Jacq loved. Including him and Tom.

Walking back to the bar to collect his pick-up, Cal thought again about the Diary. Perhaps there's something in there?

CHAPTER SEVENTEEN

Back at the homestead, Cal was glad he could go straight to the Diary, without having to tend a horse. Pleased to be able to start his search straight away, he was unprepared to find a personal letter addressed to Callum MacCready in his mother's handwriting.

"My darling son, Callum,

It is difficult to explain to a child why their parents act certain ways, *react* certain ways. I always wanted to explain things to you, but now I won't get the chance. You are not yet ready to accept things, son. I hope, by the time you find my Diary, you will be able to understand. Understand a little more anyway, of the life we lived when we three, your father, Jock and me, were young.

Be kind to Jock, please son. He has given up so much to stay here, suffered so much to stay here. We are all the family he has, well, … all the family he knows. My father was real mean to him. Let Jock enjoy some Paradise while he can, my son.

Be patient with your father, too. He bore so much, so bravely son, and because of it he cannot tell you, … cannot tell you how much he loves you. He suffered as others suffered in that and other orphanages, but he would never speak about his time there. Never! Never joined the protests, never sought compensation. Fate, he would say. It was fate. Who knows, perhaps we'd not have met if he'd been allocated to another orphanage, some other place of torture for young children torn from their homes. That would have been a tragedy too, in it's own way. But he was sent to the Charleville Orphanage, and then on to Paradise.

Your father always said life here at Paradise was sweet. That gives me some understanding of his life before he arrived in mine. But Life was hard then, Cal, and you needed to be tough to survive it. Our childhoods toughened us up, and your father thought you would need to be tough to hold on to what we had.

I know, I know, son, that it doesn't excuse his beatings, but my father spoiled his only son, and Collum didn't want to spoil you. It would have been so easy to spoil you, arriving as you did with the start of our better lives. And too, we'd waited so patiently, tried so desperately. Anything, everything that was available then, to help childless couples. You'll be surprised to hear we even spoke about a pilgrimage to see if that would help. But, … well, we never had the time. And then it was too late. But your father never complained about that either. You were our golden child, our miracle baby. Wanted, oh so desperately wanted, and loved beyond measure, but perhaps Col overcompensated? No doubt some fancy city slicker could explain it better.

This is all the information I have about your father, and Jock. I've tried to write it as he told it to me. Your Dad seemed to cope better talking as if it had happened to someone else, …several other people. I still think that the pain was so bad, he could only deal with it by pretending it happened to someone else. So that is how I wrote it, but I only heard it once or twice at certain times, when we'd had other setbacks, and Col was depressed. Col didn't dwell on the past. In a way that was one of his strengths, but it was also a weakness.

It is also all the information I have about my own parents, about the previous generations who lived and loved on Paradise. I never, ever knew my mother's name. We never had time or energy to spare for sitting and chatting. Never had any relations to visit, bringing tales of other people, other lives. Without books, I'd still have no real idea how people, *other* people, manage their lives. Isn't that amazing?

To me she was always Mum, or what Collum, Jock and the drovers called her, Mrs, or Ma MacCready. I never even knew she had a Christian name, until she died and I found their Marriage Certificate. That's why her marker is how it is.

I hope this will enable you to picture our childhoods, our young lives.

Treat your wife well. Treat your own children differently, son. Let them know how much you love them. Show them how much you love them. I am sure you will have children. Be a kind loving father. The kind loving father Collum would have been, could have been, had life not treated him so badly. Take this legacy son, and make it better for your family, when you have one.

I would be so happy to know that you at least are happy. Paradise has been a sad old place for long enough.

Having read the first few paragraphs, Cal turned impatiently to the story Mum had written in the book. Only once he'd finished that, did he read his mother's letter right through.

❋ ❋ ❋ ❋ ❋

"The fourteen year old stared boldly back at the mounted man. Collum thought he didn't fear anyone or anything. He'd survived the worst life could do to him, and was free to leave now. Free! Free! To do whatever he wished. Except... except... here was this man peering and poking at him, as if he were a pig at market.

Didn't matter. Didn't! Even if they sent him away from Charleville, he could still escape. He'd not have been able to stay here anyway, would he? It's just a case of escaping from somewhere else. Collum looked back insolently, knocking aside the cane probing his thin body.

"You haven't quelled this one then Father? He's still mighty belligerent."

"Honest, hardworking."

Collum listened to the conciliatory tone. The bully was afraid of the newcomer. Well, ...that had to be a good thing, didn't it?

"You didn't mess with him, did you Father? 'Cos if you did, I'd come back and belt you senseless."

The old man who had made Collum's life so miserable since he arrived ten years ago, cowered before the fierce glare of the out-of-towner. "No... none of that happens here. We are all god fearing...."

"Ah shut your mouth."

Collum flinched when the stick fell, but it fell across the old priest's back not his own. A look of triumph appeared fleetingly on his face. How he longed to kick the old man while he was on his knees. Exact some vengeance while he could.

"What about you boy? Got nothing to say? Did they interfere with you?"

Slanting his eyes sideways at this man who might be his saviour, Collum nodded, just once. He'd not known much, but surely the priest wasn't allowed to touch your private parts? Surely? Nor should he expect you to touch him there, or there…

Collum's head came up angrily when the newcomer said, "Well, no matter if he did. You won't get no more of that where you're going. I daresay he'll confess his wrong-doings, say a few hail Marys, and be forgiven. As many before him have been."

In his teenage arrogance, Collum didn't feel this was sufficient punishment, but was wise enough not to voice his doubts.

"Name's Red MacCready. I'm looking for drovers. Can you ride boy?"

Ashamed to admit he couldn't, worried that his future was disappearing, Collum shook his head. Just the briefest of shakes. The older man snorted.

"You'll learn. By God, you'll learn. Come 'ere boy. You can come now."

Collum looked up in amazement. "What about my stuff?"

"Stuff? Hey what d'y know? We got a wealthy boy here." The old man laughed mirthlessly. "Get it, and be back in five minutes boy. I'm not waiting."

Breathlessly back within the time limit, Collum spared a thought for six year old Sarah. He'd not been able to say goodbye. Wouldn't have been able to speak to her any case. The boys and girls were carefully segregated, apart from mealtimes, but even so the younger child had attracted Collum's attention. More importantly she had captured his concern, and was no longer intimidated by her peers, although he was powerless to stop the priests. She could read now, maybe he could write, when he got wherever he was going? Knowing that no one at the orphanage had received any letters in all the long, weary, painful years he'd been there himself. But, he could sure as hell try!

Red MacCready indicated a poor looking horse, trailing head down behind his own stallion. Collum got on any old how. Not fussed to display any skill. Just wanting to get away, get away, anywhere, as long as the priests didn't come for him.

Before their first campsite had been set, Collum was beginning to wonder if he'd made a mistake. Doesn't matter, he thought again. I'll just escape from wherever I end up. Ain't no one gonna catch me.

The stick fell across his shoulders. He'd been too stunned to notice they had stopped, too stunned to notice his boss had dismounted and was trying to hand him the reins.

"Here boy. See to the horses."

Sighing wearily in response to the blank look on the boy's face, Red added, "See you do a thorough job. Ain't too far out, we can't take you back again."

"Errm, what 'xactly... sir?"

"Take off their tack, hobble 'em, clean any sweat off them, then see to yourself. Now mind they don't wander. It's a good long walk to Paradise."

The old man gave another mirthless cackle before setting up a fire. He soon had a pot of coffee going, which was making Collum's face ache with longing. They only ever had water at the orphanage. Not always fresh either. Sometimes the smell of the priests' coffee would set up such a longing, Collum felt he would break something, break anything just for a taste of it. Good hot and strong. But he didn't. Of course he didn't. He'd been there too long not to know what rebellion like that would get you.

Hanging from each pommel, Collum found a short piece of rope in a figure of eight. Fixing this over the horse's front legs, he was pleased with the idea he should slide the little loops tight, prevent them falling off, and presumably prevent the horses from wandering.

"Glad to see you're a quick learner boy."

Eventually, Collum sat just on the outside of the fire's glow. Far enough not to earn a cuff, but not near enough to gain any warmth, either.

"Come nearer boy. Help y'self."

Collum risked a look at the face in the firelight. Bright red hair framed the entire face. From the top of the head to the tip of his beard, all was the brightest red Collum had ever seen. Flushing slightly under the other man's intense scrutiny, Collum reached for a mug, pulling the sleeve of his shirt down to cover his hand as he poured coffee. Not too much. Might be some sort of trick. Hugging both hands round his mug he sat on in silence. The old man continued to stare.

"Have a chaw boy. Don't need hot food on the trail. Jest a slice of dried meat."

Collum took the offered meat quickly, like a beaten animal. Snatching and retreating, with one hand still on his mug. He wrenched a mouthful of meat from the slice, chewing relentlessly until he could swallow it. He'd never had anything so tasty anywhere before. He was absolutely convinced of that.

Not that he could remember a life before the orphanage in Charleville. He had very vague dream-like memories of a rolling rocking ship, someone sweet-smelling, but nothing more substantial. Hell, he didn't even know his full name. People called him 'you there' or Collum. The priests mostly called him abusive names he had no way of rebutting, as he didn't know their meaning. Rebutting only earned you more cuffs, or more of the cane, or even worse, the punishment room. No, Collum had long ago learned what rebellion brought in its train.

"Would you recognise me again boy?"

Collum shifted his gaze, just slightly, but sufficient it seemed to quell the tyrant who had taken him.

"Name's Collum MacCready. Same's yours boy. They call me Red on account of my hair. Reckon they might call you the same, if you're beard's same colour as your hair." Again that mirthless cackle.

"Listen up boy. I've got something to say."

Collum nodded hopefully, without looking directly at the older man. His brain hurt with the idea they shared a name. He'd never belonged to anyone or anywhere in his whole life, and now this stranger was saying they shared a name.

"My sister was coming out to Australia. She took and died on the boat. Taken me a good long time to track you down boy, but now you're gonna be living at Paradise with my family. You'll keep your name, but you will be a hand, same as the rest of them. You hear boy?"

Collum nodded breathlessly. He belonged somewhere. A place called Paradise. Hell everyone knew about Paradise, even semi-literate orphan boys.

The old man nodded forcefully. "Don't get no fancy ideas, boy. You'll be one of the hands. Got me my own son to inherit."

After that, Collum couldn't sleep for excitement. Didn't do him any good though. He was just as stuck as he had been at Charleville. Here he worked harder, was hit harder if he didn't respond quickly enough, and still had no money of his own.

Red paid the other hands off after each drive. Keeping Collum on to take care of the spread between whiles. Giving him his keep and some second hand clothes, but no actual cash money Collum could spend.

Mrs MacCready prepared all the food, which was dispensed with a generous hand. That, and the feeling of homecoming which had swept through Collum as they trotted their horses up the driveway, on the eighth day of their journey, was all that mattered.

Two years later Collum was still trying to make up his mind whether to leave, to go on the tramp or stay here. Paradise? No, this wasn't the paradise he'd had in mind back in Charleville, but it was better than going on the tramp, surely?

But a couple of years later, when the little yellow haired girl came back from school, Collum's mind made itself up. Collum had driven Mrs MacCready into the railhead to collect her. Megan. She'd been a spindly little thing when she left, but Megan had returned this year to her own family. Back from school for the long summer holidays, although in fact, she never returned to school.

The previous year she'd been at some school friend's estate down south. The gossip had been all about that trip. How Red expected great things. The school friend was from a rich family, had an older brother too.

Collum was astonished to find the girl washing and rinsing the drovers' clothes. The daughter of the house, washing their rags? Megan's eyes flickered everywhere when Collum marched up. Took him a while to get to know her.

She seemed a nervous, flighty thing, until Collum heard Red roaring at her. In a flash he understood what her life was like. Mrs MacCready had no power over her husband. Was helpless before the tide of his anger. The little girl was helpless too, and unprotected from the bully and his swaggering son.

At twelve, young Collum MacCready showed every indication of becoming the bully his father was. Scornful and brusque with his sister and mother, he very often reduced them to tears.

Col had been soaking up family history with his gravy so it seemed. Jock MacAvoy, slightly younger than Col, had been here all his life, he said. He was fond of gossip. Any time the two of them were together, he'd set to whispering more and more about the folks, as he called them.

Seems he was an orphan too, but had been reared on the cattle station after his mother collapsed and died over the laundry. She'd been earning her keep. Red MacCready was fond of people earning their keep. To him life was simple. You worked, you ate. Didn't work, didn't eat. Simple.

In their whispered conversations, Megan let slip that the rich friend wouldn't marry into an Outback family. Col's skin crawled to imagine Red's response to that. He'd heard enough of the abuse Red snarled at his firstborn child because she wasn't the son he'd expected, to be able to visualise some of Megan's life. Red returned from the showdown with the other family, if possible in an even worse temper.

In vain did Mrs MacCready try to reassure him. Megan was too young to be married. Fifteen was way too young. It was better to keep her here, where she could be a help to her mother. There'd be other families, when Megan was older.

Her black eyes took a while to fade from her face, and even longer to disappear from Col's mind. Hell, Mrs MacCready was so sweet. She'd give you extra pie or potato soon as look at you. Why'd the old man have to be so hard?

Jock used to say, "Must be called Red on account of his face." Only quietly of course, wouldn't do to be overheard.

Arriving home from checking the fences outby, Col found Jock in bed. No one but no one, not even Mrs MacCready herself, stayed in bed during the day.

Cautiously, he prodded the prone figure. Groan.

"You alright Jock?"

"He will be soon as his back heals. Pa whipped him." Megan's eyes were over-bright as she approached. "I gotta put some more of this on your back, Jock."

Groan.

"I'll kiss it better after, Jock. Promise."

Col backed up. Would it be worth a whipping if Megan kissed it better?

"What d'he do?"

Megan shook her head, and her tears fell on Jock's back. Col rushed out of the cabin at the sound of Red's angry roar.

Megan was excited. Red was due back from Charleville today, said he had a surprise for them. Mrs MacCready took it in her stride, she'd had surprises before, learned not to trust them. Col, Jock, and Megan were watching unobtrusively, when Red rode along the dirt track towards the homestead. The pack mule, trailed by a lead rein, seemed only to have the normal sacks piled on it.

These three had a solid friendship kept hidden from Megan's brother. Wouldn't do if he suspected anything, but often they joined together, as now. The son of the house was taking his ease before the fire, while the other three were outside in the rain, fixing and mending as instructed before Red set off, three weeks' ago. Young Collum never pulled his weight, except under his father's benevolent eye.

Red roared for his wife, Megan, anyone, someone, dammit. To take the horses and let him get out of the rain. Jock and Col ran, leading the horses into the barn. A good substantial well-built barn, Red had nothing faulty on his station, no way. It was in the barn much, much later they discovered his cache of money. Money which enabled them to build Paradise into a going concern.

Unloading the sacks, Col was surprised when one of them squirmed. Lowering it gently to the floor, he tipped it up. Expecting a puppy, perhaps, or a kitten maybe. A surprise for Megan. What else could the old man mean?

A small bundle of bones fell out of the bag, and lay unresisting on the floor. Sarah!

"There boy. Told you it was a surprise. No reason for you to make great sheep's eyes at Megan now. Got your very own plaything."

Sarah stayed in bed for a week, curled into a tiny, tiny ball, whimpering in her sleep. Red issued instructions she wasn't to be moved, wasn't to be spoken to, just left. But how could Megan and her mother just leave such a small, helpless bundle of humanity?

Gently, slowly, their loving concern drew the young girl out of her shell. But nothing could retrieve her from the deep, dark well in which she lived and moved.

Col had known to his personal cost what the priests did, but that didn't prepare him for what had been done to Sarah. Red had brought her back to Paradise, understanding one of the priests had raped her. Knowing she was 'with child', the euphemism the priests had used to cover the horror swamping Sarah's mind. Unwilling, and unable to accept any blame attaching to the situation, they had simply organised this solution.

The priest himself was still at Charleville, still at the orphanage where he could and would perpetrate similar horrors for years to come. But Sarah, ...Sarah, the innocent victim of his assault, had been banished as far away as they could. Had been left to fend for herself, had, indeed, been blamed for the whole episode.

None of the people on Paradise were left in any doubt Red also believed the girl had tempted the priest.

At twelve, she was ripe, she was prime and therefore a useful addition to a homestead with three growing boys. Children too would be useful, cheaper than staff, and easier to bend to your will.

Oh yes, Red had his own reasons for helping the priests cover up this little… … problem.

Sarah was six months gone before she ventured out of the homestead and into the yard. Only going out then, because Mrs MacCready was ill again, and there was no one to feed the chooks.

Young Collum's eyes lit up when he saw her. He'd been waiting for this moment ever since she'd arrived. Wanting to be first of the three boys. He too had raped Sara, banging her head viciously against the floor of the barn when she resisted. Red caught them in the act, wrenching the fourteen year old off the limp body.

Sarah lay where she'd been abused, too sick, too weary to do anything. She lay there, semi-naked, with her skirt hoisted over her head, waiting for oblivion to return. Meg rescued her, while Red was whipping his son.

He knocked the boy's head against the wall, repeating, "You are a decent lad. Brought up decent. Have you no shame? To go with that trollop. You can catch diseases from trollops. If you want sex, go to a proper place where the girls are at least clean. To use this … this… slut without knowing what diseases she carries… You disgust me. Get out of my sight!"

The boy had slunk to his room, sobbing and weeping. This was the only time his father had beaten him and he had no way of coping with the violence. Col or Jock would have withstood the same beating. Had withstood similar beatings. Had become inured to the pain, accepting it as part of the price they paid for working here, at this place called Paradise.

Red caught his breath, clutching his head in agony. Keeling over, he lay in a huddled mass. Megan had slipped away, carefully leading Sarah back to the homestead. She glanced back briefly, but was engrossed in calming the hysterical girl in her arms.

Adding a spoonful of her father's brandy to a glass of milk, she sat patiently until Sarah had finished it. Leaving her apparently sleeping quietly, Megan slipped back to the barn. She wasn't bothered about her brother, his screams and cries were being attended to by her mother.

Back in the barn, Red lay undisturbed where he'd fallen. Nothing could disturb him now. Unable to react, Megan had simply stared at the body of her father. The only father she had ever known, was a storming, ranting, bully, who loved to plague weaker creatures. She glanced nervously about. No one in sight.

Sighing heavily, she knew she should fetch Ma. Knowing her mother would have hysterics, Megan stayed where she was, turning the problem over and over in her mind. Searching for some solution, which would cover all angles. Wearily she sat on the nearest straw bundle. Her head ached but still she had no solution.

Jock and Col came in. Ready to wash. Ready to eat. No food had been prepared today. Rising slowly as if fifty years had been added to the seventeen she'd already spent on the earth, Megan said, "Bread and Cheese. It'll have to be bread and cheese."

Jock took her hands. "You're cold, little lass." His glance rested momentarily on the body.

"Did he have a seizure? 'Twas only a matter of time. Good riddance. Shall us carry him indoors?"

His words seemed to re-vitalise Megan.

"That's it. That's it!" Standing straighter, she added, "Yes, could you and Col bring the body over to the house. Then errm… Mum and I can lay him out. Can you manage to dig a grave for him? Wait for the rain to stop, obviously. The ground will be softer. No hurry."

She laughed hysterically, drawing their eyes to her. "See, if we say he had a seizure, no one will query it. We don't have to say he was whipping Collum. Do we?" Megan looked at each of them in turn.

They knew nothing of this morning's events, so she drew several deep breaths and led them into the house. She explained everything to them and her mother. The child Sarah was still sleeping peacefully, as was the young bully, who had been dosed with some of the medication Ma used for her own problems.

Col and Jock were happy, glad to repay the little lass for her past kindnesses. Her mother nodded her head slowly. If it would save her beloved son from a murder charge, then it was fine with her. Patting her mother's hand, Megan led her briskly out of the room.

"Go sit with Collum, Ma. I'll call you when we've finished."

Checking on Sarah briefly before washing and re-dressing her Pa, Megan went over their story.

"We need to stick together. It was an accident. We don't need to mention anything else. Once we've held a service, someone needs to ride into town. But they won't investigate. Accidents happen all the time, don't they?"

The following morning Ma MacCready shrieked hysterically from the barn, where she'd gone to feed the chooks. Young Collum was hanging from the main beam. A tipped over ladder showed how he'd achieved his objective.

Megan couldn't believe it. After all their efforts yesterday, now this. How was she to explain Collum to the authorities?

In the end, they buried both bodies in one single grave, during a respite from the rain.

Two days' later, taking his own sweet time, Col rode into town for the constable. He was a day overdue on the return journey, but then he'd never been in town before. Never been able to wander freely about. Oh he still couldn't buy anything, but he could see the things for sale. Could see the shops and houses, the Church they'd started to build, the people. So many people walking about, did they have no chores to do? Imagine that. No chores!

Constable seemed happy with the idea the two MacCreadys were dead from a sudden fever, which had left the weaker members of family still standing. Nothing was mentioned of doubts he might have experienced, ... and the family breathed a united sigh of relief.

Knowing his local community thoroughly, the Constable suspected they'd killed each other in a fight, but no one at Paradise would change their tale. Eventually he shrugged, noting the cause of the two deaths as fever. Wouldn't be the first time, or the last, something like this happened. Maybe in the future it wouldn't, but right here, right now, there was nothing more he could do. Anyway, what would it achieve? Even if he could get any evidence to support his theory... ...

And,... if the family stuck to their guns about the fever? Nothing he could do, was there? No great loss, he consoled himself. Red was a bully, so was his son. The idea the other people might have revolted, coming together to commit murder was dismissed irritably. Wouldn't happen.

It was Megan and Col who held the homestead together that first winter. Struggling and striving to maintain the roof over the heads of the rest, this was the one time they were pleased to be only five people about the homestead. It was hard, but then life was hard, wasn't it? They had each learned that in their various ways.

Sarah was safely delivered of her child, but wouldn't look at it, slowly willing herself to die. The child too, as if knowing its antecedents, had not lived more than a dozen days in this cold unforgiving world. They too were buried together. United in the hereafter, as they had never been in life.

Mrs MacCready took to sitting by their grave, talking, talking, talking to the girl, Sarah. Telling how she would have looked after the baby, would have loved them both. Life would have been better for Sarah at Paradise, if only she'd lived long enough to find out. Sarah and her baby could have been, *would* have been happy. Happy at Paradise... ....

Megan never had time to listen to her mother. She was too busy keeping things going. Struggling with the books and paperwork. Cleaning the house. Chooks, washing, it all took time, and she too was bone weary. Bone tired of the damp, and the dirt trekking endlessly through her clean kitchen.

Col found her sobbing despairingly. "Don't cry little lass. It'll all come good now. We just need to turn the corner."

She'd clutched convulsively at his shirtfront. "Will it? Will it ever come right? Won't God punish us for what we've done? For helping to hide all these deaths? Won't he? The all seeing God, won't he have seen it all?"

Scooping her into his arms, as he had longed to since the first moment he'd seen her, Col sighed. "The all powerful, all knowing God, will know what has been done to us. Aye, what has been done to us in his name too. Do you think he'd want us treated like this? Wanted Sarah to be raped? No, he'll be glad we did what we could. I'd like to get hold of that priest tho'. Wouldn't his old teeth rattle in his head? Just give me five minutes alone with him. That's all I ask. Five minutes."

Staring direct into his eyes, Megan sobbed. "No Col, promise. It's over. Promise me please? I couldn't bear to have any more harm done. Hasn't there been enough suffering? Why can't we just live in peace, as we have done since... since..."

That day was a turning point in their lives. Ma MacCready found Megan's tears unbearable, and sat cuddling her daughter on her lap, as she had long years before. They'd not had time to relax like this since the girl could toddle. There was always so much to do. So many men, and only the two of them, Megan and Ma to do all the 'women's work' about the homestead. Finally Mum stood up, shook out her skirt and smiled.

"Right my lass. We shall continue. We shall be happy. We owe it to ourselves and to Sarah and her unnamed baby to drain every drop of happiness we can out of this. Let's make a feast."

The impromptu feast tightened the bond between the surviving four. Col and Jock declaring nothing had ever tasted as good before, even though it was the middle of winter, with barely sufficient foodstuffs or money.

Slowly, over a period, it became accepted that Col would run the outside while Megan, the only one with any formal education, would organise everything else. The re-building of Paradise had begun.

Things would only improve once they found Red's stash of money, hidden behind the main beam in the barn. Money enabling them to build up the business, and expand slowly over the years.

CHAPTER EIGHTEEN

At the back of the 5-year Diary, Megan had written out all the recipes she used on the homestead. In fact, although Jacq had called it a Diary, as Cal found, it was not a diary in the strict sense, that is a daily record of her life. Megan had used the book to record what she could of their memories.

Having felt the frustration herself of knowing so little about the people who had gone before them, she hoped that by writing down what she could, Cal would come to a clearer understanding of his family. Would understand why she wanted the place to be happy.

Megan had even written out the recipe of how Cal and his father preferred their coffee. No wonder Jacq's coffee always tasted just right!

Cal smiled, hugging the thought to himself. Jacq must have wanted to please him, yeah! She'd followed the recipes to the letter. She might even have read Megan's letter addressed to "Cal's love!"

Cal had frowned at the phrase, and then at the contents of the letter. Accepting finally that his mother had been right, right all along about Diane not being the one for him.

Megan had known she was dying, had known nothing would help her. She had seen her mother succumb to the same strange malady, but even so had wanted to provide what assistance she could for her husband and son. Knowing they would struggle with the office side of the business, she had written them some handy hints. Oh Ma!

Megan was right to say he wouldn't have understood had he found her book any earlier. Cal still didn't understand Megan's comments that writing down her thoughts and feelings helped with the pain.

He was extremely glad to have this private record, and more than grateful to Jacq, who had not only discovered its hiding place, but had kept it private for his own personal consumption. Not counting Jacq, of course, who had obviously read it, and then used its contents to help Cal with Paradise. Yeah, paradise regained! Well, would be soon as Jacq was back. Too right!

Reading through his mother's account of her husband's childhood moved Cal to tears. No wonder the old boy hadn't been able to express love. In public you'd not have known how deeply he cared even for Megan. From inside their little triangle Cal knew it. Could feel something of the pain of unexpressed love in himself, especially with the frustration of not seeing Jacq all this long, long time. Working was the only thing to take his mind off Jacq's absence.

He also read Megan's letter properly. Not just scanning, just skipping through the painful parts. Cal carefully read the awesome information that his own childhood mumps had been passed to Col.

The mumps he'd had aged six, had prevented his parents from having the brothers and sisters Cal had so desperately longed for. Brothers and sisters who would have diluted his feelings of loneliness. Diluted the sense of isolation that still swept over him.

Cal remembered that illness. Remembered the haunting loneliness. Hadn't realised it was the contagion itself that isolated him. Thought it was just another aspect of not being loved enough. Older and immeasurably wiser, Cal apologised to his father.

Never by so much as one word had his father ever blamed him for their tragedy. Even when he was beating his son black and blue, Col never cast any blame for his sterility. The beatings had all been related to some fault in Cal his father needed to rectify.

He'd been rude to a tramp once. Mum had tried to explain, but Cal only heard the rejection he saw in his father's beating. He wasn't good enough to be loved, like the other kids were. Other kids had toys, or sweets or such like when their fathers came home. Not Cal. Never Cal!

Recalling her words now, Cal was ashamed, deeply ashamed of his treatment of Jock. Until Jacq had told him about Jock's background, Cal would have cast him aside at retirement without realising the only family Jock had, the only *home* he had ever known was Paradise! This place, that in Cal's memory had been bleak interspersed with only rare bursts of sunshine and warmth. Yes, Cal would have condemned Jock to the life of a tramp but for Jacq. Oh Jacq sweetheart, you make me normal, come back soon my love.

Recalled from some childhood memories of his own, by the sound of childish laughter, Cal was glad to find the youngest MacGregor children playing on his verandah. Taken outside his own concerns to notice the haggard expression on Tam's face, he invited the boy up to the verandah for a drink.

Jacq's sobs also echoed through his head, with the words 'love you'. That's all, but the day glowed.

The air was fresher, colours were brighter. Even the flowers smelled wonderful. Sure, he could sit and listen to Tam's problems, anyone's problems, while Jacq still loved him.

He let the boy talk himself to a standstill, interjecting a word here and there when he dried up. Relaxing and listening to this young man, trying to help him through the maze of life still before him, Cal was hoping Jacq would be proud of him. Pleased and proud that he'd tried to help. He patted the younger man's arm as they parted.

"Glad to help." Hell, he meant it too. Wish someone had helped him.

But they had, hadn't they? Jacq had. A complete stranger, ...but she'd helped him and now couldn't stay because there was still some danger to him or others because of her. His face grew grim and determined.

Nothing, but nothing was going to stop Jacq returning. She belonged here, with him. She did. He knew it. Knew beyond question, beyond any doubt. What he'd felt for Diane had not even been a pale, pale shadow of this love.

Looking up at the moon, while grooming King, Cal knew he wanted to connect with Jacq. His mind dwelt on other lovers, historical, mythical, didn't matter to Cal. As far as he was concerned, that moon was also the one Jacq might be looking at. Somehow it connected them, even though they were miles apart. Surely he could find something to say, something Jacq would understand, and hold to while they were apart? Something that he too could hold to, until Jacq could come home again. *Home, here*, where she belonged.

CHAPTER NINETEEN

The information gleaned from his mother's diary enabled Cal to face up to some of the problems besetting him. He took charge properly. No longer did he leave anything he himself didn't want to do. He went through Jacq's spreadsheets, silently blessing her thoroughness.

Cal had only to read the spreadsheets, study the work in progress, keep an eye to the stores delivered, to realise how lax he had been. Yes, lax. If he'd concentrated more, then no one would have been able to cheat him. It certainly wasn't Diane who had set up the phoney suppliers, was it? He checked Jacq's notes again.

Dialling the phone number given, he introduced himself to a Researcher at the Head Office of his Bank.

"Ms Tregissick said you'd call. How can I help?"

Trying to ignore the surge of happiness at this evidence of Jacq's faith in him, Cal asked for an update.

"Well,..." the girl cleared her throat. "It's taken a while, what is it fifteen months, since you brought this to our attention? But we have been able to track down three intermediary accounts. We're hoping for a breakthrough fairly soon for the last one."

A tinkling laugh greeted Cal's enquiry as to how they'd persuaded the other Banks to co-operate.

"We all do. All do it, all the time. No point letting fraudsters get away with it. Might be our turn next. As long as people point it out to us, we can usually track crooks down and reimburse the monies."

Cal silently blessed the absent Jacq again. She'd been on the trail of the fraudulent Suppliers from the first. Highhanded? Yes, guess you could say that. But if she'd drawn any attention to it – with the homestead bugged and all – would they have achieved anything?

Amazed Jacq had still got people beavering away behind the scenes, Cal attended a meeting with the Prosecuting Officer. The Trial Date had been set.

Eighteen months, …a whole year and a half, after he'd last seen Jacq, he now had a date for the beginning of the end. It was still some months' away he found. Churchill's well known speech sprang to mind, and he remained in his seat by sheer will power.

Working on Firefly and King impartially that evening, Cal whispered his news. Jacq could soon come home. Home, where she belonged. Listening to the dragging footsteps, he nodded welcome to Jock.

"Don't go taciturn on me now, boss. Seems ladies like conversation. You'll need a mite of practice before my lady fella comes home." The chuckle turned into another coughing spell.

"October, old timer. That's the start of the trial. She'll be back after that, OK? You need to see a Doctor?" The upward lilt drew the expected angry expression and violent rejection. "I have to look after you. Jacq'd have my guts if anything happened to you, Cookie."

Tears filled the old eyes. "She reminds me of your Ma. She was just like that. I loved your Ma right from when I was a young'un but she married Col. Didn't even look at me. She was always real kind, real warm. Col offered to set her free when he had mumps. Said she should marry again, have more kids. I kinda hoped for a while, she'd say yes. Then her and me coulda fixed ourselves up. But, ... she wouldn't leave him. Desperate as she was for kids, she knew what it would do to a man. To feel cast aside. And it wasn't his fault, after all. Life, Jock, she used to say. Just life. Sometimes it's tough, and sometimes it's not." Jock shrugged eloquently.

"Not that I blame her. I was a bastard. Got no birth certificate. My ma died at the washtub. I was setting out some clothes on the back porch. Don't know if I was more terrified of being thrown off Paradise or being allowed to stay." He coughed again.

"Listening to your Pa's tales, not sure it was better here. Paradise? Mind, he knew, always swore it was better here. It has been, and could be again, maybe."

Cal hunted for something to say, something to show how he empathised with the old man's childhood, but could think of nothing. What can you say to someone who has worked so hard, all through his life? Nothing, that's what.

"Feeling my age. The past is clearer to me than what happened yesterday." He reached for Cal's arm, patting it roughly.

"Reckon you don't know how much she loved you. Over ten years they waited for you. They thought they'd never have a family to bring them some joy. Then, well, Megan couldn't express it clearly 'cos it hurt Col."

Wiping a bit of fabric over his face, Jock added, "Megan loved you. She'll love Jacq too. I've hung on this long for you to be happy. Ain't gonna quit now. I'll be here to see Jacq, back where she belongs."

Comforted by the old boy's words, Cal thought again about Jock's working life. Hell, he must have started aged five or six. I'd never have known but for Jacq.

Sitting by his computer later, a sudden impulse took him. Didn't need to be a genius to guess how the old boy felt.

It took a frustrating three weeks to finally uncover all the evidence Cal needed. He filled in the form, together with his card details. Yeah, amazing thing this world wide web.

❋ ❋ ❋ ❋ ❋

"Hey old timer, post."

"Jacq?"

"No, sorry, Cookie, not Jacq. Something better maybe?"

Fumbling with the envelope, Jock fingered the official stamp on the corner. "Tax man?"

"Nah. Open it."

"Sure?"

At his repeated nods, the old man eventually opened the brown envelope and withdrew the certificate.

"What is it boss?"

"Birth Certificate for Joshua Arnold MacAvoy, born 1930 in Charleville. Parent's names…"

Unprepared for the scornful look in the old man's eyes, Cal stumbled to a halt. "What?"

"D'you make this up? Think you could fool an old fella who can't read?"

"No, Jock. No! Looked it up on the Internet. Found the details, sent off for a copy. Look, here are the official stamps. Feel, see, embossed into the paper? Can't nobody forge them."

"You mean it boss? *My* birth certificate. Like I was real all along. Not a bastard?"

"Not a bastard, old man. Valued member of society. Gives your parents' names too. I've even seen a copy of their marriage certificate. Hey, you want a copy of that too?"

"All them years boss! All them years when the girls laughed at me. I could have been wed. Could have been a father, …a grandfather. All them years wasted, 'cos old Red MacCready called me bastard, and everyone believed him. Oh boss." Tears stood again in the old eyes, trickling slowly down the wrinkled face.

Ashamed of his grandfather's treatment of this old man, and too, remembering how Jock had loved his mother so much, he had stayed for her sake, Cal hugged the mess cook. Not a gesture he was prone to making, and he nearly snorted derisively at himself.

Took a while for Cookie to resume his normal demeanour, but worth it, Cal reckoned to see the delight on his face these days. The pride in his step, as Jock stomped about the place. The proprietary way he slapped the fences and checked the stock. Yeah, sure was worth it!

❋ ❋ ❋ ❋ ❋

Evenings were the worst time, Cal decided. Normally he'd have been happy, tacking up King, going for a gallop. Quick swim at the waterhole maybe, then back to a solid night's sleep. But now, well now… he was haunted.

Or, maybe the waterhole was haunted? No matter where he sat, he could see the image of himself and Jacq together. All those wonderful feelings flooded through him, again and again. No matter where he looked, he could feel her presence. Feel the intensity of their love.

He no longer experienced solid sleep. Something would disturb him, and he'd reach for her. Nothing. Always the same …nothing. Jacq had never slept with him at the homestead. They had only shared that one brief night together, and yet, now it felt so wrong… so wrong to be sleeping alone.

He tried to resist thinking about her, unwilling to torment himself with thoughts of her. But always something, some little tiny thing he'd never even have noticed before, would remind him of Jacq.

The smart newness of the paintwork was beginning to fade. Cal started to paint it himself, visualising Jacq as she lovingly restored the old homestead. Flowers bloomed again in the tubs along the verandah, as they had when Mum was alive. The tap and clatter of her heels on the hardwood floors, … … The hard standing where her neat and tidy trailer had stood, .. Oh yes, many things brought Jacq instantly, vividly to mind.

Thoughts of the neat trailer sent him back to his computer. Staggered … … astounded even, as he tracked down those little pieces of glass Jacq had so loved. The little ornaments he had broken so thoughtlessly, were worth so much. She'd never rebuked him, never even mentioned them again. And yet, they were costly. He gulped as he read the reply.

Some were irreplaceable. Oh Jacq, sweetheart, ...irreplaceable!

The glass was issued each year, it seemed. A collector's set, started at the beginning of her life perhaps, continuing in an unbroken chain to the present day. And, he'd just swept them brutally off the shelf. Cal reflected on the pain Jacq had borne for their loss. Knowing he'd not have reacted so well to such an act of carelessness. She must have been collecting them for years.

Discussing his discovery with Tom, he was surprised at his reaction. Hell, Cal was beginning to like the older man, but to laugh at Jacq's loss? How could he?

"She said she didn't know whether to hit you or hug you."

Cal's hands curled into fists, and Tom made a quick placatory gesture.

"Seems when Dave left, he said she could keep them. Jacq never liked the blighters. She often said to me she didn't like 'em. Far too fancy for her taste. Dave kept on buying 'em year after year. When he left, he told her to keep 'em. Said they were worth a fortune. About the only thing of value he did leave, if my guess is right. She didn't know what to do with them, so she carried them around with her. Felt too guilty to throw them out, 'cos they were expensive. Then too, if they were valuable, you know...? Then you broke them. Simply swept them off the shelf. She sat there," Tom pointed to the chair Cal was using.

"And laughed. I've not heard her laugh like that in years. My poor Jacq, always there for other people, picking up the pieces, helping them out. But they all stood by and let her be deceived when they coulda helped." Tom sighed deeply.

"My aunt's husband was a right basket case. Couldn't stand Jacq. Eva was married before ... ... her husband died in an industrial accident. Jacq was their child, named for him." Tom sighed again, studying the past in his head.

"Eva re-married," nodding at Cal, "re-married for love, but it didn't work out well for Jacq. She ended up with our grandparents. Oh, we all loved her, but she knew deep down she'd been rejected, not just by her stepfather, but by her mother too. That's gotta rankle, hasn't it? She was only little, three thereabouts. She's been looking for love ever since." Tom shook his head.

"I think that's why she stayed with Dave. She convinced herself she'd finally found love."

Tom sighed again. "Poor kid. Still, she sounds as if she's really blooming now. I can hear a sort of undercurrent of happiness. Not before time. She'll be too old soon to have the kids she longs for. Had better get a move on."

Cal kept his mouth shut, busy suppressing the jealousy which had taken him unawares at the prospect of Jacq blooming somewhere ... ...without him.

CHAPTER TWENTY

Although he didn't have to, Cal attended the pre-trial Hearing. Simply to hear with his own ears that the Trial Date was soon. Diane had been staring at him ever since she'd been brought into the Dock. Their eyes met briefly and he was puzzled by the expression hers contained.

Defence Counsel stood to request an Adjournment. Prosecuting Counsel argued vehemently against it, saying their witnesses had the right to live their lives freely. Defence Counsel queried his choice of phrase.

"Your Honour, one of our witnesses has been subjected to Death threats. We had to move that Witness into protective custody. The Defendants have been granted bail, are free to come and go within certain constraints, whereas a witness is not free to come or go. Cannot contact home or loved ones, waiting for this Trial to commence. Surely Your Honour, our witness deserves some thought, some consideration. She has been incarcerated, although she is blameless."

"Threatened? A witness threatened? Why haven't I heard of this before?"

The sudden silence in the Public area, became overwhelming as the Justice spoke quietly to the Barristers at the Bench. A brusque irritated gesture waved them back to their places.

Meantime Cal had worked out the threatened witness had to be Jacq. Had to be. That's why she was so cagey. Protective custody. How boring. That's what she'd said, boring, boring, boring. Hell, she could get real cosy with the guys protecting her in a year ... or two.

His stomach churned at the prospect of Jacq being in danger and him oblivious to it. He felt someone pat his arm.

"She's alright. Honest."

In nodding his head, Cal caught again the look on his ex-wife's face.

Her hand moved expressively across her throat, and she grinned evilly. Diane was threatening Jacq? Why? It wasn't Jacq's fault they'd been found out. Wasn't Jacq's fault they faced a lengthy sentence for defrauding local people, was it?

The gavel banged, restoring order. Cal vaguely heard the Judge deny the move to delay the Trial. It would commence next Monday, as scheduled. Cal watched Diane cautiously as she was led away. Bail had not this time been renewed, in deference to the witness the Judge said. Uncertain whether that was good or bad news, Cal sat on, while the Court cleared.

Some of the victims had clubbed together to form a Support Group. Viv Blackstock came over. "We're having another meeting this afternoon if you want to come. We're also meeting our own Lawyer. We can talk about that witness."

Cal nodded blankly. Too right he'd be there. Supporting Jacq anyway, anyhow.

Pru and Nick were sitting together when Cal arrived at the Blackstock place. Not their old spread, but the small semi-detached they'd managed to buy with the remains of their estate. They waved him over and he sat next to Nick.

"Is Jacq OK?"

Nick nodded. "Yeah, she's alright. Been in touch with Tom. I sorta assumed you'd be there when she's allowed to phone."

Cal nodded. Yes, recently he had been, but inhibited by not knowing Jacq's whereabouts, and also by her cousin's presence, the brief five-minute chats once a month had been unsatisfactory. Quenching the unwelcome thought they had nothing in common, Cal missed the look on Nick's face.

Pru patted his arm again, "She's fine. Be back soon."

Cal made the standard contribution towards the Lawyer's fees. Hell, if he regained the old spread, and some of the money, he could afford it. Could afford to get Jacq something too.

Oh hell and damnation! Her life's in danger and I've still not paid for her work! Putting that thought aside, he tried to concentrate on the Lawyer.

Actually, it was difficult to concentrate on the formalities of the trial, when all he really wanted was to get a good look at Jacq. Twenty-two months, how had they stood being apart for so long?

CHAPTER TWENTY-ONE

Eventually Monday arrived, and Cal took his place with the Victims Group, ahead of the media and rubbernecks. He felt very conspicuous. He'd never minded before, when he was young, rich and capable, but over the years of his marriage, and the loss of Paradise, he'd become uncomfortable at being the centre of attention.

Gradually he'd changed, become taciturn and uncommunicative. Silent and morose were two words commonly linked with the name Cal MacCready. It seemed so long since he'd enjoyed the warmth, the open companionship of his youth that he'd almost forgotten how it felt to be open and receptive; to give and receive love as an equal with another human being. The changes wrought by Jacq's presence were beginning to be eroded by her absence. His normal character had been struggling to re-assert itself, but could still be easily swamped by too much exposure, or a harsh environment.

But Cal wasn't given to introspection, and certainly today, the first day of the trial that would mean Jacq's return to his life, was not the day to start. He would keep his head down and hope that not too much would be revealed about the intimacies of his life, ….or his marriage, ….or his divorce either come to that.

Certainly Cal didn't want the townsfolk he'd known (and who had known him) all his life to be privy to the nitty-gritty of life on Paradise. With a bit of luck, nothing important would be laid bare for inspection by this close-knit community.

It seemed to Cal that the trial started very slowly, as the selection of the Jury seemed to take forever. Then Prosecution and Defence outlined their arguments.

Jacq would be the first witness, once all the background had been covered. She was the Prime Witness, which was partly why she'd been given protective custody.

How she had chafed under its restrictions. Now though, she just wanted it all to be *over*. Once and for all, *over*, so she could get on with the rest of her life. Not that she could see Cal or Tom until the final day of the Trial, but just to know it was that close, that near to finishing was good.

Smiling at the image in the mirror, Jacq spotted the look on the face of her bodyguard.

"Get lost Tucker. Too hot for you."

Much to his chagrin, she treated him like a kid brother. Rob Tucker felt they'd become good buddies, since he'd replaced the earlier guy, and once the Trial was over, Tucker had plans. Their friendship was a good basis for a future, once Jacq was free.

Once she was free of this case, they'd shake the dust off their heels and head for the bright lights. She'd had little enough fun over the past year, nor had he. Both were eager for a change in their routine. Sure, Tucker knew he shouldn't get too close to a witness, but hell, Jacq looked all right. He was congratulating himself on having finally picked the right girl as they walked into the Court Room.

The Public had all been vetted. Had all been manually screened, no one had a weapon. Security was real tight. Not only was this woman the cousin of the local police sergeant, she'd also had Death Threats, hence the protective custody.

Secure in his presumptions, Tucker sat confidently in a chair, as Jacq took the stand behind him. He spotted the look on Cal's face, but didn't relate it to Jacq. No challenge there.

His eyes roved the Public space. He didn't stop to analyse the sound as a safety catch snicked back.

Was already getting to his feet, saying over his shoulder, "Down Jacq!" She was his last thought before the bullet whipped into him. Pandemonium broke out. All around him people screamed, and he slid to the floor at Jacq's feet.

"Oh Tucker. Tucker!"

His head was on her lap, she was soothing his face, stroking back his hair. When Jacq leaned closer, he whispered, "Kiss?"

Forgetting for a moment that this was not his role. Not the part he expected to play. The numbness spread slowly through his body. He had to... had to have a kiss before...

Jacq's hands gripped tightly. "You hang on Tucker. Do you hear me?"

He nodded slowly, her grip tightened. "Tucker, stay with me buddy!"

"Kiss?"

"Hey, what makes you think I'm so desperate I have to kiss semi-conscious men? I'm not kissing you 'til you're more compos, buddy, so hang in there."

But in the end, Jacq did kiss him. As the paramedics arrived, she kissed him quickly, before giving up her place beside him.

Cal had vaulted over the rail, and was waiting when she stood up. Had watched the scene play out before him. Remembered again the kiss he'd received while semi-conscious.

Jacq peered round blankly. Uniforms, uniforms, a hug, she needed a hug. Cal's arms swept her up, holding her close while she sobbed.

When her arms remained outstretched, Cal's heart froze. Yes, she'd been real friendly with her bodyguard. That's obviously why she couldn't hug him back.

Tom pulled her round fiercely. "Sweetheart? You're safe darling. I've got you."

Jacq looked blankly from Tom to Cal, to her bloodstained hands, to the paramedics wheeling the trolley away. She sagged alarmingly.

Tom said again, "'S OK, honey. You're quite safe sweetheart." Tom stroked and soothed, but Jacq still didn't respond.

A band of Police gradually surrounded the stunned witness and her cousin, and Cal was manoeuvred out of the way. Out of the Court Room, out of doors with the other distressed members of the Public Gallery.

Court was adjourned for the day. Cal sat on outside, unsure what he should do now.

Where was Jacq? Where was Tom?

Nick rushed over. "Look at you. How did you get covered in blood?"

Jacq's blood? *This* was Jacq's blood?

Nick shook his head. "Tucker's going to be alright. They're operating now. Took a bullet in the shoulder. Saved Jacq's life. She's safe, so is Tom.

They're being taken out of town. You will stay with Pru and me."

Cal nodded, nothing was registering. He'd held Jacq in his arms so briefly, but she hadn't responded.

Didn't last then, did it? This thing called love.

❋ ❋ ❋ ❋ ❋

The Trial re-started a month late. Once the fresh charges had been sorted out. Once Tucker was out of danger. Once Jacq had recovered enough to go into public spaces again. Once she had been reassured all her loved ones were safe from harm, she testified to what she had discovered. Not just about Paradise, but about the other spreads too.

Each one followed a similar pattern. Invoices from ghost suppliers drained the properties of funds, the owner became confused and uncertain in his dealings, unable to fight the spreading rumours of insolvency. At this point most of them took to drinking in the Pub owned by Blaumfelds, and their disintegration followed rapidly.

Some, like MacGregor, took their own lives, others became drifters and vagrants. Some, like Col MacCready tried to halt the torrent draining his life's work, by handing the property over, but the end result had always been the same.

Blaumfelds offered less than the current value, once the owner became dis-spirited and disorientated. Snapping up many properties at bargain basement prices.

Cal had been stunned by the treachery revealed to the world. His ex-wife and her brother had been behind every scheme. Had been *trying* anything, *doing* anything, to obtain land so that the Development Companies fighting to expand, would have to pay premium rates for their building projects. It seemed Denis and Diane had been accumulating wealth anyway they could. Too stunned to think straight, Cal was astounded by what he heard.

Surprised by the breadth of Jacq's knowledge, Cal shook his head in disbelief. The various ruses used to obtain funds by deception, the cunning trails she'd followed so meticulously, were a mystery to him. How had Jacq known what to look for?

Finally, sickened by her investigation and seriously worried by the implications to her employer, Jacq had contacted the Fraud Section of his Bank. They had called in Government Agencies, and the whole thing snowballed in a frightening way while Jacq was visiting Brisbane. Those meetings were the reason she had avoided Nick, had tried to evade his dates, his trips out. Not wanting to mention how she was spending her days.

Staggered that Nick had lied about Cal's involvement in that trip, Cal shook his head. No wonder Jacq didn't know who to trust, but Nick had also been on the trail. Had been trying to find out what Jacq knew, whereabouts she fitted into the whole messy business.

Nick too, had fought through the dust storm set up to obscure the origins of the whole hateful mess. In trying to restore Paradise to Cal, and the MacGregor place to Pru, he wasn't sure who was who. Hadn't known about the bugs Jacq found while spring-cleaning.

Spring cleaning, Cal thought again. Setting that short phrase against the whirlwind rampaging through the homestead. Restoring it bright, beautiful and clean to him. It now again resembled the home of his youth. Oh not the big homestead of the original Paradise, but a smaller, happier place Cal looked forward to being.

Friends helping him, and he hadn't realised what they were doing. Hadn't realised how deeply mired his world had become. Hadn't realised the solution had been so close to hand. Hadn't realised that the heart of the whole damnable business had been centred on his ex-wife and her brother. How could Cal *not* have known what was going on around him? Would anyone believe that he had been caught up, ... *innocently* caught up in this vast web of deceit?

Confused and sickened by the treatment Jacq received at the hands of Defence Counsel, Cal sat numbly through her evidence. Had not glanced at Jacq, had not looked at Diane. Reeling from the belief Jacq no longer loved him, he retreated into the hurt child he had been. Retreated beyond the happy companionable teenager he liked to think he was, back to the taciturn, irascible boss Jacq had first met.

All the evidence had been heard, all the cross-examination had been finished, all claims and counter-claims mooted and refuted. The Jury received it's final instructions from the Judge and retired to consider the verdict. But Cal had seen enough, had heard enough. He returned to his homestead.

He'd had enough of sleeping on the couch at Nick's, listening to him and Pru explore their passion. Heartsick he wouldn't now be progressing his relationship with Jacq, he limped back to his little homestead, to lick his wounds.

Back where he knew he was doing a good job. Back where he was accepted at face value, on equal terms with his crew. Knowing he could match them strength for strength, task for task.

Mustering the crew, he took them out on the next drive, leaving Steve at home in his place.

This was what he knew and understood. Honest, open, hard work, …under God's beautiful sky in this beautiful wilderness. Yes, this was where Cal belonged, not in a world of deceit and distrust. Here, where what you see is what you get. Wysiwyg, he muttered under his breath.

Not the two-faced beauty of his ex-wife, not the double standards other women operated by. Good, clean work. *Honest* toil.

CHAPTER TWENTY-TWO

Three weeks later, Callum trotted up the homestead road, weary, hot, dusty and tired. Wanting only a shower, a shave, a proper meal and a fresh smelling 'proper' bed. As he'd hoped, he'd been too busy to think about the trial, too busy to think about Jacq, too busy to think about… well, anything.

Hell, too busy to worry about the cold way his crew were treating him. The sudden silences when he joined any group. The sullen way Tam filled his coffee mug. None of it reached the core of Cal. The great gap where his heart had once been.

The figure reclining in the shade on the verandah surrounding the homestead, brought to mind another figure in another life. His heart lifted momentarily. Perhaps it was Jacq? But no, no it was Jock. Casually lifting a hand as he passed, Cal received no answering acknowledgement. Odd. Oh, he was probably asleep.

Tending his horse, Cal watched the reclining figure rise and move slowly inside. Yup Jock, *and* he'd been awake too.

Checking on Pru on his way to the homestead, Cal was surprised at the lack of warmth in her smile. Things not going so well with Nick now, he thought. Hell, didn't I say nothing lasts forever?

Jock stalked passed him as Cal entered the homestead. Cal pulled him back.

"Hey old timer. No greeting. No hello to your boss, returning from a drive?"

"Huh. No great shakes as a man, my boss! Was I younger I'd show him a thing or two. My Boss!" Jock snorted disdainfully.

"Whadya mean?"

"Leaving that girlie camped by the waterhole for a week. Huh! Not even man enough to tell her he was through. Just left her there, by herself for a week. Left her to work it out…"

"*Who* sat by the waterhole?"

"Jacq, sitting up there, waiting and waiting. Like she's been doing for a year and more. She's got your message boss. Loud and clear."

Jock hauled himself out of Cal's hands, saying over his shoulder. "I'm leaving. Was only waiting for you to get back. Tell you to your face. Goodbye Boss." Jock stomped over to his little runabout.

Jock was leaving? Why? Cal placed a hand on the open window, preventing Jock going.

"Why?"

"'Cos you ain't man enough to lick that girlie's boots, *boss*. If she's moving on, then I'm going with her. She and her littl'un need a man. You may not give a damn about 'em, but someone sure as hell does."

Jock revved the engine, and Cal's hand retreated. Standing in the dust swirled up by the little car, Cal tried to get his head round the old boy's comments.

"Reckon I'm going too boss."

Cal turned round at Tam's words. "Wha…? Why?"

"Jacq don't deserve what you did to her, boss. If you can treat her like that, maybe you'd treat us the same. Best to clear out now. I'll be back for my stuff. Leave tomorrow."

Cal spun him round. "I've no idea what you're on about. You got something to say, tell me plain."

"Jacq risked her life for you. And that of her son…" Tam hesitated in response to the anger flaring in Cal's eyes.

"Hell, and you didn't even have enough decency to see her. She waited up there for a whole week, while you was out droving. Too cowardly to tell her to her face, too mean spirited to tell her you'd only been using her to get your property back."

Turning round to mount up, Tam added, "She's leaving Sunday. Tom's real cut up about it. Not the only one."

Standing under the shower, Cal's face was inscrutable. His mind was working overtime, trying to sort something out, something from all this mess.

He didn't now want the big spread, not if it meant giving up Jacq. But… but… the baby?

Must have been the bodyguard's baby. She made enough fuss over the bodyguard, didn't she? Hell, must have gone straight from the waterhole into his arms. Well, let Tucker take care of his own child. Didn't make no difference to Callum MacCready.

Why then, had he felt so numb since learning about Jacq's son? Still felt as though he was wading through treacle. Still dealt with things at one remove. Holding himself together, but only just. Afraid if he let go, he'd vanish in a storm of weeping. Splinter into a thousand shards like her glass ornaments. Glass ornaments! Hell and damnation!

Pru poured him a coffee to go with his meal. Not as good as Jacq's cooking, but still, a man can get over anything, can't he? Even discovering the treachery of the love of his life? Yes, even that.

"Did you ever see Liam? He looks just like his father. The similarity is uncanny."

The expression on Cal's face said, so what?

"Look at the photo in the lounge, that's Jacq's boy to the life." Pru turned away to serve the guy behind him.

Cal picked up his tray, taking it with him back to the desk in his office. The crew's attitude seemed to have hardened through the routine of showers and changing. They had been surly and unresponsive before, but now…. Hell, you could cut the atmosphere with a knife. Where were the usual jokes and banter flying round at the end of a successful drive? Where had it gone?

His mind tried again to work out why Tam and Jock would leave so precipitately. Absentmindedly he wandered into the lounge, picking up the photo of the two year old he had been, way back when.

Way back, …when he hadn't known how tough life could get. Hadn't known that the love of your life could walk away, have someone else's child, and come back as if nothing was different.

Back at his desk, Cal picked up another photo, replacing it abstractedly. He chewed one, two, mouthsful of sawdust.

Distracted by a knock on the door, he grunted. Patience brought in the tray of little pay packets.

"Err, boss?"

Cal grunted again, apparently concentrating on his food.

"Could I have a half day tomorrow? There's a party for Jacq. I'd really like to go…"

She'd certainly caught his attention.

"Party?"

"Farewell party from the victims… … Say thank you and good luck. They've been planning it since the verdict."

Cal grunted again, winded by the thought that Jacq was leaving. Leaving the Outback, continuing her wanderings. She'd be free to help other people. She'd said that at the Trial. That she liked helping people. Her Christian duty, she'd said. To help others in need.

Defence Counsel had been pressing her to say why she had stayed, why not just drift on? Cal remembered her smile as Jacq replied, "I found I loved the Outback. Didn't want to move anywhere else. Felt I'd come home."

Prosecuting Counsel kept springing to his feet with a protest at the questions, but Jacq had calmly dealt with all the probing. Defence Counsel pried continuously into her private life, her previous life. Unhappy to have her life laid bare before the little Town, Cal had been too embarrassed to consider Jacq's feelings.

"We are trying to establish that Ms Tregissick had an ulterior motive. That she planted evidence to incriminate my client. That she was worming her way into the affections… …

Cal had blocked out the rest of the Defence reasons for pushing, pushing, pushing. Not wanting to hear again Diane's claims.

He'd not heard any of Jacq's replies either. Didn't yet know why she had stayed, why she'd put her life on the line to recover homes and property for the victims of the Blaumfelds.

Hell, he'd never had any explanation from Jacq for the happenings of two years ago. Didn't he deserve one? Sure he did. And ... here she was planning to leave without telling him? Yeah, he'd heard *why* she helped, disbelieving her faith would sustain her to help. Got to be more than that, hasn't there?

At the time, in the Courtroom, convinced he was an object of derision, of pity, Cal had thought he wasn't listening, wasn't paying attention, but his memory retained more than he'd expected. He'd been bent on displaying no emotion, not wanting the townsfolk to be laughing at him behind his back. He'd therefore sat stoically each day in the same position. Playing the part of someone uninvolved with all the mess being revealed, someone simply concentrating on the evidence in order to reach a satisfactory conclusion, while trying to keep a blank mind behind the blank face he wore.

Today, paying out the little pay packets, he discovered most of the crew would remain in town for the party, only returning Sunday.

Someone had to stay to take care of the cattle, didn't they?

"Not me," said each one.

Catching up on events with Steve later, Cal was disconcerted by the good humour in his friend's eyes. First sign of solid friendship he'd seen in two weeks.

"Letter for you, boss."

Did that explain the twinkle?

No. The letter was from Diane, Cal recognised the writing. This must be the eight or ninth letter she'd sent him since the pre-trial hearing. Sliding open the bottom desk drawer, Cal threw the letter inside, slamming the drawer as if to shut out his thoughts.

Steve picked up the photo. "Liam's a nice boy. Shame he won't be around after Sunday. We'll miss him."

Snatching the photo back, Cal said slowly, "This is Liam?"

"Yup. Nice kid, shame he looks so like his father. But then he can't help that, can he?"

"But... but... this is me, isn't it?"

"Always were slow on the uptake, weren't you Cal? Don't tell me you still haven't figured it out?"

Steve walked away chuckling. "I got some drifters in to look after the cattle. That's if you want to go to the party. Eh boss?"

❋ ❋ ❋ ❋ ❋

Tired as he was, Cal was unable to sleep. Rummaging through old newspapers, he found the one he wanted, the one with details of the verdicts.

Hmmm, justice seemed to have been served. Sentences had been set, restitution had been ordered, the paper was happy to report all the Victims had been compensated for their losses.

That stabbed at the central pain, which was all Cal felt these days. How could anywhere be Paradise, if it didn't contain Jacq?

CHAPTER TWENTY-THREE

The unfamiliar engine noise came nearer. Convinced the rustlers intended to run him over, Cal schooled himself not to flinch. Not to groan. Not to scream. To bear up as best he could while they ran over... what? An arm? A leg? Well, ...whatever.

The manoeuvring stopped. Moving his head slightly shifted the shirt, and Cal half opened one eye, as the driver climbed out of the other side of the vehicle. Jacq's Landy!

The relief was so great he missed – no, it was unlikely he fainted, he just missed that's all, - the next few minutes. Coming round however, when Jacq tipped disinfectant into his leg wound.

Sheesh! That smarts.

Gentle hands brushed rapidly to clear the hurting fluid from his leg. He was only semi-conscious when she kissed him, but was aware that each stitch in his thigh was set with a kiss.

Worth getting hurt, if Megan kissed it better. Where'd he heard *that* before? Oh and Megan was doing a good job of the kissing, no doubt about it. Would she kiss his lips again?

Pulling himself out of his dream, Cal found he was lying in a bed clammy with sweat. He padded out to the verandah to cool off, slipping onto the daybed without conscious thought, lost in his dream of what Jacq had done for him two years ago. He'd have died out there, if she hadn't happened by. Only she hadn't *happened* by, had she?

She'd deliberately set out to track him. In case he was hurt, in case he needed help. The memory of Jacq's tears on his injuries caused his own eyes to moisten. Cal MacCready didn't cry, certainly not over some woman.

Unable to return to sleep, Cal replayed the events of that long ago day, adding in the information he'd picked up since then. Yeah, Nick and Steve thought he was a might slow, but he got there… eventually.

Tugging open the desk drawer, he removed all the envelopes. Slitting them carefully with his penknife, he spread them across the desk. It was patently obvious that the first, the anonymous letter, was also Diane's handiwork. Why hadn't he pursued it earlier? Perhaps if he had, Jacq wouldn't have been in so much danger? Perhaps that guy mightn't have been shot?

Reading again Diane's excuses, Cal considered her words. She wanted him back? Had planned to get Paradise in revenge for his father's treatment of her, but thought if she returned it to Cal, he'd come back to her. None of the other men had been as good in bed as he was? Whaa-at? One in the eye for Nick. And all the others. Not one of them could do what he did!

Momentarily Cal puffed up his chest, sinking back almost instantly at the memory of the last time he'd made love. Yes, not sex, but made love. Even Cal MacCready knew the difference… now. When it was too late to help him.

The sound of high heels tap, tap, tapping across the floor drew him away from his desk, away from the letters. Rushing to Jacq's room, he stood aghast in the doorway. The tape recorder was back on the desk, playing the tape of Jacq's movements. Where had it come from?

Disturbed and upset, he left it playing to itself, going directly to King in the paddock, just for the comfort he normally received from this old friend. Firefly and her filly were nearby. The three horses always stayed together these days. King whickered softly, as Cal leaned against the rail. Firefly... Firefly looked to be in foal again. Foal. Cal's fist beat a tattoo against his forehead.

Running back to his office, he rummaged for a calendar. Switching on his computer, Cal checked. Then he re-checked. Sitting in stunned amazement as the sun rose in a cloudless sky for another beautiful Outback day.

The day of Jacq's party. Her leaving party. Hell and damnation!

The tape had reached the end, and the machine was now whirring silently, but Cal ignored it.

Cal dressed in a hurry, tacked up King in a hurry. Had to get to Jacq. Had to.

Steve's hand reached for the bridle, holding it near King's mouth because of King's well-known tendency to nip anything within reach.

"Where're you off to?"

"Emm. Town."

The sound of Steve's chuckle followed him along the drive.

CHAPTER TWENTY-FOUR

Reining King in, Cal slipped out of the saddle intending to creep across the verandah and surprise the figure on the day bed. The screen door slammed.

Out front was a rental car. Who else was here?

Tom raised a hand, beckoning Cal over to the day bed.

"Best to stay here, son. She's a might riled up at the moment."

A sleeping toddler was curled across Tom's stomach, face down, fast asleep, a little thumb resting near his open mouth. Boy was he cute. Jacq's baby stirred slightly when Tom's stomach rumbled with laughter.

"Listen!"

Cal squatted at Tom's side, fascinated by Jacq's baby ...and his bright red hair.

"That's awfully good of you, Dave. I find I'm totally underwhelmed by your solicitude."

Cal listened carefully to the cool tones. He'd never noticed how very English Jacq became when angry.

"You find you made a mistake? My, how likely is that?"

The reply was mumbled, causing Jacq to say, "Tom has supported me throughout, he is unlikely to be upset by hearing me now."

Another rumble.

"Oh, I can, can I? Come live with you and be your love? Bit late for that now. Don't you think?"

The two antagonists seemed to have moved nearer, for Cal distinctly heard the reply.

"I need you Jacq. You're the only one for me. Come home darling. We can start afresh."

"Is that so, old chap? What about your *wife*, Dave? What does she have to say to your plans?"

"Not married, Jacq. Never was."

The derision in Jacq's snort was obvious.

"This is *Jacq* Dave, not some little bimbo, who doesn't know or care what day of the week it is. I've grown up a lot since you walked out. Did some checking of my own, Dave darling." The darling was drawled out almost lovingly.

The anxious voice started to plead.

"You really thought I was a fool. Didn't you? Thought I didn't know about your wife and girls in Newcastle. I found your marriage certificate."

"Couldn't have traced it Jacq."

Unimpressed, the bitter voice continued, "Oh I admit I was a fool. But I grew up fast. Looked through the Registers, Dave, for that month long holiday you had with the lads. Do you remember Dave? The month on the Greek Islands *with the lads?* The month I paid for? That holiday, Dave. When you wanted to re-charge your batteries, after your 4th year Exams. Just you and the lads, I think you said. No birds. That's when you married her. What was her name, now? B… began with a B. B B Brenda. What line did you spin her, *my love,* to explain your absences? Why did you marry her, Dave?"

"Mistake, all in the past. Jacq look, old bean, I have these marvellous contacts. We can syndicate your story. The story of your time out here in the boondocks. Make a fortune."

"Huh! Thought it was too good to be true. Just want to make a quick buck. Typical Dave. Why am I not surprised?"

"Jacq, please, re-con…"

"Re-consider living with you again? You were a selfish bastard. You probably still are a selfish bastard. As if, right? Go away. Fly home. Whatever. Just get out of my life, and stay out."

"But Jacq I've already spent the advance …."

A tight bitter laugh interrupted Dave's explanation that he'd already spent the advance, flying out to persuade Jacq to come home. Come back to him.

"No change there then, Dave. Always spent your money faster than you earned it." The tone changed, became more sympathetic. "No, actually, that's unfair, isn't it? Poor Dave, fancy me being unfair to you."

Jacq gave a deep sigh, adding, "What I should have said, was spending *my money* as fast as I earned it. Go. Go. Just go. I'm not in the mood today for your whining and whinging. Get out of my life."

"You'll be sorry Jacq, when you can't find work, or good baby care. And you'll need to work, won't you Jacq? Single Mum, wandering the Outback. Fine life for your son, eh Jacq? Never amounted to much did you Jacq? You'll never amount to anything without me. Never have, never will."

Unconsciously Cal had risen in response to the threat he heard in Dave's words. Tom put out a hand. Holding the baby steady with the other, he shook his head.

"Listen."

"Get out. Get out. I can live without you and your threats. I can make it wherever I am. You, …you worm you! Crawl back to your wife. Back to the girl you married while living with me. Back to the woman who had your babies, while you were explaining why I shouldn't have babies. Go run her down. Make her feel inadequate. It was the only thing you were truly any good at. Making other people feel inferior. Is that why you act so superior? Because you know it intimidates others? Well, it won't work now. People here accept me for what I am. They don't give a stuff about you, all the things *you* use to calculate your worth. Go, go, go!"

The raw anger in Jacq's voice did stop Cal. She wouldn't want him to know the pain she'd suffered. This then, was what had caused the hard bitterness he'd seen when she first arrived at Paradise. This, this …bastard, had hurt Cal's wonderful Jacq. His hands formed themselves into fists.

"I'll take the paperweights then, Jacq. They're not in your storage items. You must have them here. Hand 'em over. I've had a bloody good offer for them. Might as well recoup my losses."

"My storage items?"

"Yeah, the bloke in the flat let me look."

"You went to my flat. *My* flat, without so much as a by your leave, and rummaged, *rummaged* through my things!" Jacq's voice rose hysterically.

Tom thrust the baby at Cal, slipping through the fly screen to take his cousin's hands.

"'S alright, sweetheart. Let me throw him out."

The listening Cal flushed with embarrassment. Boy, glad Jacq doesn't know I was in her trailer! Hell, how'd she feel knowing I sat in her lounge?

He'd finally given in to an urge to be near her, to see her things even if he couldn't see the girl herself, and consequently sneaked into the trailer while she was away. He didn't know Jacq had spent a considerable part of their separation pondering the reason for his intrusion, followed as it was by Terry's search through her belongings.

Indoors Jacq shook her head. "One thing, let me watch him, while I say one more thing. Please?"

Tom nodded.

"*A real man* broke your bloody fussy little ornaments. He trashed the whole lot. They were no good to me then, and they're certainly no good to me now. I'm glad you lost money on this. Glad! Do you hear?"

The bully subsided, groaning. "Trashed! Trashed! You let some thug trash them? They were worth thousands! Thousands! You had a complete set. I bought you the complete set over the years we were together. Do you know how rare that was? A complete set of paperweights. Do you know? You stupid, stupid woman."

A burst of laughter rang out. "I think that summarises our relationship pretty fairly. Every year you bought me something I didn't like. Didn't want even, because it suited you. I wondered why you left them with me, until I saw your house. Saw your wife. Saw the mess your children made. Were they safer with me, is that all it was? Did you always plan to get them back, once they'd risen in value?"

"Saw my house? Saw my wife? I don't believe you. How? I made sure you couldn't…"

Jacq's angry voice cut over Dave's comments. "Oh yes, I knew you didn't want me to find out. But, let me tell you, *my love,* I did track you down. Brenda's parents were only too anxious to help me find my old school chum. Gave me her new address *and* photos of her kiddies too. Brenda herself was only too pleased to help out a Market Researcher. Told me all about her wonderful, wonderful husband. His marvellous job as a Radiographer."

When Jacq paused for breath, Dave interrupted, "Can't have! You…, you…, little Jacq…? Too stupid to know I was living hassle free. Too stupid to know when I was living with someone else. Too stupid to work out why I stopped making love…"

The hard bitter voice cut in again. "Stop right there. Quite frankly I'm with Rhett Butler on this. Just go."

"Rhett Butler? Is that the name of your son's father? Is it?"

Turning away from the angry man, Jacq laughed, a glorious, carefree laugh. One Cal had never heard before.

"See Tom, something else wrong with our relationship. He never picked up a book in his whole damned life. And… just for the record… my son's father is a marvellous guy. A *real* man who could knock spots off you any day of the week."

Tom manhandled the man out of the door and into the rental car.

"Rhett Butler is a character in Gone with the Wind. In it he says, "My dear, I don't give a damn!" If you want more information, buy the book for your flight back to the UK. I'll be putting out an alert on you, so don't think you can stick around here."

The little boy stirred restlessly in Cal's arms. Slipping him back onto the day bed, Cal kissed him and retreated. Jacq had certainly had enough scenes for today. He pondered her parting shot. Did it hold out a crumb of comfort?

First thing he'd do, would be cancel that order. Damned glad he'd not sent a deposit as the seller requested, even while stalling about a delivery date. Cal had been ambivalent about the glass ornaments following Tom's comments. Had wavered first this way, then that, especially while trying to come to terms with the idea Jacq had slept with someone else. Had given birth to someone else's baby.

Chuckling as he rode along, he got an answering whicker from King, which lifted his spirits momentarily. Despite the odds, despite Dave's apparently blatant attempts to hide evidence of his deceit, cover his tracks, Jacq had traced him. *Had* discovered the double life he was leading.

Yeah, it might be funny to think of Dave's reaction to this news, but it wouldn't have been much fun for Jacq at the time. Cal's habitual scowl reappeared, with the dawning realisation Jacq viewed their liaison in the same way. Cal was just some other bastard taking advantage.

Cal pondered how his own actions would look, …could look, to someone who had previously investigated and uncovered so much treachery in someone who had been loved and trusted. What's more had been loved and trusted for a damn sight longer than the six months' she'd worked on Paradise!

Why even the drovers thought he'd treated Jacq badly! Jock and Tam were prepared to quit because of it. Hell and damnation, what could he do now?

Cal looked at things from Jacq's point of view. She couldn't have told him about the baby. Couldn't. Not only would it have jeopardised her position, it would have been construed as collusion. Proof that he and Jacq had been more to each other than colleagues, which they hadn't, not until Cal had insisted on seeing her alone.

Cal had been the fool trying to jeopardise all Jacq's hard work. *Cal* had been the one who would have sacrificed other people's livelihoods for the sake of a few more minutes with Jacq. Jacq went through the pregnancy and birth alone rather than worry him. Oh Jacq!

How could he prove he wasn't some bastard taking advantage? He needed something, ...*something* to restore him to her good books. Cal as sure as hell didn't want to be on Jacq's bad side!

CHAPTER TWENTY-FIVE

Opening his e-mails back at the homestead, Cal raised his eyebrows, whistling silently. *Here* was something he could do. Dressing carefully, he drove the best pick-up back to Town. Back to the Hotel.

Ringing the Reception bell, he said to Tom's daughter.

"Hi Jan. You've got an English guest, I think. He's waiting for me. I'll be over there."

Cal watched the lift, waiting for his seller to appear. Settling himself at a low table set for four, Cal carefully positioned himself, so that his guest would have to sit opposite, where he'd be facing the desk, and the entrance doorway. Little realising that his guest had as much interest in facing the public area as Cal had in wanting him to. He was looking forward to hearing this. It had got to be good for the guy to fly out from England without an invitation and without a firm offer on the items for sale.

Accepting the offer of tea, Cal sat stony-faced, listening to Dave explain that he hadn't brought the ornaments with him, but would release them as soon as he received a good faith deposit of five thousand dollars, Australian.

Cal sipped tea, apparently considering his options. Dave seemed pretty nervous, wouldn't meet his eyes, twisting his hands together, watching the main door apprehensively every time someone came through. Yep, mighty nervous. Wonder what would happen if I took him up on his offer? Would he simply disappear with the money? He watched the other man squirm, wishing someone else could share his delight.

"I feel a trifle guilty," Cal said, in his best Australian twang. "I wanted them for a friend, to replace the ones I broke."

Dave's head jerked round to Cal's face, looking directly at him for the first time since they'd met.

"But,... ... she tells me she can't stand the things. So now I don't need them."

He watched Dave assimilate this information, watched him gauge the broad shoulders, the height and weight of his opponent, the quality of the clothes, the gold ring and watch. Waiting for him to finish his assessment before nodding politely.

"I hope you haven't come over specially. No, I'm sure an entrepreneur like yourself, will always be travelling the world. Not like us Outbackers. We tend to make and keep our friends for life. Good day to you."

Cal rose and walked away. Saluting Jan as he left the hotel, he picked up the camera he had lent her.

Bumping into Nick on the sideway, the two shared their normal back slapping hug, moving off arm in arm. A quick glance showed a stunned Dave still sitting open-mouthed where Cal had left him. Cal took another snap through the window. Goodo. That was for you, Jacq.

It was too good a moment not to share, so he told Nick about the glass ornaments. How the seller kept raising the price, changing his tale. Had received other offers, would perhaps put them up to the highest bidder, etc, and then turned up, out of the blue, offering the non-existent items for a five thousand dollar non-returnable deposit.

Nick stopped in at the Police Station with this information, and Dave was escorted out of town by two police cars with wailing sirens. Felt good. Felt really good.

Still chuckling, Cal rang Tom with the news, saying as they finished up, "Seeya tonight."

"Don't think so old mate. Unless you want bits chewed off you in front of the whole town. She's still pretty mad."

"I thought it was sorted."

Tom gave a derisive snort. "You may well think it's been sorted, but you're not the one who camped by the waterhole for a week, are you? An apology won't cover it this time. Have to think of something else. You're going to have to suffer some before she'll forgive you."

"She will forgive me though, won't she?"

"Depends what the arrangement was, I guess. Jacq didn't say. I sorta thought, perhaps… you'd agreed to meet at the waterhole. Say, have you been in touch with her privately?"

Feeling small, Cal shook his head. Jacq was right, the agreement had been to meet at the waterhole the day after the verdict. Not for Cal to chase off after some fool cattle, leaving Jacq alone. He'd not even attempted to contact her. Not asked how she was coping with the Trial. Not bothered about her, or her bodyguard.

"You OK?"

"What time's she leaving Tom, did she say?"

"Yep, real early. Says she'll stop at midday. They'll both have a siesta, go on again after the heat."

"Which way is she heading?"

"Don't know old son. Says she'll let me know from her first stop. I agreed. I can't bear to see her sitting here grieving like she is. Oops here she comes. Seeya."

Restlessly pacing back and forth on his verandah, Cal couldn't think what to do, what to say, to correct his appalling mistake. Tom was right, apology wouldn't cover this!

He compared the two snapshots he had. One of himself, one of his son. He'd no intention of losing his son. OR, his love either, …come to that.

CHAPTER TWENTY-SIX

Dressing carefully for the second time today, Cal prepared for a Dance. Parking his pickup behind the hotel, he took a deep breath. Better get this over. Jacq wouldn't bawl him out in front of the whole town, would she?

She didn't. It was far, far worse than that. She blanked him.

His eyes picked her out immediately he pushed through the doors. The vision he had first seen two and a half years ago was dancing with Steve.

When the music ended, Cal was at the side of the Dance Floor talking to Sheena. Taking Jacq out of Steve's arms, he swung her back on to the floor as another waltz struck up. Glad that the three-piece band was playing for once, rather than the disco the youngsters had at the Social. Nice reasonable dance music.

Jacq's head came up, and her eyes assessed him coolly, while he settled himself into the dance.

"Ah! Mr MacCready, isn't it? Sorry, didn't recognise you for a minute there."

Pleased to have her in his arms, Cal moved closer, running his hand over the bare skin of her back. Unsurprised by his erection after all this time apart, he was startled by her reaction to it.

She trod heavily on his foot, moving back to say with a grim smile. "Sorry. I'm quite clumsy with the waltz. It's not my favourite dance."

"Jacq, I need to talk to you. Need to explain, sweetheart. Please?"

"I can think of nothing we have to say to each other, Mr MacCready. I'm sure all the talking was done long ago."

"Jacq please? Let me explain?"

Her eyes raked over his face, but still she shook her head. The tight bitter look was firmly in place.

"We ... we need to talk about my son, Jacq. You can't just take him away."

"I was unaware you had a son, sir. So much has changed since I was last here. Congratulations. Perhaps you'll introduce me sometime, ...before I leave."

"Liam. Liam is *my* son." The confidence in Cal's voice faltered under the withering look she gave him.

"Oh no, I don't think so. I have it on excellent authority that the paternity of *my son* is not a subject for debate."

Cal stared in blank amazement. Yes, the Judge had said that at the Trial. Had also declared unequivocally that Ms Tregissick's personal life was just that, personal and had no bearing on the case under trial.

It was when the Defence were pressing for answers to the bombshell they had just dropped. The bombshell that, in the intervening period, Jacq had given birth. She now had a child.

Cal had taken her refusal to name the father as confirmation she had slept with someone else. After their magical time together at the waterhole, Jacq had slept with someone else! His calculations had proven this was not the case.

In a flash he understood why she'd kept quiet. Understood how Jacq had taken his silence after the trial.

Understood what she'd worked out, sitting alone by the waterhole, waiting for Cal to show up as they'd agreed.

Shaken out of his complacency, his heart stopped beating, and his thumb stopped tracing round and round her back. He'd thought he simply needed to turn up, and she'd be all over him, ready to forgive, ready to start afresh, ready to set out on the dream they'd talked about. Now, …now he knew that it would take more, much, much more. As Tom had said, apology wouldn't cover what Jacq had suffered over the last few weeks, or the last two years either.

The bitter tone of voice was firmly in place when she said wearily, "You're probably right. We didn't know each other. Have nothing in common. *Had* nothing in common, except a desire to find out who was causing your problems. Best to move on, before you realise what an appalling mistake you nearly made."

The music stopped, and Jacq stepped out of his arms on a sigh of relief. She smiled again, that cold artificial smile, showing beyond all doubt Cal was merely a casual acquaintance.

"I'll say *goodbye* and thank you Mr MacCready. I hope I didn't tread on you too hard or too often." She slipped away from him, before he could draw her back into his arms. Her words remained suspended in the air between them.

He grabbed a beer from the bar, and stood to one side, watching her. How had she picked up his doubts? Why voice them today? Here? Now? Did *she* have doubts? Did Jacq doubt Cal? Doubt his love?

Jacq moved easily around the townsfolk, talking to each of them, these people Cal had known all his life. Gliding effortlessly through the throng, wearing a straight sheath slit to the thigh, which hugged close to her marvellous figure. Cal, who never noticed women's clothes, looked again. It had no sleeves or back either, only tiny little straps to support her breasts. The neckline draped at the front, revealing the swell of that marvellous bust. The one he had spent so long kissing at the waterhole. Had visualised many times in the interval.

Jacq never glanced in his direction. Swooping across the front of the bar in someone else's arms, Cal heard her laughter. The bright happy sound she so seldom made.

"Told you not to come," Tom said. "You should have left her to cool off, first."

"But Liam's…"

"Not if Jacq doesn't say so. At the moment, he's her son, and hers alone."

"You can stop her leaving, can't you?"

"Nope. I love her, want to see her happy. If she can't be happy here, I'd rather she moved on again."

The two men stood silently together sipping beer, watching Jacq. A commotion at the door heralded new arrivals.

Jacq flew across the floor, and Cal thought he'd die from the pain in his heart.

"Rob! Rob! You made it."

The hug and kiss Rob Tucker received, was the one Cal had expected. The one Cal wanted.

With his arm no longer in a sling, Tucker took advantage of the happy vision in his arms. Jacq was very flushed when she finally slipped out of his embrace. The crowd closed over the gathering by the door, and Cal had another drink.

"Better not get too drunk, if you want another crack at Jacq."

"Hmmm?"

"You know how she was when she phoned? She'll be madder than that, if you fall over now, son."

Cal arched his eyebrows at Tom, who sighed.

"She was worried about me. Knew I was drinking. Knew I wasn't coping at all. Persuaded the powers-that-be to let her make one phone call. When I didn't answer, she spoke to Nick, then you at his place. Remember?"

Cal remembered making her cry, making Jacq cry when he couldn't hold her or comfort her. Adding to her problems rather than helping her. Hell and damnation! He stamped up and down, feeling a twinge from his ankle, and a tingle in his thigh wound, as he slammed angrily about.

"That's not helping, is it?" Tom nodded in Jacq's direction.

Her head had come up at the noise by the bar. Slipping her arms round Tucker's neck, they glided onto the floor for a good old-fashioned smooch.

Hey, nobody but *nobody* messed with Cal's girl like that! Tom held his arm.

"Don't start a scene. Wouldn't do if you were in the slammer overnight, would it?"

Cal reddened; he'd spent many a night in the slammer because of his inability to think things through. But, if he spent tonight there, he'd be unable to prevent Jacq leaving. Better cool off.

"Thanks, Tom. I'll cool off, I think."

Wandering absently outside, Cal bumped into Nick and Pru just arriving. Nick had finished his shift and was eager to boogie with his new wife. Cal thought again about the constancy of their loving. Sounds of their ecstasy had marred his nights at their place during the trial.

He should have gone home. Why had he stayed at Nick's? 'T was obvious he was in the way. Wait a minute ….

How did the guys know Liam? How could they have met Liam? Why would Steve know more about my son than I do?

Because … Jacq and Tom stayed at the homestead. Of course! It was the only thing to make any sense.

Jacq had to be somewhere she felt safe, while the Trial was in recess. Made sense to be the homestead. All the folks there liked her, would do anything for her. Cal knew that at least, feeling again their cold disapproval on this last drive.

The image of the child sprawled across Tom's stomach this morning, drew him back to the Dance.

Nick's hands roamed over the bare back he held, while dancing with Jacq. They weren't talking. Just swaying to and fro to the music. Eyes closed; seemingly content to be together like that.

Hell and Damnation!

Pru's chuckle disturbed Cal's thoughts.

"Dance?"

She chuckled again. "I don't dance with a thundercloud. You should try what Jacq's doing."

Disconcerted when Pru only chuckled again at his glare, he was surprised she added, "Making you jealous, of course. Sauce for the goose, don't you think?"

Jolted, Cal looked again at Jacq. She wouldn't be, would she? Making him jealous? No! Trying to make him realise what he'd thrown away? Yes, that was only too likely.

She was far too relaxed, far too happy. He'd never seen her like this before. Cool, confident, poised, elegant, totally unlike either that first glimpse or the vision. None of the images of Jacq Cal carried round in his brain, were anything like the woman before him tonight.

"Thanks, love to." Cal's arms encircled Pru and they danced onto the floor. Swirling across the room, apparently in earnest conversation with his friend's wife, Cal watched Jacq under his eyebrows. No reaction, hell no reaction. He flirted with two or three of the single women congregating at one end of the hall. No reaction.

Circling the floor with Rob Tucker again, Jacq's eyes slid slowly over Cal. As if she didn't see him. Or anyway, not anyone she cared to recognise. She'd been looking at him that way every time he felt her glance on him.

He nearly stamped his foot with frustration, feeling again that tingly sensation in his leg, where she'd kissed the stitches.

The woman in his arms giggled. "I'm Rob's wife, by the way."

Peering more closely at the woman in his arms, Cal said, "Sorry?"

"Rob's wife. Rob Tucker. The man who was shot."

"The bodyguard?"

"Yeah. We split up a year ago. Nothing seemed right. Constantly rowing. It was awful, I can't begin to describe it." Tears clouded her eyes. "He was offered this residential job. Cushy he called it. Said it would give us space. Space to think about what we wanted. They got real close what with the baby and all. Rob's wanted a family for a long time, but I didn't. I wanted a career. I met Jacq and Liam. He's so cute. You just want to eat him up, don't you?"

Sue gulped at the look on Cal's face. "Then Rob was shot. Defending Jacq. And I just knew that no matter what, I couldn't live without him. I wanted his babies, well, eeerr before it got too late. Before he was shot in the line of duty someplace else. He loves his job, y'know? I decided to give it all up. Just be with him, whatever happens. Just us as a family." She brushed ineffectually at the tears.

Cal took her outside to recover, but not before he heard Jacq say, "Yeah, Cal MacCready enjoys making women cry. Brags about it."

Offering his hanky, Cal reflected on Jacq's words. That was the old Cal MacCready, not the one who loved Jacq. And, …he'd never told her, never spoken aloud all the things he'd been thinking during their time apart. So, how could he blame her for thinking he'd not changed?

Sue whispered, "Jacq made it OK between us. Rob says she helped him get his head straight. Yeah he likes the action, likes to fight for Law and Order, but not at the expense of losing his life. He's going to study Law. She's a great friend. They talked and talked, apparently. Rob says he'd like her with him in a tight spot."

Adding, in response to Cal's growl, "No, no. Not like that. She's cool and calm, even when she's frightened. That's what he meant. So tonight, when she asked us to help make you suffer, he agreed. I'm sorry now tho'. I wouldn't want anyone to feel what I felt, while Rob was protecting Jacq. What did you do to her to make her like this?"

Sitting on a bench in the Town Square, Cal told Sue all that had happened. Finding in the telling, that he could see things more clearly. Could, in fact, see things from different perspectives. Jacq's, Jock's, Tom's. He could recall clearly all Jacq's help, especially in the Bush. Yeah, she'd been frightened, but she'd seemed cool and calm. Cal only knew about the inner turmoil because he'd felt her shaking.

But, none of it helped him get Jacq to stay. Persuade Jacq to stay here, as a family with Cal and Liam.

"I don't know what to do. How to persuade her to stay."

"If she won't stay, you'll just have to go with her then, won't you?"

It sounded so simple. Why couldn't he go? Why shouldn't he go? He'd follow Jacq and Liam, protecting them even when she didn't want him to. Perhaps if he hung around, she'd forgive him eventually? If he hung around, he'd find some way to prove the depths of his love?

Escorting his confidante back to the Dance, Cal retreated to his pick-up to plan his next move.

He didn't see Jacq slide past the queue of men waiting for the Last Waltz and into the arms of her cousin, Tom. Didn't hear the shared confidences after they'd said goodnight to the townsfolk. He was far too busy.

CHAPTER TWENTY-SEVEN

The side door of the trailer opened, and Jacq pushed two containers of water onto the step. She went back for two more. Manhandling them into position, she fastened them down ready for the journey. Leaving the door open, she headed back indoors.

"Hold it right there."

The gun in her side encouraged Jacq to follow instructions. A small gasp the only evidence of her distress.

"That's it. Get in and drive."

"Keys, I left the keys, to pick up the water." Jacq stood her ground.

Terry weighed up her comments, eyeing her by the low lights from the verandah.

Jacq waved her hands, repeating, "No keys. Going nowhere without the keys, are we?"

He grunted. "No funny business. I'm not fussed who else I hurt, OK?"

Jacq bowed her head as if defeated, blinking back tears to say, "Inside the door, on the chest."

The gun jabbed. "Fetch 'em."

Drawing a deeper breath, Jacq cautiously opened the screen door, balancing it against her outstretched leg to open the inner door, and reach her keys off the chest.

"Right, come on."

Turning about, Jacq marched head high, towards the driver's side of the trailer.

"No, this side, you can crawl over." Terry gestured again with the gun. "I'll use it if I have to."

Jacq didn't doubt his words. Didn't doubt either, that Tom would rush to her defence, as he had throughout her childhood, if any sound woke him now, or disturbed the baby still sleeping.

She fumbled with the keys, dropping them in a clatter on the floor. The gun jerked quickly against the side of her head. Smothering a gasp of pain, she reached for the keys, turning her head to look along the floor of the trailer at the same time.

Cal saw her flick the switch hidden in the floor near the gear lever. Caught the look in her eyes before she straightened up and turned forward again.

He had spent a pleasant night asleep on Jacq's single bed. Enjoying the feeling of being this close to her. The scent of her hair on the pillows, the knowledge she'd slept in these sheets. Bliss!

Shocked awake by the sound of the door opening, he was still not fully awake until she returned with the second pair of bottles. Surprised when she'd slammed the door without bringing Liam on board, he'd been taken aback by her decision to climb across the full width of the cab, until Terry's gun followed her in.

The door to Jacq's room remained fastened back, as it had been when he first broke in. He'd had no problems with the lock, same as the last time he'd sneaked in for a look round. Slipping to the floor, Cal hoped Terry wouldn't check everything was properly secured before leaving.

It looked as if Jacq had secured most things yesterday. The work bar, normally separating the kitchen and lounge, was now locked in place over the shower door, leaving the whole floor area clear. The chair in which he'd been placed after breaking the ornaments, was also secured. The books and other loose items had disappeared from sight, presumably beneath the benches.

"I'm going to enjoy slapping you around Missy. You and your sharp tongue."

"Touch me mister, and they'll know who you are. Will know who to track down."

"Dead men, ...well in this case, dead *women* tell no tales."

"Forensic science is wonderful. Can catch villains from very little discernible evidence."

Cal marvelled that she could sound so assured, even while praying she'd not irritate Terry too much. Jacq don't rile him up, please love.

At the end of Tom's lane, she said, "Where too?"

"Right. Make for the waterhole on the MacCready spread, seems you have a reputation for sitting up there."

She nodded, driving silently through the pre-dawn birdsong towards Cal's place. Her silence seemed to grate on the gunman's nerves.

"Thought you'd got away with it, did you?"

"What?"

"Cal MacCready."

"You're obviously behind the times, Terry. Cal MacCready is old news."

"Diane says you want to marry him. She'd not make a mistake like that."

"Is that why you're doing this? 'Cos of Diane?"

Terry nodded, apparently wary of saying too much.

"Well, she's wrong. Cal MacCready has no time for women. No time at all. Yeah he has the odd itch, which he scratches with whoever is convenient. Not permanent. No way."

The bitterness in her voice stabbed at him, as Cal tried to work out some options. It seemed Terry didn't know they had a stowaway, but Jacq did. She'd also left Liam. Wanted him safe no doubt.

A pick-up passed them. The gun swiped at the arm holding the steering wheel.

Jacq swerved left and right twice before getting back on track. She fought the wheel every step of the way.

"You'd better watch your step, shit-head. You could have killed us both."

"Why'd you leave that light on? Driving around like a bloody Christmas tree, all lit up. Hoping someone'd see us. Turn the bloody thing off, before I hit you again."

"Like I said, shit-head. Do it again, and I swear I won't save you next time." Jacq sounded as if she meant it.

"Just turn the bloody thing off."

Cal was plunged into darkness, and it was a while before his eyes adjusted. The two in the cab were reflected eerily in the faint glow from the dash as they drove along the highway.

Jacq seemed her normal self, but Cal knew she'd be working out survival methods. He made a few contingency plans of his own. Hoping he'd be able to pick up and run with whatever Jacq had in mind.

Cal needed to get out before he could tackle Terry, hoping and praying there would be enough leeway to do that without harming Jacq.

The rest of the drive passed in silence. Parking at right angles to the waterhole, Jacq pulled on the hand brake. Cal's brain fumbled for a reason. Surely it was more sensible to leave it on the track?

But she hadn't. She'd parked it as naturally as if she were on a shopping trip. Swinging right-handed into the area left of the bench. The side door was now away from the waterhole, towards the bush.

The keys were snatched out of her hands.

"Get in the back. You can get down from there."

Climbing through the space between the cab area and the lounge, Jacq seemed to stumble. The gun caught her head again. Jacq sprawled on the floor.

Terry checked her roughly. Resuming his seat in the cab, he swung it round to face the trailer.

Terry started cleaning his nails with his penknife. This habit had always irritated Cal and now, with Jacq unconscious on the floor, was stoking up a real fierce loathing.

Cal watched Jacq on the floor, waiting for a glimmer of life. Her eyes opened slowly, looking directly at him across the trailer. He nodded, relieved when she winked. Thankful too for the grin appearing briefly before her eyes closed, then re-opened. Knowing whatever happened they were in this together. Whatever happened... *together*.

Jacq winced and groaned noisily as if coming round. Sitting up she said casually, "Real gentleman, aren't you Terry? Is that the way Diane likes it? Rough and ready?"

She slipped out of his reach, turning and standing in one graceful movement.

"Was it her idea to bug the bedroom? Or yours? Hear anything to turn you on, Terry?"

Don't Jacq, don't rile him up.

As if she could hear him, Jacq stopped. "Coffee?"

She filled the kettle, setting it on the stove. Having tried to light it, she said, matter of factly, "Have to turn on the gas. Do you want to come with?"

"Nah. Nowhere you can run."

"Switch on the outside lights, there's a good fellow. That switch by your knee, there. That'll turn on the outside lights."

It did. To Cal's relief it switched on overhead lights on the right hand side, not the door side. Understanding why Jacq had parked like this, he hoped he would be able to sneak out, creep up on Terry later. No sense sitting here, hoping to take a swing at Terry in the confines of the trailer.

Terry swung his seat round, following Jacq with his eyes as she strolled from the door round to the lit side of the trailer. He remained watching her in the wing mirrors, so Cal slipped silently out of the side door. He wondered briefly if he should let Jacq know he was out, but she was taking an age to return, so he melted into the shadows. Dawn had still not arrived out here.

The door clicked into place behind Jacq. Cal remained where he was, near enough to see what was happening, far enough not to be seen by someone in the doorway.

Inside the trailer, Jacq said, "Do you want damper? I can soon mix up a batch."

"Yeah. You can stall as much as you want. The end result is not in doubt."

Shrugging, Jacq set about the damper. Pouring coffee into a mug she walked slowly forward.

"Set it down there."

"Don't trust me not to throw it at you?"

Jacq returned to her tea, sipping the cooling brew carefully. "So why? Why did you bother, when Diane's in jail for ten years? Why bother with me?"

"Diane wanted rid. She's still paying me. Anything I can turn up which can be used for the Appeal. No prime witness – proof she was lying, was in collusion with MacCready the whole way through, Diane will be free and available. She says she'll offer him the original Paradise, if he re-marries her. He's so besotted with the old place, she says he'll agree." Terry chuckled.

"She's been working on this ever since they divorced. Poor sap. Doesn't know what he's missing."

"You do though, yeah?"

Pausing to take another bite of damper, Terry nodded.

"Sure do. I like 'em feisty. Hey, I told you that before. You smacked me down. I'm gonna enjoy this."

He rubbed the front of his trousers graphically with his gun. "Just you and me missy. No one to hear the screams."

"Got a little problem there. Period."

The distaste on Terry's face lightened Jacq's heart, but she schooled her face not to react. Thank God she'd heard about that ruse somewhere. Had never believed it would work. Hey, it still might not.

"Say, turn off the outside lights, please. Don't want to drain the battery."

"Battery condition won't matter to you." But he did reach for the switch.

Jacq watched him cautiously. Perhaps she hadn't used enough stuff?

Having finished his damper and with a beautiful dawn continuing all around them, Terry said, "Better get ready for a swim. Save me taking your clothes off."

"Hey, nobody ever tell you the English don't do skinny dipping?"

Terry lurched down the trailer in her direction. Jacq retreated, pushing open the side door quickly.

"Not so full of yourself now, are you?"

Galvanised by Jacq's whimper, Cal leapt forward.

Fortunately, Terry had already fallen headlong over the step, sprawling in an untidy heap on the ground. Cal leapt on him, to find he was already out cold.

"Jacq, I need some rope. Rope love. Tie him up."

"Jacq sweetheart. Rope?" Cal turned towards her. This time he took in the shock, which had her frozen to the spot.

Standing before her he said, as gently as he could. "It's alright sweetheart. You're safe now. Quite safe."

Deep black pits yawned in the eyes before him. Gone was the expression of love he had glimpsed back at Tom's. Cal stroked her arms gently, repeating his words, to no avail. Even safe within Cal's arms, she didn't respond.

"Everyone in the trailer come out with your hands up. You are surrounded."

"Tam! Darling, it's Tam."

Jacq gave a great juddering sigh, looking about her as she came back to the present. By the time Tam arrived she was back to her normal self, well almost, Cal thought.

The noise of a helicopter overhead, brought a further relaxation, although Cal had not been able to hug her again.

Terry was handcuffed to the bumper, while Jacq made fresh coffee and fresh damper.

"What d'y do to him?"

The giggle sounded slightly off-key as Jacq replied, "Knockout stuff. Natives gave it to me couple of years ago. I wasn't sure how much to use."

"Good job you still had it."

They had an impromptu breakfast, seated round the bench at the waterhole.

Tam had been sleeping under the Landy when Jacq switched on the transmitter in her trailer. He'd called the police before following them at a safe distance.

Jacq grinned lovingly. "Good job Terry didn't use the wing mirrors, eh?"

Tam blushed and Cal thought about this boy, only eighteen, but already man enough to follow a kidnapper rather than risk his friend.

The police confirmed they had heard all the conversation from the radio Jacq had also managed to switch on.

The Senior Officer eyed the bruising. "You look a bit washed out Jacq. Take it easy, get Cal to drive back."

Their prisoner was still unconscious when they loaded him into the helicopter for the ride to jail. The Police went off with a cheery wave.

Cal spent ten minutes trying to catch Tam's eye to indicate he should take himself off.

"I'll come with you Tam, Liam will be worried about me."

"You'll come in the trailer." Cal growled, wishing he hadn't, when Jacq flinched again.

"It's faster. They'll both be worried."

"Tam can say we'll be there soon. Can't you?"

Eyeing the boss, now back to his old form, Tam wasn't convinced he should leave Jacq behind.

"I'll take her boss. Make sure she comes to no harm."

"She's staying with me and that's flat." Cal waved his arm to indicate the mess cook was dismissed. "She'll be better in the trailer. More comfortable. With a head injury she shouldn't be jounced around in that old crate."

"Hey, less of the old crate, please." Jacq's head came up defiantly. The bright red marks from the gun showed luridly against the skin now so pale beneath the tan. Taking Tam's hand, she nodded.

"I'll be alright, Tam. Tell 'em to expect us about an hour after you. If we're not back, you still have the tracker, right?"

Kissing his cheek, she saw him into the Landy. "Thanks for all your help. I'll be fine. Seeya in a bit."

She watched the youngster rattle off in the old vehicle, seeming unaware when Cal moved to stand behind her.

"Need any medication on that bruising?"

Her hand skimmed her face, but she didn't turn towards him. Apparently transfixed by the retreating vehicle, her head shook. He marched round in front of her.

"Seems we always meet here for explanations, doesn't it?" Taking her hands, he gently drew her into a hug. Jacq's arms remained by her sides, but her tears soaked through his good shirt.

Sitting abruptly on the bench, with Jacq on his lap, Cal waited for the tears to subside. Gradually, her hands moved towards him, hugging him back. His inevitable erection caused a blip, but his precious Jacq peeked out of the grin. Cal sighed, content just to sit with her in his arms until she was calm again.

Some time later, Jacq sat up, taking in her surroundings to say, "We'd better get going. Tam will be there soon."

Recognising she wasn't yet ready to deal with any other problems, Cal nodded. Her arms circled his neck, and she pulled him down for one marvellous, marvellous kiss. It felt so right, so perfect to be kissing Jacq again.

"Thanks, boss."

"I've missed you Jack."

"Yeah boss. I noticed."

The giggle wasn't quite right, but Cal was too busy looking seriously into Jacq's eyes to recognise the stress it showed.

Neither spoke on the drive home.

Helping her out of the trailer, Cal was surprised Tom stayed on the verandah. He'd come through the screen door as the trailer stopped, and now, just stood watching, with Liam in his arms. The baby squealed, calling with his arms outstretched, wanting his Mummy.

"Please, don't leave until we've had a chance to talk, please sweetheart. I need to explain. There's so much I need to say to you."

The pause while Jacq considered his words caused Cal major breathing problems.

"Need?"

"Need, sweetheart. To explain, to thank, to apologise, to tell you. I... I... really need to..."

"Talking's cheap enough, boss. Anyhow, won't be able to go until the Police are through. Be here for a couple of weeks easily, I guess."

Although she sighed, Jacq shook his hand briskly, moving off towards the house.

"Y'alright honey?"

Nodding, Jacq said, "How're my two boys? Did you miss me?"

Once she was safely indoors, Cal strode off to his pickup. He'd go to the Police station, then home. Come back to see Jacq this aftie.

CHAPTER TWENTY-EIGHT

Pleased by the impulse, which made him to stop at the florists this morning, before driving home, Cal hitched King to the fence Jacq had been painting way back when. Grinning nervously, Cal took the gift-wrapped parcels off the pommel.

No answer. Hell, no answer!

He leaned on the bell and was rewarded by movement from inside.

"Wait a minute."

A tousled Jacq came down the hallway, tightening the belt on a bathrobe. She faltered nervously at the shape blocking the light, so he called.

"'S me sweetheart. Cal."

"Thanks, boss." Opening the door, she beckoned him in. "Errm, tea? Coffee?"

"Where's Liam… er Tom?"

"Jan's. Tom wanted me to sleep." Jacq drifted back down the hallway, stifling a yawn, and indicating Cal should precede her into the lounge. "Tea?"

The injuries to her face had swollen and she now looked rather like a lopsided hamster with food in one cheek. The flowers were sitting in state on the coffee table.

Flushing, Jacq said, "Oh thanks for the flowers. It was kind of you."

"Let me make some tea."

"Hey, like you'd know how?"

"Let me dazzle you with my prowess." Cal held out an inviting hand.

"If you're trying to butter me up, I tell you now, it won't work."

"Also, I hoped you'd let me give your son a welcome home present."

"One present?" Jacq nervously eyed the boxes he was offering, while weighing up his choice of words.

"Well, I started out with one present, but couldn't decide, so I got two or three…"

"He already has a wagon load of toys, boss. I'll need to get a bigger trailer at this rate."

"Tea," was said decisively before Jacq could retract the hand she'd offered him. "Come on."

Yawning and stretching, Jacq pointed out the makings of tea.

"Scones, anything? I baked yesterday." She chuckled. "Enough to keep Tom going until next month."

"Some scones won't go amiss. Unless they've got that mystery ingredient in?"

Shaking her head, she chuckled again.

Cal carried a laden tea tray back to the lounge. Jacq sat on the couch, seeming surprised when Cal took the armchair, but he wanted to be where he could see her. Watch her reaction to what he had to say.

Buttering a scone, he watched her cautiously. She'd leaned against the back of the couch with a weary sigh.

Sipping her tea Jacq spotted him watching her and smiled. Not the smile of the rescue, but no longer the grim smile she'd used at first.

"Thanks boss."

"Jacq?"

"Yes boss." She nodded helpfully, while he played with the buttered scone.

"I don't know where to begin, sweetheart, and that's the truth. I owe you so much... so much... and then treated you appallingly."

Her left hand made its usual stop motion.

Setting down the scone he had only been mangling, Cal held on to her hand. "I have, sweetheart. I honestly have. I want to make it up to you, if I can."

Jacq pulled away, her face freezing into the bitter expression he'd seen right at the very beginning, when she'd worked miracles in two weeks.

"Seems to me, we made a bargain, boss. I accept that's all it was."

"No Jacq. Please sweetheart? I need to explain things, ...and I'm not very good at explaining. Cookie told me I'd need to practice for when you got home. Shoulda believed him I guess."

Cal removed her teacup, capturing both her hands. Moving to the edge of the chair, he gazed intently at her.

"Please sweetheart?"

Tears glistened in her eyes, but she nodded.

"Why did you do it, sweetheart? Especially once it got so dangerous?"

"That's not explaining, that's asking questions. You said explain."

Cal watched the boot-faced Jacq take over from his sweetheart, recognising another defence mechanism when he saw one.

Grinning cheekily, he said, "Yeah, but I was kind of hoping you'd help me out, sweetheart. Like you always do. You have the right words to put in my correspondence, the right words to say to all my Suppliers, my Bankers, my whatever. I just thought you'd help me explain myself."

Tears slid down her cheeks as she said the one word, "Nope."

"Okay. Say, you comfortable right over there like that? Would you like to sit on my lap maybe, while I explain?"

"Nope. Too many things take over, once I sit on your lap."

Retaining her hands, buoyed up by the fact that her face had relaxed somewhat, Cal proceeded to tell Jacq all he had worked out for himself. Feeling better with each unburdening, Cal even confessed to the break-in at the trailer.

"I'm sorry sweetheart. Shouldn't have done it, but I missed you so."

Jacq nodded silently, not mentioning the CCTV footage, …not helping him out.

Cal moved on, to how Terry had diverted him away from the homestead with the money, that long ago day. Her hands tightened in his.

"But why? Why didn't you drop the money in first? What was more important than the money?"

"You were! He said he'd seen you heading off into the bush. His horse seemed to be lame. He said he couldn't follow you, but you were riding hell for leather across country. I just lit out… … eerrm…"

"You lit out after *me?* Thinking I would be so foolish as to do something harebrained like that? Would be so reckless with Firefly?"

They struggled for possession of her hands for a few minutes, while Cal tried desperately to think of something else to say.

Eventually he said, "That's what you did though, isn't it? You were heading out after me, just on Firefly until Tam stopped you. Weren't you? Then you went back for the magical Landy."

"That's different! I knew where you were going."

"How can it be different, lady?"

Jacq blushed. "Well, ...I had a tag on King and another on the money. Knew which way you'd gone."

Firing up again she added, "But you didn't, did you? Just lit out, not thinking. Barge in first, throw your weight about, *then* think about things. Bah! Men!"

"So, how does it differ from what you did?"

"I... I... knew where to look. Knew which direction you'd taken. Had the receiver. Had a voice disguiser programme on the loud hailer. Was confident I could get away in a chase..."

She wound down again, as Cal started laughing.

"Oh lady, you slay me. Trackers, voice disguisers, Computer programmes, banking, home doctoring. Is there anything you can't do?"

"Are you taking the mickey?" She asked it angrily, before subsiding against him. "Yes, actually there is."

"What?"

"Something I'm no good at."

"As if, right?"

"I'm no good at personal things. I... I... don't like to get involved. I... always pull out before I can be hurt again."

Cal pulled her into his arms for a passionate kiss.

Eventually he said, "Same here, sweetheart. Maybe we should practice together?"

"But… I'm too bossy to love. Always have to be right."

"Same here sweetheart. I think that's why we've had a few fireworks. But I love you, want you in my life always."

Sighing happily, Jacq settled on Cal's lap for the rest of his explanation. This time, she interrupted with bits of information he hadn't known or couldn't have known.

Cal laughed to learn Jacq had kept guinea pigs when young, …had assumed all critters were the same. Perhaps bigger, but basically required the same care. She's not that wrong either, he thought.

The whole plot took shape as they talked. Sundown came and went. Jacq fell asleep leaning against Cal. He sighed, happy to be this close and hopeful for a brighter future.

He was coming out of her bedroom, when the door opened to admit Tom, with Liam asleep in his arms.

"Which room?"

Startled by the look he received, Cal waited blankly for a reply. Holding open the door of the baby's room, Cal watched Tom settle the sleeping babe in his cot.

Shoved roughly back into the lounge, Cal expected the hard bitter voice saying, "Where's Jacq? If you've harmed that girl…"

"Hey fella. I was just putting her to bed. We've been talking all afternoon. I wore her out. Look for yourself."

He tugged a reluctant Tom back to Jacq's room, where she had settled down with a smile on her face. Sleeping peacefully at last.

Surprised by the tears in Tom's eyes, Cal said, "What?"

"She doesn't get too many nights when she can sleep like that. Sorry I bawled you out."

"I deserved it. I'm going to make her happy. I promise you. Whatever it takes, Jacq is going to be happy in the future."

Reluctant to leave the sleeping woman, Cal hesitated on the verandah.

"You intend to marry her, you'll have to do some proper courting. None of this modern stuff. Baby first then marriage." Tom's chuckle echoed after Cal as he re-mounted King.

Yeah proper courting, too right. But marry before she hightailed it out of here in that dainty trailer of hers.

Christmas in two weeks, ideal time. Maybe, if he was *really* good, she'd let him adopt her son for his own.

CHAPTER TWENTY-NINE

Callum trotted up the homestead road, weary, hot, dusty and tired. Wanting to get home to his wife of eight months. Get back to the unique state of happiness enveloping him these days. Couldn't imagine wanting to go droving for much longer. No way, not with Paradise all around him.

He'd slipped away from camp, ahead of the dawn, ahead of the herd, just wanting to get home. To get home today, …now, … right this minute. Wanted to see his wife, take her to bed, then… well maybe *then* he'd see to his horse, see to the men, and come back for seconds.

He'd passed the ride thinking about this year. About the times he'd wondered if Jacq would ever agree to marry him. It wasn't until he'd organised a picnic for the two of them, at the waterhole, that she had finally succumbed to his persuasion.

Although she'd agreed to marry him, Jacq resisted his efforts to get her back to bed until after the wedding.

"Nope, I've been caught that way before. Don't handle the goods, boss."

Cal chuckled aloud, remembering the scenes as his hands had started roaming across the vision that was Jacq.

They'd spent many happy days together, the three of them, happy family days out. Cal and Jacq had also spent many evenings together, dining, dancing, or simply watching TV. Cal had even persuaded her to ride with him again. But …Jacq always resisted his attempts to return to the waterhole, shuddering at the memory of Terry and his gun.

Encouraged by the way Jacq called him Mac rather than boss, Cal wandered round in a daze.

By the end of January, Jacq was muttering about finding a job. She needed to fill her days, she said, hated sitting around doing nothing. Cal didn't want her working anywhere else, but she refused all his attempts to create a job on the homestead.

Eventually Cal decided to remind her of happier times spent at the waterhole, in particular one specific sundown. Cal organised a picnic for the two of them. Valentine's Day. He could propose, get her agreement to marry, then she wouldn't go off again, or if she did, they'd go together.

Jock and Tam were only too eager to help, setting off to organise things at the waterhole, while Cal checked his plans and collected Jacq.

"Trust me. It'll be fine."

His hand caressed hers gently. Jacq smiled nervously in his direction.

❋ ❋ ❋ ❋ ❋

Sitting her in one of the chairs set up in the shade of the shelter, Cal offered her a single long stemmed rose, going on one knee to propose. Shocked to receive the old stop motion of her hand, even while she blushed and shook her head.

"No Mac. Please?"

"I love you sweetheart."

"I saw your face love, at the trial. When the Defence made the announcement about Liam. Saw the rejection. I..."

Stammering, Jacq traced his jaw-line with her finger, smiling sadly into his eyes, before adding, "It seems I may be too old for more children. You need an heir, I accept that. It cannot be Liam. You know that, don't you? That Liam has *no father*..."

Cal interrupted quickly, not wanting her to have to put into words the pain his thoughtless rejection had caused her.

"I love you Jacq Tregissick. Need to have you in my life. I was a damned fool at the Trial Jacq, a damned fool. It's a lot to ask I know, but I'd like you to forgive me. I've been a damned fool for a long time. I understand what you're saying about Liam, truly. I know what I gave up, but Jacq, you're the one who keeps me normal. Please Jacq... please... at least think about marrying me? You don't want to leave the Outback, and this way you could stay. Bring Liam up here, in the surroundings you love. Help me with Paradise. You helped me get it back, now I want you to help restore it, please Jacq, please?"

"You did that before, Mac. Married just for Paradise. Don't make the same mistake again. Your Mum wanted you to be happy. Said your happiness would restore Paradise."

"She was right, Jacq. Paradise will only be restored if you stay. If you go... well, if you go... I will follow. Wherever it is, wherever *you* go, that's where I'll be. Even if you don't marry me, I shall simply stay on the edge of your life. Waiting... waiting and hoping that one day you'll forgive me for being a damned fool."

Taking his face between her hands, Jacq stared intently into his eyes.

"What are you offering then, Callum MacCready? What do you expect to gain?"

"What I am offering and hope to gain is a partner. Someone I love and trust, who will love and trust me in return. Going forward together, to whatever the future holds. But that someone has to be you, Jacq. Has to be. You alone make my life complete. If you won't stay, then I must come with you."

Tears trailed down Jacq's face at his words.

"You'd leave... leave all this..."

The expansive gesture she made, intending to embrace the waterhole, the homestead, and the whole of the outback, swept the glasses off the table. They bounced softly on the picnic rug.

"Hey, mind the glassware, please. Thought it was only me got destructive with glassware."

Cal hugged her, wiping her tears gently with a serviette.

"Mac! Don't change the subject. You're saying you'd leave all this for me?"

He nodded humbly. "Everything. Glasses, china, cutlery... As long as I have *you*, my life *is* complete. Everything else is just trappings." He kissed the tearful face in front of him. "Actually there's no rush, sweetheart, is there? *My* mind is made up. If you don't stay, then I shall come with. No worries. Let's leave all that. Just enjoy the day, huh? Would you like a swim before lunch?"

"No swimmers," was said slowly.

"Oh I think so, lady. Everyone knows the English don't do skinny dipping." He smiled lovingly, handing over her swimsuit, smuggled out to him by Tom. "I can stay and help you change, if you like?"

Shaking her head, she pushed him away. "I'll change here. You sit on that bench watching the waterhole. I'm trusting you here, right?"

"OK, but give a shout if I can help with anything."

Trying to work out a change of strategy, Cal was startled by two arms twining round his neck.

"Hey there big boy. Do you wanna swim?"

"You'd better go. I'm just waiting for my girl. She'll be back any minute."

The happy giggle was more what Cal had expected. Slipping off his cut-offs to reveal swimming shorts, Cal turned towards Jacq and whistled.

"Wow, you're gorgeous. I might just have a quick dip with you before she turns up, OK?"

Hand in hand they went for a swim. Swimming and splashing happily, Cal decided to leave matters alone. He'd said all he could, and... and well, if she really couldn't stay, then he'd follow. Wherever she went, that's where he needed to be.

They ate their picnic, and drank the champagne, dozing replete, curled together in the shade of the shelter.

Happy to have his girl back in his arms, Cal was quite decided. If Jacq moved, then he did too. This was what he wanted, the bliss of holding a sleeping Jacq in his arms again.

Having finished off their picnic, they decided to swim again as sunset gilded the water. Both were reluctant to turn for home after such an idyllic day.

Smooching his girl on her doorstep, Cal was aware of the lights in the lounge, showing Tom was still up. Giving her one last kiss, he pushed Jacq towards the verandah.

"Better go sweetheart. Don't need an audience."

"Thanks for a lovely day, Mac. I've had a great time." Jacq kissed him one more time. Giggling into his mouth as his erection nudged against her. "Seeya tomorrow."

She waved from the verandah as Cal slipped back into the pickup and started the engine.

Cal was in the Store Room, stacking the freshly delivered feed, when he heard the Landy pull up. Wiping his hands on a clean rag, he loped to meet her.

"Hi. Wasn't expecting you this morning."

Cal was used now, to seeing the vision that was Jacq, rather than the workmanlike Jacq he had first employed. It was the vision standing in front of him, smiling.

"Hi. Is the boss about? I heard there was a good job going up here."

Stunned, Cal shook his head. "Eeer, job?"

"Yeah, met your boss yesterday, told me about a good job. Is it still available?"

Cal's hands automatically slipped on to the tanned body scarcely concealed beneath the wispy top.

"Hey, the boss might not want you handling the goods."

"I *am* the boss, lady. Can do what I like." Pulling her closer, Cal gave in to his desire.

When she could speak, Jacq said, "Seems the job has fantastic perks. Is it still going?"

"Open to all-comers until noon."

Giggling, Jacq checked her watch. "You open to a little bribery?"

"Depends."

"Huhhuh. This maybe?"

Jacq kissed him as she had at the campsite. Cal shook his head.

Jacq kissed again, but this time as they had at the waterhole, the first time they'd stayed there. Cal shook his head.

Dropping her hat, Jacq linked her arms behind his neck to pull herself up level, and kissed him as he had never been kissed before. He staggered, putting both arms around her to deepen the kiss, and support her mid-air.

When she pulled back, he muttered, "That might just do it lady. I need to check your references." This time he kissed her.

"Yup, you're hired."

"Hey, what's the pay, boss? And the hours?"

"The hours are simple, 24/7. The pay's negotiable. Depends how good you are." He leered.

"OK, I'll take it."

The crew came a-running when Cal's whoop of joy was over-ridden by Jacq's squeal as he tossed her into the air, catching her again for another kiss.

Yup, Cal would not forget his proposal, ...or Jacq's acceptance.

CHAPTER THIRTY

Smiling broadly now, Cal remembered their honeymoon. They'd taken the little trailer back to the waterhole, making it off-limits to the rest of the homestead. Liam had stayed with Tom.

Not because Jacq or Cal hadn't wanted Liam with them, but because Tom had assumed he would look after the boy and neither wanted to disillusion him. Tom seemed to have taken on a new lease of life with the return of his cousin and her child.

Cal didn't want to be the one to dim the brightness on Tom's face these days. He wished it had been possible to give his own father a new lease of life after Megan's death. Wished that, like Tom, his own father could have been re-vitalised by a beloved cousin at such a traumatic time. Remembering again fleetingly that neither his mother nor his father had any other family, except each other and Jock. Liam already had more family than Cal had. Lucky boy! Cal certainly didn't want to upset the applecart.

Besides which, he was very conscious he had forfeited any rights to William. Although Jacq had named her son William, Liam had only ever referred to himself as 'Liam and so now that's what he was called by everyone. Even the crew, who loved to see the toddler round and about the homestead.

No, as long as Jacq was his wife, and Cal could cherish her *and* Liam, then he was happy. In truth, Cal felt he didn't deserve such happiness. Wasn't going to sacrifice one minute of it for the sake of something he didn't deserve. And, if.... as she'd said, Jacq couldn't have any more children, well that was his fault too.

Because he hadn't been there for her. Hadn't trusted her or loved her enough when push came to shove. So ... he'd settle for what he did have. A wife he loved passionately, and her son whom he loved with equal intensity.

Cal sighed now, recalling the passion. Yeah, it was still like that, but his honeymoon had been something else. Say, did Bunyan ever write a sequel to Paradise Lost?

❋ ❋ ❋ ❋ ❋

The group of figures on the verandah cheered as he came into sight. A bent old man and a little boy set off for the stockyards hand in hand, but the other figure remained where she was on the recliner. Jacq – his wife.

Sighing happily, Cal headed for the stockyards. See to his horse, see to his men, then see to himself. Oh yes.

"Hiya boss. Good trip?"

The small boy hid behind Jock's jeans as Cal gave a quick update on the latest drive, while walking the horse towards the paddocks. Watching Liam carefully, Cal wondered why he was acting so shy. Wasn't usually. Usually gave a great shout of glee before stumbling unsteadily towards him calling, "Cal, Cal."

"If you was to come off your horse, get down to his level, he'd know who you are. From his height you look like a giant. Hell, he can't even see your face properly, way up there."

Stepping stiffly off his horse, Cal chuckled at his assumption he'd see Jacq before anyone else. Squatting before the toddler, he smiled, holding out his arms.

"Daddy! Daddy!"

Two chubby arms wound round his neck, holding him tight. Liam started the babbling sounds only Jacq and Patience understood.

Standing up with the toddler still clinging to him, Cal hugged him right back. Blowing the squeaky noises Liam loved all along his neck crease, caused the boy to wriggle and giggle delightedly.

"He's saying how much him and Jacq missed you. Says you've been gone too long."

Cal shook his head. When had Jock picked up all this baby stuff? Seems Jock could understand Liam nearly as well as Pru and Jacq herself.

Liam reached two hands towards Jock. "Granpy."

"Granpy?" Cal's eyebrows rose sharply. The mystery deepened. Liam was calling Jock Granpy?

Liam nodded. Pointing along the drive he made a car noise before saying, "Granpa."

Taking the child back, Jock chuckled happily. "Jacq suggested it. Calls me Granpy and Tom Granpa. Knows the difference too. Real smart kid. Takes after his Ma."

Mention of Jacq caused Cal a real problem inside his jeans. Jock grinned knowingly.

"You'd better see if the Missus can do something for that, boss. Liam and me'll see to your horse. Might take us a while, not so spry now as I was."

Liam crowed with delight when lifted on to the saddle. Clasped firmly by his loving Granpy, they set off together.

Cal too was off, heading for the verandah. Didn't need a second telling, no sir! Off to his wife, quick smart!

Jacq was sauntering casually towards the stockyards. "Hey boss. Good drive?"

Swooping her into his arms, Cal swung her high in the air.

"Hey, careful. Don't handle the... You stink! Put me down. I don't play with people who smell of cattle. Go have a shower."

Jacq struggled free, indicating the homestead. Cal tugged at her hand.

"Nope. Check on the meal. Be back when you've finished."

Disappointed, Cal reluctantly headed for the shower. Stripping off his dirty trail clothes, he stood letting the fresh water run over his hot, tired, sticky body. Lathering up, he concentrated on cleaning his hair first.

With shampoo in his hair, on his face and hands, Cal was surprised to feel two arms encircle his waist. They reached for the soap, and started to work on his shoulders and back.

Rinsing soap from his hair, so he could at least open his eyes, Cal gasped, as the hands gently caressed between his legs.

"Hey boss! Didn't know you were into multi-tasking. How'd you do that?" Jacq chuckled at his response to being soaped thoroughly. "Would you like your Christmas present?"

"So happens I have yours on me right now, lady. Yours first, right?"

"Mmmm." Her wet body slid the length of his, as Jacq settled to her knees. Kissing the old scar always drove him mad.

Groaning, Cal hoisted her up to where he could kiss her face, muttering his love into her hair, while she continued to soap him.

Rinsing off the soap, Cal stepped quickly straight out of the shower into bed, taking Jacq with him.

"Clean now, lady."

She giggled into his mouth with the next kiss, sighing happily.

❋ ❋ ❋ ❋ ❋

Cupping one of her breasts in his hand, Cal settled contentedly on his side. The slight movement woke Jacq, and she smiled lovingly into his eyes.

"Welcome home boss."

"Best welcome home I've ever had.

"Mmmmm."

"That all you can say?"

"Figured out your present yet?"

"Yes, wasn't wrapped, but felt real good."

He tweaked her nipple gently, before kissing it lovingly.

"Silly. That was my present, not your present. Can't you guess?"

Jacq moved his hand lower, so it was stroking her belly. "Actually, you'd better not do too much of that, or we won't be able to help with the meal." Carrying his hand to her lips, she kissed each finger.

"I'm not hungry. Might stay right here."

"We have to feed the men, sweet. Don't we? Do you need three guesses?"

Reaching up casually, Jacq kissed and stroked his chest. "Do you know I wanted to do that the first morning? When you came out to the critter? I had this almost overwhelming urge to touch you, to kiss you."

"You could have given in to it lady. I wouldn't have objected. Don't now either."

"Hey you. Meal, right? Wait until later."

"More of this later? Promise now?"

"Yup, much as you like, *if* you guess your present correctly." Jacq slid out of bed, reaching for clean pants.

Watching the line of her body as she stretched to fasten her bra, Cal held his breath. Boy, she looked so good. Slipping behind her, he covered her hands with his calloused ones. "Wow! Look what you did."

Jacq giggled and wriggled. "Can't see from here. Can only feel. That you boss?"

"Yup. I love you Jacq MacCready."

"Yeah me too. Glad you married me, aren't you?"

"Hey that's not fair…"

Cal was interrupted by shouts from Jacq's son, as he came along the hallway.

"What's he saying?"

"Oh gosh, you'd better go. Seems his Daddy is home, and the men are coming up the drive. He's been helping Granpy groom his horse."

"Daddy?"

"Yeah, you'd better go before he gets here. Liam's Daddy has a real bad temper. Ask anyone."

"Nah, Liam's Daddy is a pussycat. Trust me. His Mummy is no pushover but Liam's Daddy… Liam's Daddy…"

Recalling the words her son had used, Cal slanted his eyes at Jacq. "Say, just who is Liam's Daddy?"

Shrugging into her shirt, Jacq said, "Some old drover I met up by the waterhole one year. Keep going back, never saw him again."

"Oh that fella? He's Liam's Daddy?"

"Yup. No other fella for me, not since I painted Tom's fence."

Swooping his wife into his arms, Cal kissed her passionately. Was she saying what he thought she was saying?

Keeping his arm round her as they left their bedroom, he pondered this new idea, adding it to Jock's words. Jock *and* Tom both to be Grandfathers to this little boy? Jacq's little boy? He felt a glow of pride for his wife. Mum would have been extra pleased by that gesture, wouldn't she just!

"Hello son. Mummy and I were just coming."

They set off for the back kitchen swinging the little boy between them.

"Up Daddy. Up."

"He wants you to pick him up."

"Me? He's calling for his Daddy."

"Yup, knows what he wants. Wants to ride on your shoulders, I guess. That's what Daddy's do."

"Wait a bit… you're his Mummy, you carry him."

Jacq slanted a quick look sideways at him, standing with hands on hips to say, "Oooh, you're a big meanie, Callum MacCready. Don't you think you should carry your first child?"

Patting her stomach she added, "'specially while I'm carrying your second child."

There was a minute or two of stunned silence, while Cal looked at the mischief on his wife's face, and worked out what she meant. Then he swooped Jacq off her feet with a holler which brought all the crew into the yard. A frightened Liam stood transfixed by their side.

Jacq smiled lovingly down at her little boy. "Daddy gets a bit over-excited sometimes, huh?"

Re-assured by her reaction, the little boy hopped up and down excitedly.

"Me too, Daddy. Me too."

He didn't stop until Cal had returned Jacq to her feet. Then Cal swooped up his son for a hug, before swirling him round and round until they were both dizzy.

Jock slipped his arm through Jacq's. "Told 'im then?"

"Yup. I guess he's pleased. You know Cal, takes a while for the penny to drop."

Other Books by Mary-Ann Simpson

Sagas
Romantic Myth

Now he has found her, Vicar Ashley Williams wants only to cherish his love, protecting her from the terrors that threaten to engulf her. But, having tackled the trauma of her childhood, Ashley faces an agonising dilemma. Is he – in fact – her Prince Charming, here at last to rescue Melissa, so that she can live happily ever after? OR, …is he the Dragon, who will extinguish her happy spirit?

The House of Bedlam   (part of the Norfolk Series)

Dr Jim Chambers has a reputation for moving swiftly from woman to woman, loving and leaving them with practiced charm. Until that is, he meets Megan Davis. But Megan is not interested in men, …*any* man, but especially not another serial womaniser. She is too busy building a safe haven for her precious boys. A secure solid base from which she hopes they will start to recover, …learn to be happy.

The Norfolk Series   *Usual Terms*

Blast from the Past

Outsourcing

Fabric of Life

Combined Forces
(sequel to Usual Terms)

Printed in the United Kingdom
by Lightning Source UK Ltd.
116112UKS00001B/19-48